HE FELT HIS POW
HIM, DRAINING IN
HOLLOW OF THE
TREMBLING RAN THROUGH

He jerked like a creature dying and a stream of white froth broke from his twisted mouth. His limbs no longer seemed to belong to him, so violent, so spasmodic was their threshing. The mare's tail on his bone mask whipped across his face as he rode out away from the man and left his body to fall empty to the ground. The flames leaped high for a moment and sank down into the dark.

Michael woke into terror, retching at the old, foul taste in his mouth, wiping his stinging eyes in a horror at what he might see – but there was nothing, only his wife sleeping beside him. And from this first drawing-in, the shaman never left Michael again.

Sheila Holligon was born and educated on Teesside, and now lives on a farm on the North Yorkshire moors near Lealholm. She has had four collections of poetry published, and several short stories, and writes regularly for American and Canadian papers about breeding rare poultry. Her novels *Nightrider* and *Bridestone* are both available in Signet Creed.

SHEILA HOLLIGON

BRIDESTONE

A SIGNET BOOK

SIGNET

Published by the Penguin Group
Penguin Books Ltd, 27 Wrights Lane, London w8 5tz, England
Penguin Books USA Inc., 375 Hudson Street, New York, New York 10014, USA
Penguin Books Australia Ltd, Ringwood, Victoria, Australia
Penguin Books Canada Ltd, 10 Alcorn Avenue, Toronto, Ontario, Canada m4v 3b2
Penguin Books (NZ) Ltd, 182–190 Wairau Road, Auckland 10, New Zealand

Penguin Books Ltd, Registered Offices: Harmondsworth, Middlesex, England

First published 1995

1 3 5 7 9 10 8 6 4 2

Typeset by Datix International Limited, Bungay, Suffolk
Printed in England by Clays Ltd, St Ives plc
Filmset in 10/12 pt Monophoto Baskerville

For Emanuel Z.

Chapter One

THE shaman thrust his fingers into the blood of the dead baby and gave it to the fire in a red string. Dropping the child to the earth he pulled towards him his wooden drum and, squatting beside it, began to beat softly on its skin cover.

He watched the fire and waited.

Out of the future the man came sleepwalking slowly through the blackness between the lines of posts at the entrance to the village, each with its staring, bloody head spiked on the top. The drumbeat quickened, pulling him towards the red eye of the fire.

The shaman looked up across the flames at him and let the drumbeat patter into silence. He rose to his feet and the firelight flickered on the running horse tattooed blue across his chest, on his mareskin cloak and the mask of bone on his head. He crackled with power: he was a smoking crystal, a transformer, a magician. He stared with pale eyes at the man he had conjured up and knew him for the chosen one. This was the one who in time to come would give his goddess life again. The shaman's own life here with his tribe was nearing its end. He had seen it coming. Before he walked away from them for the last time there was much he must teach this stranger.

The shaman came through the red ash and billowing smoke to stand beside the man. He could smell the fear-sweat on him, acrid and bitter. He reached out and pulled the stiff figure towards him, staring into the white face, then spat into each of the closed eyes. Fastening his mouth tightly over the cold lips he breathed into him as if he were gentling a young horse. He felt his power pouring from him, draining into the dark hollow of the man and a sudden trembling ran through him as he emptied and began to move out into the night. He jerked like a creature dying and a stream of white froth broke from his twisted mouth. His limbs no longer seemed to belong to him, so violent, so spasmodic was their threshing. The mare's tail on his bone mask whipped across his face as he rode out away from the man and left his body to fall empty to the ground. The flames leapt high for a moment and sank down into dark.

Michael woke into terror, retching at the old, foul taste in his mouth, wiping his stinging eyes in a horror at what he might see – but there was nothing, only his wife sleeping beside him. And from this first drawing-in, the shaman never left Michael again.

At the top of the house Alice Denby opened a window. Below her, at the bottom of the world, lay her rag-doll daughter Cat, offering her breasts to the sun. Mother and daughter; flesh and yet not. Alice stood and watched.

In the room below, her husband Simon wrote blackly on a large sheet of paper. On the other side of his desk the three Arab women, black as crows in their robes, perched uneasily on the edges of their chairs. 'Where was this pain?' said Simon, writing busily without lifting his head. The three faces in their beaked masks swung as one to the interpreter. He sighed heavily. Surely the good doctor had been listening?

'It was in Saudi Arabia,' he said.

Down one floor again, the breast specialist looked at the right breast of the rich American woman and soothed her with the words, that it was most probably nothing,

nothing at all. He thought, as he had done before, that women were made like unexploded bombs, all with the timer ticking silently away. He patted her reassuringly on her slim brown shoulder before going to his desk to begin the complicated procedure of admitting her to the London Clinic. He glanced out of the window as he picked up the phone and for a moment thought that one of his patients was lying on the grass below, waiting to be examined. He blinked at the bare breasts, then smiled with relief. It was Simon's daughter – and a very healthy body he was looking at, too.

On the ground floor the receptionist in her white coat crossed over to the row of phones on the hall table and, as she picked up a receiver, wondered why it was so quiet in the waiting room.

Out in the little garden Cat lay in the grass and closed her eyes against the dust-flecked yellow light. Further off along the gardens a bird was singing. A police car punctuated the afternoon with a high-pitched scream above the sound of traffic in Marylebone Road. Beside Cat in the grass lay her sketch book. She was supposed to be working in it, but all she had produced so far was a page with Harry's name scrawled over and over. Harry. She'd known him for four months now, since she'd met him at Caroline's party. She wished that she'd never gone there, never met him.

It had been hot and stuffy in Caroline's flat. She'd drunk too much and felt depressed. For once she wasn't wearing jeans, and the low-cut black dress she had on felt like drag. Her high heels were crippling her and why anyone should choose to wear stockings and suspenders was beyond her. Leaving seemed like a good idea. She was making her way to the door when Harry walked through it. Tall and fair, every cliché in the book walked in with him. He glanced round and came straight over

3

to her. 'Can I take you away from all this?' he said, laughing, and she had let him.

She let him take her out to dinner and then back to his house in St John's Wood. They ended up in his bed and the sex was good. He knew how to please her and he was generous, taking his time. He liked her stockings and suspenders. He liked her – so much so that he asked her to move in with him, then, that night; but that was going too fast for her. She went home in a taxi and realized only then that she didn't know his name, only that he was Harry. How could she have gone to bed with Mr X? She rang Caroline to find out who he was but got no further. Caroline knew him only as the friend of a friend.

Cat spent forty-eight hours wondering if she'd see him again and then he rang her. He wanted all of her time from then on, that was the problem, and he didn't like it when she wouldn't give him it. There was a hard edge under that charming smile when she wasn't instantly available and the fact that she had her classes at art school meant nothing to him. He closed himself off from her so that she couldn't find out anything about him. 'Cat Denby, age twenty-two, art student, London born and bred. Living at home with Doctor Dad and Mother Hen. How about you?'

He shrugged and kissed her. It worried her that she knew so little about him. How did he make his money? And there was a lot. She could see that by the house and the presents he tried to give her. It was one of the presents which had brought things to a head last night. Harry had taken her out for a meal, then back to his house and straight to bed. It had been as good as it always was and he had kissed her, then reached under the pillow and pulled out a box. He took something from it and dropped it between her breasts. It was cold and glittering with points of fire.

'For you,' he said.

'It's a diamond necklace.'

'Yes,' he said, grinning. 'I had noticed.'

'I can't take this,' she began and his face changed, became as cold as the diamonds.

'You can't refuse it.'

Cat picked it up and sat up to look at it. She held it in her hands for a moment, then got out of bed and crossed to the long mirror. She fastened the necklace round her throat. Who had worn it before her? She knew women were supposed to love diamonds but it felt all wrong, dead against her skin. He got out of bed and came and stood behind her, running his hands across her nipples.

'You should always wear it like that,' he said. 'With nothing else.'

She could feel his erection pressing against her as he bent and kissed her throat. She unfastened the heavy clasp and turned to push the necklace into his hands. 'It's very beautiful but I can't take it.'

'I don't think you understand. I got it for you.'

'Where from?' she said without thinking.

'That's none of your business. Why don't you want it?'

'It won't go with my jeans,' she said flippantly, wanting to diffuse the anger she could see in him.

'Then you'll have to wear a dress and try to look like a fucking lady, won't you? Instead of dressing like a grubby little lad as usual. Always got paint under your finger-nails, haven't you?'

'It's my work.' She pushed past him and began to pull on her clothes.

'You don't work. All you do is play at being an artist. You still live safely at home with Mummy and Daddy. You still go to school.'

'That's not how it is. You don't know me at all if you see me tarted up in diamonds. It'll be a fur coat next.'

'Why not?' he said. 'I can get you a nice mink. No problem. Wear it like the necklace. Nothing under it but your knickers.'

He was running the diamonds through his fingers. 'Diamonds are a girl's best friend,' he said, smiling, and came towards her to put the necklace back round her throat.

'No,' she said, pushing him away from her.

'Don't you say no to me, bitch.' His hand came up to hit her hard across the face. She staggered back, tears running down her stinging cheek, horrified at seeing how aroused he was by hitting her. As he came towards her again she turned and ran. She heard him shout something after her as she slammed the front door but it wasn't until she found a taxi and slumped into the back seat, with her heart pounding, that she realized what he'd shouted.

'Run home to Mummy like a good little girl.'

Cat thought now that she never wanted to see him again. She'd been more frightened than hurt but she wouldn't let anyone treat her like that. Next time it would be worse. She'd seen how turned on he'd been by hitting her. Next time she might not get off so easily. The necklace wasn't important. His violence was. What was worrying her now was how easily would he let go of her? He knew where she lived. He'd picked her up from this house a couple of times although he would never come in for a meal. He said he wouldn't know what to say to a doctor. He needn't have worried. Cat couldn't imagine her father finding anything to say to Harry. And her mother would have found too much – it would have been a non-stop stream of questions which would have slid off Harry as if he hadn't heard them.

But if he came here looking for her? Cat shivered at the idea and sat up. The sun had gone behind a cloud and the house loomed over her, black and shadowed. She stared up at it and saw her mother leaning out of the window watching her. Cat felt that her mother was always watching her, as if her entire purpose in life was to spy on her daughter twenty-four hours a day. She would want to know why Cat wasn't seeing that nice fair young man any more. She was waving at Cat, pointing at her. Cat frowned and looked away from her towards the window of the waiting room. To her dismay, she saw a line of interested dark faces, staring at her. 'Oh shit!' she said softly and, reaching for her shirt, pulled it down quickly over her heavy breasts. She'd forgotten that there were patients in this afternoon – at least she'd taken their minds off their troubles. She ran her fingers through her ruffled spikes of black hair and, snatching up her sketch book, tore off the page covered with Harry's name. She crumpled it up crossly.

In the waiting room the group of Arabs sighed regretfully and, murmuring among themselves, went back to the flower-patterned sofas and the old copies of *Country Life*.

Through the open window at the top of the house, Cat heard the faint shrilling of the phone. 'Harry,' she panicked. 'It's Harry and what do I say?' She felt the hard crack of his hand on her face again and, bending her head, began to draw quickly, slashing at the paper with thick black strokes. She'd covered most of the paper before she realized what she was drawing. She stared down at Harry's handsome face looking at her and wished she was anywhere but London. She wanted to be out of reach of Harry, out of reach of her mother. The phone had stopped ringing. She held her breath in the silence and sat with bent head, waiting.

'Catherine,' came her mother's voice floating down from the high window. 'It's for you, dear!'

Chapter Two

'YORKSHIRE?' said Alice faintly, sitting down on the edge of the bed. Cat was packing sketch pads and pastels into a bag. Alice sat and watched her. Why was Cat going to Yorkshire so suddenly? For Alice, it was somewhere wild and bleak, far up on the northern thrust of England, covered in a blue crackle of ice. 'Who do you know in Yorkshire?'

'Fen. That's who the phone call was from. She's been working up there at a stables since Easter. She rang to ask me to go up and stay with her.'

'In the stables?' said Alice fearfully, imagining her only child sleeping in a hay loft.

'No, of course not, Mother. Don't be stupid. Fen says there's a small cottage that goes with the job. It's okay for me to stay there with her.'

Alice was pleased. Cat and Fen had been friends for years, ever since they were at boarding school together. Yorkshire was a long way away, but Cat looked very pale today. There was a black bruise starting to show up below her eye. Alice wished she knew how it had got there but she didn't dare ask that. A holiday would do Cat good. Alice opened her mouth to say so, then closed it again. Perhaps it wasn't the right thing to say – she said a lot of things these days which weren't right for Cat. Alice sighed, remembering when Cat had been Catherine and such a good little girl, with long dark hair and pretty dresses. That was before she went away to school and turned herself into Cat, with hair exactly like a golliwog Alice had as a child. All black spikes. And

8

three silver earrings in one ear. Why did she want three, wondered Alice. She watched Cat push a sweater into the bag. 'When are you going? And how long will you stay there?'

'I'm going up tomorrow. I'm getting the InterCity from King's Cross, arriving York 12.19. Then I change for Scarborough. Fen says I can stay as long as I want. I don't have anything to keep me in London until September and I can do some work up there. I'm supposed to be working on a project on landscapes.'

Alice took all this in. What did Cat mean, that there was nothing to keep her in London? What had happened to that nice boyfriend, the fair one who came for her in that beautiful big car? 'Is there a phone at this cottage?' Alice sounded all innocence. 'Then if anyone rings here for you, I can give them your number –'

Cat swung round to her. 'Don't you dare! Don't you give the number to anyone who asks for it!'

Alice was startled at how angry Cat looked. 'But I'll need to know it.' She twisted her fingers together. How could she let Cat go off for the summer and not be able to ring her?

Cat groaned. 'Calm down. I'll leave the number and address but just for you, okay? I really do need to get right away for a few weeks.'

Alice nodded. Cat pushed a pair of mirrored shades into her bag and her mother frowned at the sight of them. She didn't like those nasty sunglasses. All she could see when she looked at Cat in them were two little images of herself. Alice had lately taken against seeing herself at all. She turned away her head when she passed a mirror these days. Mirrors had started lying to Alice. She didn't believe the reflection they gave back to her now and two of herself shrunk to doll size in her daughter's eyes made her feel very odd. Cat had such beautiful

9

dark eyes; it was a shame to cover them up at all. Alice thought of the first time she had seen Cat when the nurse brought her to her after such red pain. Alice held the baby close to herself and thought that she was safe then, that she would never be unhappy again. But the years had taken Cat away from her. 'You weren't wearing your shirt in the garden again. Your Daddy will be so upset if he finds out.'

Cat struggled to zip up the bag. 'Don't tell him then. As if it matters. I'll be glad to be away from here and up in Yorkshire. I won't have people watching me all the time there.'

She was angry again. Did she mean she wanted to be on her own now? One of the hot flushes which so disturbed Alice these days was prickling at the edges of her skin. She'd better go. There was a lot to think about: Fen working as a groom in Yorkshire and Cat going to stay with her. Would the cottage be damp? And would the pair of them eat properly? Alice got stiffly to her feet and, smoothing her dress down over her heavy hips, smiled vaguely and left the room.

Cat closed the door after her. Between her mother's cross-questioning and her father's vagueness it would be a relief to get away from both of them. Getting away from her parents was nothing compared to the relief she felt at the chance to get away from Harry. She wouldn't feel safe from him until she was on the train heading north. It would be good to see Fen again. They had the sort of friendship which was always there, even if they didn't see each other for months. Fen was beautiful – tall and leggy with a thick plait of fair hair. She never seemed to realize how attractive she was: she was so placid and self-contained even Cat found it difficult sometimes to know just what she felt. The phone call had been a perfect piece of timing. Fen had spent most of it talking about a horse, as usual, but then she'd begun to talk about someone called Michael. It wasn't often Fen showed much interest in a man. Cat was looking forward to meeting this Michael.

Cat spent the train journey mapping it for herself in a spiral-bound notebook with a fine, black fibre-tip pen. Houses gave way to fields and by late afternoon to moorland, to dry-stone walls, black-faced sheep and half-derelict stations where weeds filled what must have once been flower beds. The journey was a succession of images, of light and shadow. By the time she climbed stiffly out of the train at Scarborough, Cat felt as though she'd been sitting in it for so long that she'd thinned and dissolved into nothing more than a pair of eyes and a fibre-tip pen. She followed the crowd going along the platform, looking for Fen. The fresh, salt-grey air washed over as she came out of the station.

Fen was there waiting, leaning on her little Mini. She was very brown, all legs in a pair of faded shorts, her long plait ripened to the colour of corn by the sun. Cat called her name. Fen gave a shout of pleasure and wrapped Cat in a great hug, then stepped back and looked at Cat's face. 'Hey! Who did you get in a fight with?' Cat shrugged and glanced away and Fen frowned at how upset she looked. She kissed her cheek and, taking Cat's bag from her, threw it into the back of the car. 'Come on,' she said. 'I don't think I should be parking here.'

Cat climbed into the Mini next to her and slammed the door. As Fen eased out into the busy traffic she said happily to her, 'I am so pleased you could come at such short notice, Cat. I was sure you would have other plans for the summer.'

'Not me. Free as a bird.'

Fen looked quickly at her face and then back at the road. 'Like that, is it? I thought you sounded a bit down on the phone. Is it boyfriend trouble?'

'Not any more it's not. I'll tell you the details later – let's talk about you instead. You look very well, something must be agreeing with you up here. It's either the horse you were telling me about or this Michael.'

'Wait until you see him. He's magnificent.'

'Which one? The man or the horse?'

'Bel, of course. Though Michael is nearly as good. He's Bel's groom, the stallion man. I've never met anyone as good with horses as he is. It was his idea to ask you here now; it's the best time because the last of the visiting mares is ready to leave.'

'Visiting mares? You do bed and breakfast for horses?'

'Idiot. Visiting Bel. He's a pure Cleveland Bay at stud. Mrs Barton, who owns him, lives at Fox Hall. She doesn't do anything in the yard any more, that's why they advertised for help over the summer. Me. It's not a bad job. I get the cottage and a lot of free time, though I don't get paid much more than pocket money.'

'Job satisfaction,' said Cat and exclaimed in surprise as the road curved suddenly. It was high tide in the bay below them, and the sea was beating white against the cliffs. On the far side a small village of red-roofed cottages clung to the steep crag. Fen pulled off into a lay-by and opened the window. 'Raven's Bay,' she said. The sound of gulls screaming rose above the water breaking far below them on the seal-grey rocks.

'It's beautiful,' said Cat. 'Thanks for asking me here, Fen.' She leaned forward and touched Fen's full mouth with her fingers. Fen turned to her, startled, then smiled and kissed her. Their mouths met, warm and soft for an instant, tasting of summer, then Fen started up the car and drove off.

Fox Hall and the cottages belonging to it lay inland from Raven's Bay, standing at each side of the one road leading up the narrow valley as if they had grown there. Behind the cottages was a field and above that a thin ribbon of larch wood crested the steep ridge of the valley side. Fen pulled the car on to the grass verge. 'Here we are then. This end cottage is ours, the other one is where Michael and his family live.' She reached behind her for Cat's bag, scrambling out of the car. 'Come on, you must be hungry. I'll get us something to eat. Fancy an omelette?'

Cat got out of the car and stretched, sniffing the cool moor air. 'Fine. I'm hungry enough to eat a horse.'

'Hey! Say that very quietly round here, would you?' Fen led the way through the little white gate and up to the porch door. She opened it and started to say something to Cat, then stopped. Cat couldn't see what Fen was staring at or why she was standing so frozen in the doorway.

'Fen? What is it?'

Fen shook her head and stepped into the porch. Cat followed her and saw what she was staring at. The floor of the porch was made of old red and blue tiles. In the centre of them someone had laid out a thick spiral of soil, curling round and round in on itself to the centre where there was the white skull of a long-dead bird. Scattered on the soil were the heads of scarlet geraniums, and a heap of broken, discarded plants lay with some empty pots under a long white shelf. The smell of bruised leaves filled the little porch and Cat could hear the buzzing of a fly, caught in a spider's web in the window. She stared at the long, fragile beak of the bird skull, at the formal patterning of soil and flower heads.

'Fen? Who's done this?'

'I don't know. I can't think who would have been in

here.' She walked round the edge of the spiral and bent to lift up the mat at the house door. She picked up the key and stood holding it in her hand, then opened the door and stood listening. She turned to Cat and shrugged. 'Must have been Patsy, the kid next door, messing about – her idea of a welcome for you. Come in, you must be wondering what sort of place you've come to.'

'But the plants – shouldn't we try to re-pot them?' Cat stepped carefully over the soil and followed Fen inside.

'I'll put them in some water in the sink and see to them later. Let's have the kettle on first.' She hurried in towards the kitchen.

Cat stood for a moment longer looking back at the dark line of soil, blood-spotted with the red flower heads and thought that it didn't look much like the work of a child to her. Too formal, somehow. It was like a maze pattern in some old art-form, she thought, and followed Fen slowly.

Some time later, Cat pushed her empty plate away from her and sighed happily. 'That was perfect. Thanks.'

'You should be thanking next door's hens. They laid the eggs for the omelette.'

'Who does live next door?'

'Michael, his wife Sally and their little girl, Patsy.'

'She's the one you think made the pattern in the porch?'

Fen shrugged. 'There's no one else. She's a strange kid. She must have done it.'

'Why didn't you lock the porch door?'

'I never do, there's no need out here. Anyway, there's no key to the outer door of the porch.' Fen got up and collected the empty plates. 'I've got a bottle of wine in the kitchen. Help yourself to some bread and cheese.'

'No room,' said Cat regretfully. She watched Fen go through the door in the far corner. She'd seen the kitchen already and at some point was going to draw the shallow brown sink with the rack of old plates next to it. There was nothing in this room she wanted to put on to paper. It was one of the gloomiest rooms she'd ever been in; it was nothing at all like her idea of a country cottage. It wasn't much better upstairs. There was one bedroom with a brass bed Queen Victoria would have appreciated and a tiny bathroom next to it, with the loo nestling cosily beside the bath, which had four animals' feet, as if it were going to gallop off downstairs one moonlit night. At least there was piped water – Fen didn't have to carry it all from the nearest well.

Cat stared round at the furniture. It was best described as big and brown. A sticky-looking sideboard with barley-sugar legs squatted opposite the heavy table where she was sitting. There was a fat, leather sofa with the stuffing coming out of one arm and a pair of matching armchairs. Even though there was a window at each end of the long room, the low-beamed ceiling swallowed up much of the light. There was one picture: a pseudo-Landseer in a gilt frame hanging above the sideboard. A depressed stag gazed mournfully down at Cat. She knew exactly how it felt. She shivered, rubbing the goose pimples on her bare arms and wished she'd kept on her jacket. The stone fireplace had a fire laid in it with a basket of logs on the hearth. 'Fen? Can we light the fire?'

Coming in with the opened wine and two glasses, Fen looked at her in mock astonishment. 'You can't be cold already. You Southern softies.'

'I'm frozen,' admitted Cat cheerfully, cutting herself a slice of cheese. 'And less of the Southern softies. You've been up here so long you've forgotten you come from deepest Suffolk yourself. Go on, light it for me. It's years since I've seen a real wood fire. D'you remember us making toffee on the one in the TV lounge at school?'

'And we dropped the pan upside down on their price-less rug. How could I forget?' Kneeling on the mat in front of the fire, Fen struck a match and held it to the paper. With a dry crackle the larch twigs filled the room with a sharp, burning scent.

Cat poured herself a glass of wine and shivered. 'Can I have a bath and get warmed up? I can't talk when my teeth are chattering. I need to talk to you about Harry.'

'Help yourself.' Fen was intent on the fire. 'You know the way.'

'I can hardly get lost. You sure you don't want me to help you clear up the mess in the porch place first?'

'No, I'll do it. Don't worry about it Cat, she won't do it again.'

'Good!' said Cat and shivered her way upstairs.

By the time she came downstairs in an old dressing-gown she'd found hanging behind the door, the fire was blazing, throwing shadows on the dark beams. Fen was lying on the rug, the bottle of wine next to her, watching the flames. 'I hope it's okay, you sharing a bed with me?'

Cat wasn't deceived by the off-hand tone. 'Of course it is,' she said, kneeling beside her and, pulling off the band from the end of Fen's long plait, began to unweave the thick strands of pale hair. 'It always is okay,' she said. 'We go back a lot of years, you and I. Nothing changes what's between us. Not even Harry – especially not Harry. Remember the first time, Fen?'

Fen and Cat at eleven. Even then it had been there in Fen, that long-legged-foal look, those startlingly blue eyes with the dark eyebrows. Cat had been small then, flat-chested, with nothing to show that in another few years she would be beautiful. She took off Fen's shorts and shirt as carefully now as if she were unwrapping a present. She touched the small high breasts and remembered how she had trembled the first time she touched

16

them, excited at the risk of being discovered together in the school showers. Fen had small breasts already then: sugar cones with soft pink nipples. Cat had stuck out her tongue and licked one and Fen had giggled, said it tickled. But for the first time Cat had felt a queer, fluttering throb between her legs as the nipple hardened.

The dressing-gown dropped to the floor next to her as she slid a hand over the soft fleecy mound at Fen's cunt; the smell and feel of her was dear and familiar. She bent and kissed Fen's mouth, tasting the swollen bottom lip like a ripe fruit. How many months had it been since they were together? It didn't matter, it was always right between the two of them. There'd never been any other women for Cat, only Fen. When she was fourteen she'd moved on to men, starting with the gardener's boy. She wondered now how Fen managed without sex when she took so much pleasure in it with Cat. Men had never taken Cat's place with her. She never mentioned any other women and Cat never asked. When they were together they made love. It was as simple as that.

They fitted well together, knowing each other's needs and desires. Cat knew this body as well as her own and, because it was another woman's, there was no rush to climax, no urgency. This was a journey they were making together and they could take as long as they liked to arrive. Kneeling astride her, Cat slid her fingers into the rain-wet valley of her. Fen's fingers stroked her thighs and, as she began to tease at Cat, the old, familiar patterns reaffirmed themselves. Cat sighed with pleasure, feeling herself at the edge of a long, slow coming and, as she did so, something inside her which had hurt since Harry struck her began to ease, and yes, yes, yes, she cried out in delight.

In the cottage next door Michael stood by the window, staring out into the garden but seeing nothing. She was here then. He'd seen her coming up the path behind Fen and she had been dark haired and beautiful, just as he had seen her in his dream. He'd always had strange dreams, brightly coloured and disturbing, but now in the night (and not always in the night) he was seeing something else, something he had no word for but dreams. They were of such a terrible reality that they were staining his days, bleeding into his thoughts. They weren't his dreams: he knew whose dreams he was having. He'd looked up the word in the dictionary to make sure he'd got the right name. He knew the definition by heart and said it over again now to himself: 'Shaman: a priest or witchdoctor. Shamanism: a primitive religion in which gods, spirits and demons influencing all life are believed to be responsive to shamans.' Gods, spirits and demons. He'd been over and over that summoning of him by the shaman but he still had no idea of what was wanted from him. There was something Michael had to do, some ceremony he had to perform but he was feeling his way blind, picking up signs through the dream-visions he was being sent. Why him? He shuddered at the half-memory of the shaman's mouth on his, of his foul breath in Michael's mouth and nostrils, of the bitter spittle on his eyes. And yet: there had been so much power in the shaman. Michael wanted some of that. He must have been chosen for a special reason. He would listen and watch very carefully and he would make the shaman's magic for him.

He had brought Fen's friend here because of a dream but he had no idea why, only that she was needed. For what? He'd understood nothing of the dream except the ending, then he knew what he had been told to do. All day he had been uneasy, waiting for something. It had been very hot, so that even the flower-scented dusk had been soft and warm. A full moon later turned the landscape to black and silver. Michael had been unable to sleep for the heat and the tension inside him. He fell at last into a light doze from which he opened his eyes to find himself in a new landscape. Everywhere was still white, but this wasn't moonlight, this was snow.

He was shivering in a bitter, frosting cold; it was biting through the cloak of skin he wore. He was in a clearing among dark-rooted trees, standing where a small spring bubbled from the frozen soil at the foot of a great oak. Crystals of ice splintered the banks of the spring and crusted the fallen twigs and reedy grass under his feet. He brought a beaker of thin horn and a small leather bag from under his robe. Pulling open the bag he sprinkled the handful of seed it held on to the ground round the rising of the spring and, pulling the plug of moss from the mouth of the horn, let the thick blood scribble at his feet in the white snow. Red on white. He studied the bloody pattern at his feet then, sinking to his haunches, gazed into the bubbles of water breaking from the ground. His body emptied and became so still that a great black bird flapped raggedly down from the trees and began to peck with a grey, horny beak at the scattered seed.

There were shapes drifting up to him through the water. He could see a woman with long yellow hair riding on a stallion. There was a face forming in the water; a dark-haired woman. She came running alongside the horse and the yellow-haired woman leaned down and pulled her up behind her. The water bubbled and the horse with its two riders was gone, but Michael knew that this second one with the dark hair must come to be with Fen. Waking fully, he knew that he must bring her here.

'Gods, spirits and demons,' he said again and wondered what the shaman would send him for the next sign.

Chapter Three

IT was very late that night before Cat and Fen were all talked out. Cat was happier now she'd told Fen about Harry and what he'd done to her. Fen didn't say much, she never did, but she had listened. She lay long and straight in the big bed now, watching Cat unpack her clothes into the battered chest of drawers. Cat piled her sketch pads and pencils on top of it. 'You've brought some work with you? I was hoping you would; I've been looking for places to take you. What are you doing at the moment?'

'It's a project I've to hand in at the beginning of next term: "Figures in a summer landscape".'

'The landscape's no problem. Figures are going to be a bit more difficult.' She yawned sleepily. 'Unless you include sheep.'

'I've never tried drawing sheep. I'll just put you in all the landscapes instead. Then in years to come, when I'm rich and famous, everyone will want to know who the mysterious blonde is. Just don't hold your breath waiting.'

'This is your last year, isn't it? Then what are you going to do?'

'I've not really decided. I'm not good enough to set up on my own. My tutor says I'm not committed enough – I don't push myself hard enough. Something in design, perhaps. Maybe Harry was right. He said I was only playing at it, that I'm still really at school, living with Mummy and Daddy.'

'Harry didn't do a lot for your self-confidence, did he?'

Fen yawned again. 'Sorry. I'm half asleep. It's with getting up so early. I've got to be at the stables before seven. There's no need for you to get up then – I'll just leave you in bed, if that's okay? Then you can get up when you want.'

'That's a relief. I thought for a nasty minute you were going to get me up in the middle of the night with you. Can I come over to the stables and see the stallion? I'd like to make some sketches of him if your Mrs Barton will let me.'

'She'll love the idea, especially if you do one for her. She got one framed that Patsy drew of him. You'll have to look at Patsy's stuff, she's really good. She's always drawing the horses, strange pictures for a kid. There's a couple of old mares as well as Bel – he's so beautiful. You wait till you see him tomorrow. You'll meet Michael as well. It's nice having you here, Cat.'

Cat pushed the empty bag under the bed. 'It's nice to be here. I was desperate to be out of London. I'm going to have a very quiet holiday doing nothing.'

'It'll be quiet enough. It's never anything else.'

Cat climbed in next to her. 'Good. Move over and let me in. My feet are freezing.'

Fen groaned and agreed as Cat wriggled down next to her. She reached out and switched off the bedside light.

The night whirled blackly about Cat as soon as she shut her eyes. Dark as thick as skin pressed in on her and behind her eyelids she began again to journey north, feeling the rocking of the train, seeing the waves crash white in Raven's Bay. She was sinking down below it all when a wild scream ripped up the dark. 'What was that?' she croaked, sitting bolt upright and clutching Fen.

'It's only an owl, silly. Go to sleep, it's nothing.'

The country dark came feathering thicker than ever

on Cat and the silence deepened. She'd always lived in London, and night to her was the lights of the city. Lying there listening to Fen's breathing she felt as if the dark outside was pressing against the small window. It was a lonely place this, and Cat wasn't sure she was going to like it. There had been that queer business when she arrived, that spiral laid out so carefully on the floor of the porch. Fen seemed convinced it was Patsy, but the kid must be weird to do that. The owl screeched more faintly now from the trees behind Fox Hall and Cat jerked at the sound. She would never sleep. She would lie here all night watching the window and waiting for morning to come. If it ever did. She yawned, pulled the quilt up over her ears and fell at once into a deep sleep.

It seemed to Cat that she'd only been asleep for an hour or so when she woke to the sound of a cock crowing, shrill and urgent. She stretched out an arm for Fen but the bed was empty beside her. She blinked lazily at the brass bars at the end of the bed and for a moment wondered where she was. She'd never slept in a bed like this one before. It was like being in a Victorian cage. It was a very serious sort of bed – the kind to have babies in. Or to die in. Cat shuddered at the thought of the long-dead women who must have slept in it. Sitting up abruptly she pushed back the covers and slid from the bed into the morning sunlight.

Pulling off the T-shirt she'd slept in, she wandered to the window overlooking the garden at the back of the house. Pushing back the curtain she lifted up the old-fashioned sash window and leant out. The patch of garden below consisted mainly of some sickly looking rose bushes and a small patch of yellow grass. The garden next door was much bigger, with an end section wired off as a chicken run. There were some big, golden-brown hens strutting and scratching in the dry soil there. The red-combed cock was with them; he had a ruff of golden feathers and a splendid black flowing tail. He stood on tiptoe and stretched his beak into the air to crow again, raucous and triumphant in the sun. Cat winced at the piercing sound. Much as her fingers itched to draw him, his voice was not as fine as his feathers were.

She looked at the garden next to the run. It was immaculate, not a weed in sight. Someone was a good gardener. The lines of small, green plants with their knots of colour were as straight as rows of knitting. Cat admired the pattern of them in the dry soil. There was a small patch of shaved lawn next to the cottage, with a child's swing in the middle of it. As Cat leant on the window-ledge, enjoying the sun, a girl of about eleven came running out into the garden and climbed on to the seat of the swing. She began to move slowly backwards and forwards, her hair fanning round her in a black cloud. A woman carrying a bowl followed her out and Cat leant forward to have a better look at her. So this was Fen's neighbour. Somehow Cat couldn't imagine Fen and this one having a heart-to-heart over the garden fence about soap powder.

The woman was in her late thirties, ripe with the strange, slow blooming which comes to some women then. There was a lushness about her heavy breasts and the swing of her round bottom as she went down the garden. It was easy to see where the girl got her dark, gypsy looks from. They had the same thick, waving hair, with a blue sheening on it like a bird's wing. So this was Michael's wife, was it? Augustus John would have loved her, thought Cat.

Sally slammed the door of the hen-run crossly behind her and, ducking down, went into the low hen-house.

Another bloody woman next door was the last thing she needed. Talk about having it on the doorstep. Michael had gone on and on about her as if she was *his* guest, not that lanky Fen's. How did Michael know so much about her anyway? And what difference was it going to make to him who came visiting next door? Sally sighed and picked up the two dark brown eggs in the nearest box. She held them for a moment, admiring the smooth, chocolate-dark shells, then put them carefully in her bowl. She slid her hand under the hen sitting fluffed up in the straw of the next box. There was a warm egg under her. Sally picked it out gently. The hen took this as a personal insult and, ruffling up her feathers, screeched and pecked hard at Sally's hand before settling herself down again with a lot of muttering. Sally checked the last box, but it was empty. The Welsummer cock came strutting up to her with his little flock as she came out of the hen-house and she took a handful of corn from her apron pocket. She bent and held it out for him and he pecked at the grains in the palm of her hand, calling up his hens as the round corn fell to the earth.

Another woman for Sally to keep an eye on.

She'd fall for Michael, whoever she was. They always did. There was something about him that pulled women to him; some queer power over them he had. She'd seen it time after time with all sorts of women, ones you would never think would be attracted to Michael. There were those three down in the village. Called themselves a Writers' Group. You'd never think they wanted Mike for anything, but he was down there twice a week helping them with their research. Research. She'd never heard it called that before. Whatever they called it, they always ended up eating out of his hand. Every one of them.

Sally stood watching the hens bob like puppets at her feet then, fastening the door of the run behind her, set off up the path, holding the bowl against the full curve of her stomach. She was uneasy about Michael. She had the feeling that he was up to something. He was off in his head somewhere, with no time for her. 'Mick the Prick,' she whispered with malice. She saw herself advancing on a spread-eagled Michael, carving knife in her hand, then frowned crossly. That wasn't what she wanted. What she wanted was him all to herself. Prick and all.

She glanced up at the cottage next door and saw her standing there at the window. The visitor from London. The one who was making her so cross this morning. There she stood, bold as brass, watching Sally. Bare as the day and would you look at the size of them. Oh, Michael was going to love this one. She sucked in her stomach furiously and the eggs went rattling round the bowl.

Cat became aware that she was leaning out of the window, with her breasts perched naked on the window-sill like two peeled Humpty Dumpties. The woman standing on the path was very angry; she was glaring up with rage crackling round her. Even her hair seemed to be all standing on end. Cat tried to duck out of sight, but the sash window slid slowly and gently down, pinning her to the sill. She struggled to lift it, but she was held fast.

The girl on the swing had come to stand beside her mother, leaning against her. She looked up at Cat and grinned, then reached quickly into the bowl that her mother was holding. One of the big brown eggs came spinning slowly through the air and cracked against Cat's shoulder. The yolk slid stickily, wetly down across her breasts. She tried again to lift the window, but it wouldn't move. She could feel it cutting painfully into the skin of her shoulders, flattening her nipples against the sill.

'That's enough, Patsy,' said the woman, giving the

girl a shake and the pair of them giggled and with their arms round each other went into their cottage. The door slammed behind them; at the sound the pressure lifted from Cat's back. She could lift the window easily now. She wriggled back into the room and stood shivering. Only the nasty feeling of raw egg clinging stickily to her skin convinced her that she hadn't imagined the whole thing. She ran into the bathroom and turned on the taps, wondering why Fen hadn't warned her that the woman next door was so strange. All that anger just because Cat wasn't wearing anything – it was just as bad as being back home. Obviously nobody ever went topless in this place. At least nobody threw eggs at her in London. Fen had said Patsy was weird but she hadn't thought to mention that she was given to throwing eggs at people. Cat lowered herself into the steaming water and began to lather off the egg. She would make herself a cup of coffee when she got out of the bath, then she was going across the road to find Fen.

The kettle boiled just as she found the jar of coffee and the sugar. She poured the water into her mug and sniffed the reassuring smell. She took a sip of the black sweetness and felt it go straight to the hollow left by her encounter with the witch and her apprentice. As she stood cradling the mug, she saw a movement out of her eye-corner. It came from the small window and she whirled nervously, half-expecting to see the woman again, hanging like a bat in the small square of light. She splashed hot coffee on her hand and yelped.

'Oh my God! It's an angel!' she breathed in horror. There was a man standing looking in at her, naked to the waist. He could have been naked further than that for all she knew, but she couldn't see below that for the window-ledge. He was more beautiful than any man – and indeed most women – she had ever seen. The morning sun made a glittering halo of the curling golden hair which fell to his shoulders. His long, grey eyes were as blank as painted ones, and the carved mouth looked as if it were never meant to be sullied by food. It was his expression which terrified her. She had seen it in old pictures; it was a face which should have been painted in oils with a gilt frame round it. He had an unearthly, holy look. He stood and gazed in at her in perfect stillness, knowing her and judging her.

The mug of coffee jerked and shook in her hand. She edged it down on to the table next to her, and began to back slowly towards the door. Her movement seemed to release him from his watching. The space he'd filled was suddenly empty and he was gone. Cat hesitated, then made herself go to the window and look out. He was running across the grass to the road. His jeans looked reassuringly normal and there were no wings sprouting from his long, brown back. He was human, then, but there'd been something very strange about him. Cat sat down weakly at the table and gulped her cooling coffee. This was all getting too much for her. As soon as her legs stopped shaking she was going to find Fen: she wanted deliverance from angels and witches.

Extract from Michael's Stallion Book

It's three months now since the shaman called me to him in the dream. Strange months. It began that night with him breathing himself into me. Then I got a phone call a couple of nights later from Abbey Carter, down in the village. I'd seen her about, couldn't miss her, her being so tall with all that long, red hair. In her early fifties. Her husband left her last year for a younger woman. More fool him. He didn't know what he was leaving. Young women are still empty, no experience of anything. Older ones are wiser with more to give a man.

Abbey told me she'd just joined with two other women in the village to form a sort of Writers' Group, working on a local project about the big standing stone behind these cottages. The Bridestone. She said the group was called 'Hecate', and she laughed. I looked it up when she rang off. Hecate was the triple-headed goddess — being three of them I suppose that's why they chose the name. Supposedly this Hecate was full of a terrible and perverse sexuality. And into witchcraft. Now I know them better it suits them perfectly — three outwardly sedate middle-aged ladies seething away underneath and sexually insatiable, thanks to their Hormone Replacement Therapy. Given them all a second bite at the apple and they are savouring every moment. Every bite. Abbey asked me to take the three of them up to the Bridestone — someone had told her I know a lot about local history. Not as much as I would like to.

The other two women are Olivia Watson, from the Post Office, and Amy Martin, who lives in a bungalow full of cats at the far end of the village. They came here in Olivia's car — Abbey rides an old bike and Amy walks everywhere. Or rides her broomstick. I took them up past the cottages through the wood to the stone, me making nice gentle conversation so as not to startle these middle-aged ladies. Them wondering how to get inside my jeans, if I'd only known it. When we got up to the Bridestone they were very impressed with it. 'Phallic!' they kept exclaiming. Saying how big it is — it is big, well over seven feet, broad as well. With a flat stone slab in front of it. I'd never thought much about this slab. I was telling the other two a bit about the history of standing stones and I turned round and saw Abbey. She'd laid herself out flat on the slab and her red hair was spread all round her.

And everything changed. I saw her through the shaman's eyes and her hair turned to blood and ran from the stone and her throat was cut from ear to ear like a grinning mouth. I saw her lying there, dead and sacrificed. Then it faded and when I looked again it was Abbey lying there, smiling up at me. But that's what the stone slab was — I know that now: it was the killing stone. Amy is as sharp as a needle. Pointy little face and long silver hair, never been married. She knew something was wrong. She peered at me and wanted to know what I'd seen to make me go so white. I didn't tell them then but I told them afterwards. When I knew that these three were important to me and all a part of the things to come. They said they were writing something for a 'performance' and needed my advice. Twice a week they needed my advice, and they looked at me oh so slyly up there under the Bridestone with their spiral-bound notebooks and their pens.

And that same week Fen moved into the cottage next door and came to work at the stables with me. Mrs Barton brought her across the yard to meet me. I was in with Bel and I heard him whinny and swing round to the door. He liked her from the start. And I looked up and there she was, like a corn-maiden, all long, wheat-coloured hair and legs in faded jeans that went on for ever. And very blue eyes. I knew she was special from the start. Not for me, though, not this one. I knew that from the start as well.

Chapter Four

For the stallion there were no seasons of desire. For him, all seasons were alike, all mares were for him to cover. Now in his prime, he could have covered forty mares this summer. He teased at the neck of the mare standing to the right of him, as ready now as he would be tomorrow or any of the summer days. Bel. It was Michael who called him that. Bel, the shining one, the healer, the sun. His stud name was Cleveland Beauty of Ramsdale but that was no name to call him by. Michael thought how fine he looked, his dark coat shining as if it were polished. It was a splendid animal, a stallion. Inside the stallion book where he wrote down everything concerning Bel, there was an old brochure from when he was being used fully and was properly at stud. There was a photo on the front of it showing a younger Michael proudly holding Bel on a stallion bridle, the horse's legs carefully positioned to show him off to his best advantage. Michael admired the photo every time he wrote in the book.

The mare was slightly smaller than Bel's great sixteen two hands and was lighter in colour. She had entered her period of oestrus two days before and would accept Bel only for a few days more. She straddled her legs now and, pushing down, urinated profusely. The man holding her head spoke softly to her and she bared her teeth and whickered at him. This was an older mare. She had had three foals by Bel already. She had taken the thrust of him before – there was no need to use the twitch on her soft upper lip, no need to immobilize her for him. She wouldn't kick out at him.

Mare and stallion were ready to bring together. Michael moved Bel carefully into position behind her, all the time talking to him, encouraging him. The stallion placed himself and reared, crashing down on the mare as if he would crush her. His long weapon slid into the mare as if it were oiled. The girl standing holding the mare's bound tail out of his way watched her carefully, but she stood accepting him, taking only a short step forward to brace herself. The stallion's tail was flagging up and down, a sure sign that he was ejaculating. Michael put his hand gently under him and by the pulsations throbbing under his fingers knew that Bel had picked up his own perfect rhythm. Ejaculation took place in just under two minutes.

Cat stood by the gate. She discovered that she was holding on to it so tightly that her fingers hurt and she let go of it stiffly. She watched the stallion enter the mare; she saw the long crouching thrust of him and it seemed to her that it was herself he was entering, her flesh he was penetrating. She felt as if she were the mare, felt herself open and flow out to that great strength. She felt the piston strokes of him pumping into her and she leant forward against the gate with her legs shaking under her. Then it seemed as if the stallion were changing shape, splitting in two as she watched him. A man was walking round the stallion's hind-quarters. He was wearing tight, faded jodhpurs and shiny brown boots and his half-open shirt showed a mass of hair on his broad chest. For a moment, he was still the stallion for Cat and she wanted him to come to her, to take her and mount her. He swung abruptly away as Bel withdrew from the mare. Only then did Cat take in that the girl standing by the mare's bound tail was Fen, and was jealous of her for being there. She hardly noticed that it was her angel by the mare's head. Bel and the man came towards her, the stallion dancing and whinnying, looking back over his shoulder, reluctant to leave his mare. They came towards the gate and Cat fumbled at the latch, dragged it open. The man nodded briefly at her and she saw how his hair was the exact colour of the stallion's coat. She moved back as the sweating horse came through the gateway in a flurry of hooves and clattered off across the yard.

Fen and the angel were leading the mare slowly across the field to the open gate. They were talking together and patting the mare's neck as they came. It was as if the performance was over and the players were moving off-stage now that the ceremony was made. It was only then that Cat saw the three women standing further along the fence from her. They were staring at her with a curious, greedy look as if she were one of the performers. Cat looked away from them and stood hesitating by the gate. She wanted to talk to Fen, but not when she was with the angel. Her body didn't feel as if it belonged to her; her head was full of shifting erotic images. Images of both the stallion and the man.

Michael. She could feel herself wet for him, could imagine throwing herself down at those booted feet and begging him to fuck her. No wonder that every second sentence of Fen's began with the word 'Michael'. Cat knew why now. She turned and ran.

Fen and Michael came across the courtyard and walked under the archway to find Cat sitting on the grass verge, hugging her knees and waiting for them. Michael's arm was round Fen's shoulders and she was listening to something he was telling her. Her face lit up when she saw Cat. 'There you are!' she said. 'I wondered where you'd got to – I wanted to show you Bel.'

'I saw him,' said Cat. She looked at Michael. He was

even better close to. Handsome didn't apply to him, his face was too strong, he was too hard for that. From the bulge in his tight jodhpurs he identified himself with the stallion as much as Cat had done. There was a rank, animal attraction all over the man and, at the same time as it drew Cat to him, something in her was uneasy at the way she was responding to him. He smelled of horse, of sweat. Of sex. Cat felt vulnerable crouching in the grass at his feet. She scrambled up and opened her mouth to say something witty and sophisticated, but nothing came out except a strangled squeak.

'Michael, this is Cat,' said Fen.

He took Cat's hand and shook it briefly, smiling at her. 'Nice to meet you. Fen's talked a lot about you. You'll find it a bit quiet for you here after London.'

His voice coaxed, teased at her. It was the voice which he used for the horses, his stallion voice, a shade lower and softer than his usual speaking voice. This was a voice which made both animals and women want to wag their tails at him and lick his hand.

'Quiet,' repeated Cat. She thought of her day so far. She'd met a witch, got egg all over her, been terrified by an angel and seen the stallion in action. And her response to Michael scared her: she had never desired anyone the way she wanted this man now.

Fen was looking at Cat in surprise. She'd never seen her so lost for words. 'Are you okay? You look very white.'

'I'm fine,' managed Cat. 'It's all this fresh air before breakfast. I'm not used to it.'

Michael laughed and, reaching out, touched Cat on the shoulder. 'I'll see you both later,' he said and strolled across the road, where he went up the path into his own cottage. Cat would have happily followed him home.

'Are you sure you're all right? Come on, let's go and

get something to eat before you pass out on me. Isn't Bel beautiful?'

'Yes. And Michael is . . .' Cat trailed off, at a loss for the right word.

'Yes, isn't he?' said Fen laughing at her. 'Isn't he just?'

Michael shouted through to Sally in the kitchen to ask her if she'd seen the proper little teaser who'd arrived next door yet – there was no answer apart from a loud clattering of pans. He grinned and got out his stallion book from the cupboard. He stroked the leather cover before he opened it and began to write. He liked the feel of this book: he'd found it in a chest up in the attics of Fox Hall when he was mending a broken window and had taken it for his own. It was an old tradition, that the groom kept a book where he wrote down details of horse management. Michael liked that idea but his book was more than that: part diary, part dream record, it was thick with cuttings and photos glued in, with his thoughts and ideas all mixed up with his care for Bel.

'The weather is fine and mild,' he wrote. 'The stallion covered Pride of Harrogate. This will probably be her last foal by him because of her age. She goes home to Harrogate in three days. Stud fees all paid up. Horse box coming for her 10 a.m. Bel made a good covering. He is very fit, as fit as I can get him.'

She was the last of Bel's summer brides, thought Michael. In the old days it would have been the other way round. The stallion would have gone to the mares, not the mare come to him. Michael would have liked that, going from farm to farm along the valley, walking the dusty roads with Bel. The men would have been out in the fields making hay; only the women would have been there to greet him, itching under their long skirts at the sight of Bel. Michael and Bel together, covering their brides. Queer how just looking at the stallion did that to some women. Not to Fen – but then it was her job and she was very professional about it. And Bel liked her – that was important. She was as deep as an unruffled pool, was Fen. Michael was sure she was still a virgin. But her friend wasn't. Michael had known by her swollen mouth and the look in her eyes how she'd responded to watching the stallion. And to him. He could have had her then when he touched her shoulder. She was a bonny lass, great dark eyes and that cropped hair. No good as a breeder, her hips were too narrow for that, but her breasts were beautiful, set high on her. Strange how women's bodies were all so different but all so beautiful in their own way. All women had it, that something special about them. Michael wanted every woman he saw; it saddened him that he couldn't make love to them all, make them all feel beautiful.

He sighed and, bending his head, began to write again. 'The new woman has arrived. I put the idea into Fen's head and brought her in as I hoped. Her name is Cat.'

Cat. Daft name, but it suited her. Dark little kit-cat.

The smell of frying bacon crept through the cottage next door. Cat sat at the table, cradling a mug of steaming tea, watching Fen.

'Are you feeling better now? You were so pale before.' Fen turned the sizzling rashers in the frying pan.

'I'm fine. I just had a very strange morning. You keep telling me how quiet it is up here but my life in London is a rest cure compared to this place.'

'What d'you mean?'

'What do I mean? I got out of bed this morning ready for one of these quiet days. I leant out of the window to admire the view. The witch next door fastened me down to the window-sill and her imp of a daughter threw an egg at me.'

'What witch?' Fen broke two brown eggs into the pan and began to spoon fat over their dark yellow centres. 'You mean Sally? She's okay. I told you Patsy was a menace. She didn't really throw an egg at you, did she?'

'The egg shell's still up in the bedroom if you need proof. And I couldn't get the window up, I was stuck there.'

Fen was looking worried now. 'It does stick sometimes. No wonder you were pale.'

'Oh that's not all. I had my bath and came downstairs and made a cup of coffee. I turned round and there was an angel standing looking at me through the window.'

'An angel? A real angel? Cat, there's no such thing!'

'I thought he was one at the time. He was with you in the field.'

'Oh, you mean Ash.' Fen looked relieved. 'Yes, I suppose he does look like an angel. All those golden curls.'

'And the expression – very Burne-Jones. That remote, holier-than-thou look. Judging me. Why was he peering in at me anyway?'

'He wasn't. He'd be looking for me.' Fen divided the food on to two plates and put one in front of Cat. 'There, get that inside you. He lives at the pub in the village but he spends most of his time over at the stables. And he helps Michael in the garden. He goes up to the Bridestone on the moor top most mornings, that's why he'd be coming down past the cottage. He wouldn't mean to startle you, he's a very gentle person.'

'So that's the angel. Then I came to find you and saw the stallion at it.'

Fen grinned. 'I did tell you he was at stud. Isn't he a lovely animal? He has quite a temper but Ash can handle him so well. Michael says in the old days Ash would have been a whisperer – one of those men who could tame horses just by whispering in their ears.'

Michael's name fell like a stone between them.

'Michael,' said Cat, pushing her empty plate away from her. 'Tell me about him.'

Fen folded her arms and leant across the table to Cat. The two heads came close and their voices grew softer.

'He's very strange,' said Cat.

'And very sexy.'

Cat looked at Fen in surprise. It was rare for Fen to get excited over anything male with two legs.

'Yes, I know. Not like me, is it. I've never met a man like him before. There's something about his voice.'

'And his body.' A grin spread over Cat's face, mirrored exactly on Fen's. 'I wonder what he's like in bed?'

'Hung like a horse I expect. Him and Bel together,' said Fen dreamily.

'That would explain the attraction.'

'Oh you know me, Cat. I'm just sexually lazy. Really, I seem to have stayed in the same place as I was when we left school. You'd been through half the male staff by then, including the window cleaner. The Italian one you claimed to be sketching.'

'I'd forgotten him. He wasn't important Fen, you knew that. You were the one who mattered. Still are.'

'At least I don't thump you in the face.'

Cat put her hand up to her bruise and shuddered. 'Let's not talk about Harry. Your work at the stables must mean you're with Michael most of the day?'

'There's feeding, cleaning out, cleaning tack. More work when there's a visiting mare, obviously. And I exercise the two old mares. Go to the village on errands for Mrs Barton. Michael does her garden with Ash and Sally cleans for her a couple of hours a day.'

'Is he easy to talk to?'

'He listens. He likes to talk about the history of this area – the Bridestone, that kind of thing.'

'What is this stone? You said my angel went up there.'

'It's a standing stone, a very big one with a flat stone in front of it. It was one of the things I thought you might like to draw. Michael says I can be off during the day when you're here. I only need help him with morning and night feeds. It was his idea to ask you here, you know.'

'Michael's idea?' Cat was startled. 'How did he know about me?'

'He likes to hear about when we were at school to-gether. Things we got up to.'

'I hope you didn't tell him all the things we got up to?'

Fen laughed and shook her head. 'No, of course not. He said to ring you up when I did. Said that it was the right time.'

'It was more than that – it was a miracle. I needed to get away from Harry. Besides, it was far too long since we'd last seen each other.'

'Yes, it was. What would you like to do now? You've had a queer start to your holiday, what would you like to do for the rest of the day?'

'Please can we go to the beach?' asked Cat with no hesitation. 'I'd like to go somewhere nice and peaceful, where there are no witches and no angels. Can we?'

'Good idea.' Fen stretched, then gathering up the dirty plates, turned to put them in the sink. 'There's a little beach next to Raven's Bay you'll like. There's only a footpath down to it, no road, and it's very rocky so not many people bother with it. And it's going to be hot. Pack your pads and pencils while I wash this lot.'

'And my bikini?'

'Of course,' said Fen gravely. 'Give the gulls a treat.'

Extract from Michael's Stallion Book

I rode Bel out on the moor this morning to stretch his legs and take the edge off him a bit. He gets very nervy when there is a mare staying with us. I took him up as far as the Bridestone. It was very early and there was a thin mist of heat up there. It made the stone look strange, as if it was floating in the queer light. Sent shivers down my back and spooked Bel. No wonder Stonehenge has a big effect on people. I will get to see it one of these days. All those bad scenes there shouldn't happen, the trouble between the police and the New Travellers. Children of Albion, who quoted Blake, determined to be allowed access to the last great source of power. There is still a link between the old stones and the people. How strong it must have been in times past.

I see this more, since the night the shaman breathed himself into me. I see how past and present are one natural stream, how the shaman could bring about a strange, collective dream state in his tribe and make them one with the world around them. I can feel something of this when I ride Bel. He's a wise creature, picking up signs when we're out that I never even see. A rabbit in the bracken, a place where a fox has tainted the path. There is no finer animal than the stallion.

Strange that I didn't first think of a horse when I needed something I could give my women as a totem, something to centre their concentration on and power-up for themselves. Then I had to go to the post office for some stamps for Mrs Barton and Olivia was unpacking a box of toys. There was one standing on the counter – it was a small plastic horse. One of those which are always advertised so much at Christmas on TV, exciting small girls. Patsy has one. She only ever wanted the horse, not the long-haired dolly and the fitted wardrobe that go with it. I picked up the toy and as soon as I touched it I knew. It burnt like fire against my skin and I knew that this was what I'd been looking for. Olivia looked at me in surprise when I bought six of them, laughing at my expression.

'Wait,' I said. 'Wait until I show you what we'll do with them.'

That night I gathered the three women together in Abbey's cottage. They knew something of what I was going to do: there was so much tension and sexual need in that room I could feed on it. Abbey switched off the lights and lit candles round the room. She said she had a surprise for me and she took the women out. I sat cross-legged on the rug in front of the fire, my back to the crackling wood flames, and stood the three little horses in a row in front of me. My head was full of images of white flesh. I've fucked a lot of women in my time but never more than one at once. Three of them.

They came silent and barefoot back into the room to stand in a line in front of me. For the first time they were wearing their long black robes with hoods, fastened only at the waist with a sash. In the firelight I could see their legs, the pale flesh of the curve of their round stomachs. They were wearing masks and I sat and stared up at them in amazement at the cleverness of this idea. The masks covered the top half of their faces and below them their mouths were slashes of bright red lipstick. Abbey was a soft-faced hare, pale-furred and long-whiskered with black-tipped ears. Amy was a crow. The shining black feathers and the sharp pointed beak swung to me where I sat. And Olivia was a shaggy-headed wolf, grey and long-muzzled. They stood and looked down at me, then slowly untied their sashes and let their robes fall open. And I saw that their nipples, too, were scarlet-tipped with lipstick. They stood and waited for my approval. 'Oh yes,' I nodded. 'Well done, my ladies.' And crow and hare and wolf dipped and nodded to me.

'Kneel down,' I said and they sank to the floor in a rustle of skirts. They looked at the little horses and waited. For a long minute I sat in silence and let them wait. 'Take off your robes,' I said then, and they shrugged them off to sit naked in the flickering light. They were rosy-skinned where the firelight touched them, pale as milk in the shadows. I let them leave on their masks above their bare skin for they helped to build up the magic — masks are very strange things, they transform and release the wearer. I needed the women to leave themselves behind. I stood and pulled off my clothes and heard the women's indrawn breath as they saw how I was already hard and erect for them. I crouched beside Abbey and stroked her heavy breasts with their blood-red nipples and she lay back against the rug and stretched out her long legs. I slid my fingers into the red bush of hair at her cunt and she was wet for me. I took one of the little horses and rubbed it there at the red cleft, rubbed the smooth back and haunches against her until she moaned and whimpered for me to go into her. I laid the little horse on the warm skin of her stomach and thrust into her. She came with a quick yelp and I could hear Olivia moaning next to her as she did.

When I turned to her, Olivia had her fingers on herself. She was on her back with the wolf's mask turned up to the shadowed ceiling. I caught hold of her hips and rubbed my thumbs across the soft skin there, stroked down the pale skin to the dark bush of hair at her cunt and my fingers joined her slippery ones as I stroked the second horse against her. She caught hold of my prick and groaned for me to go into her, coming with a long cry as I slid in, holding me to her as if she would never let me go. I waited until she was still again and kissed her, left her grieving and came to the last one. Amy.

I knew she'd never been with a man and I wanted it to be good for her. That's why I left her until the last, until she'd seen me with the other two. She was crouching on her heels with her arms round her knees, crow head on one side, beady eyes glinting in the firelight. I stroked her throat and she cawed at me, harsh and mocking as if to say she was not so easy. I sat back and watched her and there was only the sound of the fire settling in the room. Then Abbey was at one side of her and Olivia at the other, kissing her hunched shoulders, stroking her curved back. She

41

rocked herself backwards and forwards, then reluctantly lay on her back, scissoring her legs together as if they were stitched. I reached out and stroked her and she was rigid with tension. Then Abbey's head bent to a breast and she began to suck gently at the red nipple, and Olivia's hands were stroking down over the soft skin. Amy groaned and parted her legs for Olivia's coaxing fingers and I saw with delight how the thatch of hair at her cunt was pure silver, strange and beautiful. I let them suck and kiss at her with their red mouths until I was ready again — it excited me watching them with her. I picked up the last little horse and touched Amy with it between her legs and she gasped at the smooth roundness of it against her. Then I took her quickly while the two women soothed and gentled her. I tried not to hurt her and I was not so hard as with the first two. She didn't come but it didn't matter, not for this first time. There would be other and better times for her. She was the same as Olivia and Abbey now and that was what was important. Then it was done and all three horses were ritualized, given their first magical power and receptive to more.

The women pulled on their robes and we sat in a ring, all four bound together with joined hands. I knew that they had all wanted me by the way that they looked at me, by the way they were for ever touching me. Making them wait then taking them all at the same time had built up their need to a high peak of desire that night. Oh, I was so proud of them and they knew it. They sat and watched me like three cats after a dish of thick cream. Licking their lips at me. And belonging to me now, all three of them. Sometimes I wonder how they talk of me among themselves but I never ask them that. That is private to the three of them.

Since that night the women have carried their little horses with them everywhere. It was their own idea to decorate them as they have, with flowers and ribbons, bones and feathers. They'd seen how the heavy horses were decorated at the village show and it gave them the idea of what to do — it's the same idea really, horse brasses and knots of ribbons for protection. And later we ritualized *the amulet bags which they hang round their necks, the fetish bags they use when they are blessing the Bridestone. I am so lucky to have these three. They are drawing on things inside themselves and day by day grow stronger.*

Chapter Five

ABBEY Carter rode her old black bicycle towards the cottages just in time to see the Mini drive off along the coast road. In the basket on the handlebars was the rabbit; it was still warm, more or less unmarked from the car which had killed it on the lane outside Abbey's cottage early that morning. Its one remaining eye stared glassily up at Abbey as she propped her bike against the garden wall. Make the new one welcome, Michael had said. Widen the ring to bring her in. Abbey grinned slyly to herself. She'd make her welcome in her own way.

She'd seen her at the stallion-mating. Abbey had seen how young she was, how her breasts sat high on her and how narrow her hips were. Abbey had been like that, once. But ripeness is all, she told herself firmly. She was fifty-six and Michael needed her, used her along with the other two in his ceremonies. The new one might be young, but Abbey had years of experience. She knew how to please Michael. She thought of his hard body against hers and shivered happily.

Lifting out the rabbit by the ears, she checked that her small, sharp knife was in the pocket of her long skirt. She opened the garden gate and went up the path to the porch – the door wasn't locked. She knew it wouldn't be.

Cat looked down at the drawing. She wasn't satisfied with it, but then she never was. It was as if there were a gap she fell down with the first mark on the paper: she saw what she wanted to draw in her head, but that first mark failed her. She'd caught something of Fen in it, the

44

way she sat so straight-backed, with her plait of hair hanging like an old-fashioned bell-pull on the brown skin. Fen was sitting at the edge of the rocks, watching the sea break below her. Cat got up and went across to her to drop the sketch pad on her lap. 'There you are. That's you.'

Fen studied the drawing. 'I look all legs.'

'That's because you are.' Cat lay back against a slab of rock and closed her eyes. The first faint prickling of the sun on her skin took her like the beginnings of desire. She loved the sun. She and Fen used to spend long summer afternoons in the seeding grass behind the old sports pavilion, hours filled with the scent of new cut grass and the dull pocking of tennis balls. The first touching of their mouths had led to a journey into unknown territory. She sighed, remembering how heightened everything had been then. 'D'you remember that time in the swimming pool?'

Fen turned to look at her in surprise. 'What made you think of that?'

'The water, I suppose. Is it one of the stories you tell Michael?'

Fen said nothing. Cat sat up and stared at her. 'It is. You've told him about the swimming pool.'

Fen nodded. 'He loves it.'

'I'm not surprised.' Cat lay back down again and behind her closed eyes, she remembered. It had been after a swimming lesson in the indoor pool, late on a winter evening. The pool lights had been switched off; the pool was empty. Only Cat and Fen with four of their friends were still in the changing room, peeling off their one-piece regulation suits. Cat held hers up in disgust, saying how nice it would be to swim bare instead, to feel the water against their skin.

'Let's try it,' said Fen and called to the other girls.

The six of them pattered back over the white tiles to the edge of the pool, where a blue dusk coming through the curving glass roof was the only light. Like little fishes they went into the water, their wet, smooth heads gleaming.

The dark and the feel of the water excited them so that they began to romp like puppies, rolling and tussling with one another, then suddenly the pool lights came on, harsh and glaring. The caretaker stood there on the edge of the pool, shouting at them to get out of the water, threatening to report them all. There had been no more swimming for them that term. The caretaker looked so slyly, so knowingly at them after that, as if he were thinking of their breasts cutting the dark water.

A gull came screeching overhead as Cat let herself fall away into a blood-red haze, listening to the crashing of the waves. Fen's voice startled her as she knelt beside her. She was offering to oil her. 'You make me sound like an old bike,' said Cat lazily.

'You'll look like an old boiler if you don't. You're already burning. It's the sea air, makes you feel cooler than you really are.'

The smell of the sun-tan cream drifted to Cat. Fen's fingers touched her feet, sending messages in braille along her legs, reaffirming patterns of response laid down a long time ago. The messages came in shorthand to Cat now, but they were still strong and reassuring. Fen's fingers stroked and smoothed at Cat's legs, brushed down her flat stomach to the cleft between her legs. She poured more cream on to her fingers and, pulling aside the black triangle of cloth began to smooth it on to the pale, shaved skin. Her fingers were pressing harder now and the gull screeched derisively overhead as Cat arched her back and groaned, feeling herself begin to come. Fen's fingers were sliding inside her to the red softness there,

46

and the sound of the waves crashing and the cry of the gull overhead ripped through her as she gave herself to Fen's fingers like a fish caught on a hook. Then there was nothing but a red blur of sun and Fen's mouth coming hard on hers.

The heat of the day was draining slowly away by the time they reluctantly climbed back up the steep cliff path to the car. They had forgotten the maze pattern waiting for them on the porch floor the first time they'd gone into the cottage together.

This time the smell hit them as soon as they opened the porch door. That and the heat. Already flies were buzzing round the gutted rabbit where it lay spread on the tiles in the middle of the floor, its innards laid out like a message round it in a glistening purple and red coil. The smell gagged at Cat's throat. She backed out to the porch door, pulling Fen with her, and gulped at the fresh air. The dead rabbit was not the only offering. There were some letters drawn with a bloody finger on the faded white paint of the inner door. Cat made them out with difficulty. Epona.

Michael padded through the soft, warm dark across the road and over to the stallion's box. Bel came to meet him and blew softly at the front of Michael's shirt before turning back to his hay net. Michael stood for some time listening to him feed, then, sure that all was well with him, came back across the yard on to the grass at the road-side. Fen's cottage was all in darkness. They must be having an early night. He stared at the blank window of Fen's bedroom and wondered why she was so important, why the shaman sent him so many images of her . . . and behind his eyes something shifted, sickening him, turning him faint. His legs shook so that he thought he was going to fall and, crouching down on the grass, he covered his face with his hands. He was looking now through the shaman's eyes and he saw Fen walking naked through a field of flowers. Her hair was loose, spilling long and silver down her back. She was the goddess, proud and regal, walking along a sandy track where green blades of wheat came springing as her bare feet touched the soil. There was a group of mares running towards her, manes and tails flying. They flared their red nostrils at the musky smell of her and wheeled to stand around her. She reached out and touched their swelling, shining flanks and, at her touch, they were in foal. She pushed through the mares and came to stand in front of him, and he saw how her stomach curved high on her in early pregnancy. She took his hand and placed it on herself and he felt himself harden at the feel of her warm, rounded flesh and then he was Michael again, crouching sick and confused on the grass.

A baby? Fen's baby? Was that what this was all about? It wasn't his child; he knew she wasn't for him. She was being saved for something else. Or somebody. He was beginning to understand that when the shaman had chosen him that night it wasn't so much for himself as for what he must do with the women. He was drawing them together for an unseen end. He wondered again whose baby Fen had been carrying and felt a terrible, sad envy that he was not to father it.

Extract from Michael's Stallion Book

Ash went with me this afternoon in the Land Rover to Thornton le Dale. Mrs Barton buys her hay from a farm there, straight out of the field, and I went over to check it was the usual high standard. It's good hay this year, plenty about now, and this was fine. Smelt right, looked right and has a good variety of grasses and flowers in it. Plenty of clover and Bel likes that. Ordered the usual amount. It's cheaper bought like this – by next winter it will be up to £3.50 a bale, like last year. Ash enjoyed himself. He doesn't get out very far. He's surprisingly good company for someone who doesn't say very much. Very restful to be with.

He's a good lad, is Ash. His father doesn't think so – Dave at the Fox and Hounds in the village. I don't often go in there but one night after I'd had one of the usual rows with Sally I went down there to get away from her. It's clean enough and there's always a big open fire going but I've never cared for Dave. He's been a bitter man since his wife died. No need for him to take it out on Ash, though. There's tales in the village that he knocks the lad about.

Ash was helping in the bar that night. He came round to collect some dirty glasses from a gang of strangers that was in – flash town gits in suits. They started to make fun of him, laughing at his long hair and calling him 'Flossy'. He just ignored them but that wasn't enough for them. One of them stuck out a foot and tripped him up, sending him flying with a tray full of empty glasses. There was broken glass everywhere and he'd banged his head on a table going down. He just sat there with these yobs laughing at him, then one of them poured the remains of his drink over Ash's head. And I looked round to see what Dave was going to do about it to find that he wasn't going to do anything at all. He was just leaning on the bar watching, sneering at Ash.

I went and helped the lad to his feet and picked up the broken

49

glasses. *The yobs took one look at my face and left, as soon as they realized there wasn't going to be anything else to laugh at.*

'Useless lump,' was all his father said when I put the tray with the glasses on it down on the bar. 'Nowt but trouble, you are. Flossy!' He tossed Ash a tea towel to dry his head with.

'I need someone to help me in the garden up at Fox Hall,' I said. 'And to give me a hand with the stallion and the stables — if you like horses.'

Ash stopped wiping his face. He had a look on it now like a dog gets when you say, 'Walkies!' 'You're the stallion man,' he said. 'You ride Bel.'

See, he even knew the horse's name before he ever came to work here. 'Would you like to come to work with Bel? The money's not very good but —'

'What does he want with money?' cut in his father. 'Have you taken a close look at him? He hasn't the brains to know what to do with money if he had any. Half the time he doesn't even know what day of the week it is. He'll come to work for you, don't worry. I'll be glad to get the useless bugger out from under my feet.'

'Ash?' I said, and waited for his answer.

'Tomorrow?' he said and smiled at me. That was when I realized how beautiful he is. I held out my hand and he shook it doubtfully, as if he wasn't used to doing it. 'Tomorrow morning,' I said, and went out, before I smashed Dave's face in.

In an old book I found a saying by some great philosopher that 'Horses are taught not by Harshness but by Gentleness.' It's true enough of Ash. I watched him very carefully the first few times he went in with Bel, but Bel took to him straight away, like he did with Fen. Some days the stallion works better for me, but often he is better with Ash. The lad is a born natural, it's as if he knows what the horse is thinking. It was the best thing I ever did for Bel, getting Ash to work here. A lot of the splendid way Bel looks this summer is due to the way Ash has cared for him.

It works with people as well, of course, that old saying. I've never shouted at Ash because I know he'll go to pieces. I leave him a lot of the time just to go by his own instincts. He spends hours in the loose-box with Bel, just keeping him company. And I noticed a queer thing fairly early on with Ash: he gets turned on by Bel. I don't mean that he's putting lipstick kisses all over the horse the minute my back is turned, I mean that he is so close to Bel that when the horse gets roused up then so does he. Sometimes I catch them with their heads close together and a certain look on Ash's face and it's daft but I feel jealous, left out.

He does as I tell him but I need more from him than that. The women belong to me and are centred on me because of the sex link which is so powerful. I need that link with Ash. I still don't know what the shaman wants of me, but I know that Ash fits in somewhere as much as my women do.

A couple of weeks ago, on one of the first really hot days that we've had, Ash was in the loose box, cleaning out, stripped to his waist. He was wearing a pair of very old, faded jeans with half the seat ripped out. I leaned over the door of the box and stood watching, and I wanted him. It's never happened to me before, this, it's always been women with me. It was his long, muscled back and the glimpse of white skin through the torn jeans. I wanted to taste him, to feel him. I went into the box and took the fork from his hands to lean it against the wall, then I took him by the shoulders and turned him to face me, so gently because I was afraid of scaring him off. I cradled his head in my hands and stroked his small ears with my thumbs and kissed him. His mouth was unmoving under mine; it was like kissing a wax dummy, he was so still. I ran my hands down his back and slid my fingers into the tear in his jeans to touch the curve of his small bottom, and for the first time in my life I got an erection with another man. I pulled him to me and hugged him hard up against me so that he could feel it.

He stood leaning against me then, very hesitantly, he put his arms round me and held me. It was strange, feeling the strength of another man like that. I licked his bare shoulder and bit him,

51

very gently, and he tasted of sweat and of horse. He grinned then, looking very carefully into my eyes. 'We're the same,' he said, and laughed.

I couldn't think what he meant and then I realized. We're exactly the same height, Ash and I, just over six feet. 'So we are,' I said and slapped him on the bottom, told him to get on and finish cleaning out the loose box. He picked up the fork so obediently that I saw that if I am careful with him and don't hurt him, I can reach him through sex. Then since I never waste a good erection, I came looking for Sally. Somehow I must use Ash with the women. Get him to have sex with one of the three on her own at first, I think. Abbey. She's the most experienced, the most motherly of the three. Amy doesn't have enough sex wisdom for him and Olivia isn't much better.

Cat is the teaser for him, that's why she's here, as an extra mare is sometimes used at a stallion mating. Led out to excite the horse before the true mare, to urge him on to cover his true bride. There is a lot of space in him to be filled up – that's why he has such a lot of untapped power. I want to teach him to use sex to make his own magic. Teach him that it's a good thing. And if I admit it, I want him for myself.

Chapter Six

ALICE Denby sat in the late sunlight spilling into her living-room and wrote to her daughter.

Dear Cat,

It seems very strange to me that your father and I spent so much on your education, yet you don't seem to be able to write a single postcard. Not that your father has noticed that you haven't written since you went away. All we've had from you in a week is that one brief phone call to say you'd arrived. I've rung you several times but there was no reply. Your father is busy with his patients. There is somehow never any time for me.

I walked through Regent's Park today in Queen Mary's rose garden. The roses were falling and the people were speaking in code as they passed me. It's very hot in London. It's been like this since you went. Everywhere I looked there were lovers lying in the grass; the grass was the wrong colour. The lovers frightened me – I didn't know the years would go so quickly. They should have warned me. I shall never lie in the summer grass with a lover now. All the living is in you. There's no air in the city streets. At night, a dog barks, over and over, in the mews. I am afraid that it is chained up, that there's something hurting it. But what can I do?

The papers say it's the hottest summer since the days of Nell Gwyn. How hot the women must have been then, in those dusty bells of skirts. All gone to nothing; the streets of London are full of ghosts. Strange that there are none in this old house. Unless of course it will be me. I often now can't sleep these hot nights but walking the dark stairs I meet no one but myself, hear nothing but my heart beat drumming the walls. There were two dead rats in the street today. I think this is a sign.

And the blood flows as if it would drain me dry. But how can you know what it is to be in the change of life? (And I am so afraid of what I am being changed into.) You are so young. I saw your breasts in the garden. Mine were like that once, when your father loved to touch them. A long time ago.

The flat is very quiet without you. I know so little of your life these days. Once you were small, and all mine. What happened between you and that nice young man? You went off to Yorkshire so suddenly. Maybe you'll meet someone up there and fall in love with him.

I'll be the old woman in black at your wedding.

I'll weep for you and tear my breasts until the blood runs blood blood blood.

Alice put down her pen. This wasn't a suitable letter for a mother to send to her daughter. She tore it carefully into small pieces and, going to the window, tossed them out. They hung suspended on the still air, then drifted down into gardens, over walls, out of sight. A piece landed on the windowsill of the room below, where Simon stood by the open window, waiting for his patient to dress. Picking it up, Simon read the word 'blood' with some dismay.

'What are you doing now, my darling, what are you doing now?' said Alice, pausing in front of the long, gilt mirror in the hall. She was clutching in one hand the piece of paper with Cat's address on it, for it was all of Cat she had for now. She peered into the mirror, uncertain as to who this old woman was, peering back. 'I'm melting,' she said sadly. The edges of herself were blurred. The flesh was moving down from her throat, her shoulders, to congeal on her hips and bottom. She turned and studied the line of herself. The curve of her bottom was elongating, pouching at the base. She lifted the hem of her dress. Her ankles were still slim, and her legs from the knee down. Yes, they were hers, but above the knees the old woman was creeping in.

It must be some trick of the light, this old woman. She was still little Alice inside herself. A much loved twelve year old. This body of a woman in her fifties could surely not be her. Leaning towards the mirror, Alice reached out a finger and touched the face in recognition. 'Mother,' she said sadly. 'Mother.' Breathing on the glass, she blurred the face until it could no longer be seen.

The phone shrilled loudly in the room behind her. She turned and hurried to answer its cross demand. 'Cat,' she thought. 'Something's happened to Cat.' Picking up the phone, she said anxiously, 'Cat?'

'Mrs Denby?'

'Yes, yes,' she admitted hastily.

'Could I speak to your daughter, please? I'm a friend of hers.'

'I'm sorry. She's not here. She's gone away to Yorkshire.'

There was a slight pause, then the voice went on smoothly, 'Ah. In that case, could you give me her phone number? I do need to get in touch with her.'

Alice didn't answer. Cat had told her not to give the number to anyone, but what did she tell this nice young man? He had a lovely voice. Dark brown, thought Alice. Simon's voice was . . . blue. Ice-blue and cold.

'Are you still there?' said the voice sharply.

'Yes, I'm still here. I'm sorry, Cat asked me not to give her number to anyone.'

'I'm not just anyone. I'm her friend, you stupid woman. Would you tell me the number, please?'

'No,' said Alice.

'You are as useless as your bitch of a daughter. Tell me, Mrs Denby. How d'you think she got that bruise?'

The line went dead. Alice stood holding the phone to her ear. If she had been worried about Cat before, it was nothing to how she felt now.

Passing the phone on her way upstairs with Fen, Cat thought briefly of ringing her mother. She felt guilty at not having rung her again, but once her mother got on the phone she'd be there for ages, wanting the very last detail. She'd send her a postcard tomorrow instead. All Cat wanted now after another day on the beach was a bath. She was sticky with salt water and sun cream. Turning on the bath taps she took off her shorts and top and studied her reflection. A couple of days on the beach had made a big difference. Her skin was darkening beautifully. Coming into the bathroom behind her, Fen laughed.

'Are you admiring yourself again? Go on, get in the bath and leave the sink for me. I want to wash my hair.'

Cat lay back with a groan of pleasure. 'At least there was nothing nasty waiting in the porch for us today. Makes a change. Talk about something nasty in the woodshed – it has nothing on this place. We still haven't found out what that word means, the one that was written on the door. Epona.'

'I've a feeling it's got something to do with horses. I'll ask Michael tomorrow. I haven't got round to telling him Patsy is up to mischief . . .'

'I'd hardly call leaving us a dead rabbit up to mischief. It's more than that. Can we go somewhere I can send my mother a postcard tomorrow? Or else she'll arrive in person to see what I'm up to.'

'Haven't you sent her one yet? Cat, you are bad. You know how she worries.'

'Makes a career out of it,' said Cat gloomily. 'I have this nightmare about my mother. Did I ever tell you about it? I can see myself on my wedding day, walking down the aisle of Marylebone Church on Father's arm. I'm wearing this long, white dress and veil, and I get to the altar and this figure steps up beside me. I lift my veil and turn to face my groom and it's my mother standing there.'

Fen wrapped a towel round her dripping hair and began to rub it dry. 'You should get away from home. You're a big girl now.'

'That's what Harry jeered at me. Told me to run home to my mother like a good little girl. I wish my mother had a job. Or a lover. She might be more like your mum then.'

'Mine gave up cheerfully on me years ago, when I left school. Turned my bedroom into a study and works there at her magazine stories. She still has James at home doing his A levels until he goes off to university. Did I tell you he's got a girlfriend now? Penny. She's nice. She writes poetry, so Mum loves her, and she's got green fingers and admires Dad's garden, so he thinks she's perfect.'

'How nice,' said Cat. 'How normal.'

Fen dropped the wet towel to the floor. 'Move up and I'll come in with you.' Fastening her wet hair in a knot and sitting down with her back to Cat, Fen folded up her long legs under the taps. Cat began to soap her back.

'When does your job here finish?'

'End of September. Then I think I'll look for something abroad. Do you want to do some riding while you're here? We could take the mares to the village tomorrow if you like. Then you can send your mother that postcard.'

'Yes. Fine. I'd like that. I'll probably fall straight off – I've only ridden a couple of times since we left school.'

'No you won't. It's like riding a bike. You never

57

forget.' Fen reached forward and turned on the hot-water tap.

Cat smoothed the soapy foam round Fen's shoulders and down over her breasts.

'That's nice. Cat, d'you remember that *Emmanuelle* film we went to see? That time we were supposed to be doing research for A levels in the British Museum? The film where they went to that bath place and the girls washed them?'

Cat remembered. It had done more for her education than the dried remains in the British Museum. Slow images flickered through her mind of a kneeling girl bending and rubbing her breasts against the back of the girl lying face down between her legs. Rubbing the soap to a thick lather between her hands, Cat covered her breasts with the clove-scented lather. Edging closer to Fen's back she leant forward until her nipples brushed down on to the brown skin, and Fen shivered and groaned. Cat pulled herself to her knees and arched over.

The line of the two women was delicate, pure; it was a tinted Japanese print in motion. The physical bond made between them years back at their first coming together was still there, the empathy between them as deep as ever. Cat's heavy breasts smoothed and rubbed the long arch of the back, at the top of the arch hanging as perfect as if they could be plucked from her, then, as she put her weight on them, they seemed almost to dissolve down the line of Fen's back from the bent nape of her neck. Water glistened and dripped in rivulets from their wet skin. There was no sound but the falling of these droplets of water and the heavy slapping of the wet flesh as Cat's breasts moved and patterned the gleaming skin. Her hands gripped tightly on the rim of the bath and Fen's hands were on herself between her legs.

Cat began to murmur to her, increasing as she did so the pressure on her breasts, slapping them down on her stiff nipples in a quicker pattern than before. Fen began to move under her, crying out in high, broken sounds, almost like a bird call, louder and louder until she came on a falling cry of Cat's name. The image of the two broke on the cry as they murmured to each other, helping one another out of the water, where they began to dry one another, first Fen and then Cat, lovingly wiping the warm drops from the brown skin.

On the other side of the thin wall Sally sat crouched with her back against it, her arms wrapped in her apron, listening. Faint and distorted as the sound was, Fen's last cry had been unmistakable. 'The mucky little pair,' thought Sally happily. Who would have thought it? Maybe they were more interested in each other than they were in Michael. Not that it made much difference: it was how interested he was in them that mattered. He usually got what he wanted, in the end.

Must be funny, doing it with another woman. She'd never fancied it, herself, though Michael had suggested it once or twice. Three in a bed with him in the middle of the sandwich. Sausage meat. She'd never wanted anyone but Michael, and she'd been a long time getting round to that because she'd been a real slow starter. What chance had she had of anything though, living in that tiny cottage right on the edge of the moor with her mam? Sally had been fat and lumpish, and the other kids had always been at her, saying her mother was a witch. Wanting to know why she had no dad. Even her mam didn't seem too clear on that one. She'd known her mam was different from everyone else's, she'd always known that. For a start, her mam had a crystal ball, even if she wasn't exactly a witch. She'd never been daft enough to tell the kids at school about it, but her mam could see things in it. Once, when she was small, Sally had run into the cottage and had seen her mam sitting in front of the ball and it was smoking, thin white smoke curling up out of it.

The summer that she was sixteen, a letter had come from a cousin of her mam's over in Pickering, asking if Sally would like to go for a holiday. The first holiday she'd ever had. Kath and Tom must have been in their early thirties then, living in a posh little bungalow with a shower. First one of those as well for Sally. One afternoon she'd been using it and Kath had come into the bathroom. Sally hadn't known where to look, standing there with nothing on, but Kath had made a fuss of her and told her she was lovely. She'd asked Sally if she'd ever done it. Sally had gone all colours. Never had the chance. Then Kath asked her if she'd like to see what a man looked like – Tom, of course. The way she said it, Sally couldn't see how to say no.

She went off to bed early and about eleven o'clock she crept round to their bedroom window, feeling stupid. Kath had left the curtains open a crack, like she said she would. Sally peered through and saw Kath come in from the bathroom with just a towel round her. Tom came in after her. Sally held her hands over her face, feeling it burn at seeing him like that. Bollock naked. The first prick she'd ever seen. She thought it was enormous. She hadn't seen Michael's then, of course.

Sally shifted uncomfortably against the wall, remembering how excited she'd got. That autumn she met Michael at a Young Farmers' Dance and after that it was as if she couldn't see anyone else very clearly. She thought it would put him off, meeting her mam, but it hadn't. Maybe it was something to do with him being brought up in that children's home in Leeds. It was as if he wanted to burrow into her family, going over all the

60

old stuff her mam had got from her old gran. He was always trying to get Sally to look in the crystal ball but it was no use — she could never see anything. Her mam said she hadn't got the power, whatever that was. Sometimes Sally thought Patsy must have it. She got a queer, old look on her face sometimes. All gone away. And she saw things, too.

Sally pressed her ear to the wall again, but it was very quiet in there now. Finished whatever they'd been up to. Wait till Mike knew. This would put his nose right out of joint. She would tell him in bed tonight — that should take his mind off that bloody horse for a bit.

'Our Mam, where are you?' shouted Patsy up the stairs. 'The cock's out in the garden, digging up the onions.'

For a startled moment, Sally had a wonderful vision of an enormous prick running wild round the garden, hurling onions in all directions. Getting stiffly to her feet, she hurried down the stairs, hugging to herself the thought of how she would tell Michael about the two next door. There'd been a time, when they were first married, when she would dress up for him, be a different woman every time. Black nights of sex. Once he'd tied her to the bed and left her, went off to the pub for a drink. She'd been so angry with him that when he finally got himself back home and let her loose, she stormed out and left him to it for a few days. Went home to her mother. He turned up there a few days later to bring her home. Fucked her on the floor as soon as they were through the front door here and that was when she started Patsy. After that, somewhere inside herself she'd always been listening for the baby. Not tonight though. Tonight she'd pack Patsy off to bed early and have a bath. She'd wear the black nightie and be what he wanted.

He was later coming home than usual. She got fed up

61

of waiting for him in the end. She left his supper on the table and went up to get ready for bed. She heard him come in and the scraping back of his chair as he finished eating. She lay and listened to his footsteps coming up the stairs and caught her breath at the sight of the figure suddenly outlined blackly in the doorway. She knew it was Michael, but the dark seemed to be all wrapped round him. He looked different. Then he was across the room, pulling off the bedclothes and on her, hard and ready for her without so much as a word.

'Give up,' she said crossly. 'Hang on a bit – what's your rush then?'

He didn't answer her, only pushed himself into her without a sound. She felt how he was changed and she cried out, beating uselessly at him with her fists. His nails raked her breasts as he tore off the black nightie and she whimpered in pain as his hand came down across her mouth. He was pushing himself harder than ever into her and she was being impaled by someone who was her husband but was someone else, someone who felt different and smelled different. All the uneasy feelings that she'd had about Michael lately came roaring into her head and she hurt, she hurt, and he hollowed her out like a knife.

Extract from Michael's Stallion Book

I frightened Sally. I don't really know what I did to her, but I hurt her. I had my supper and went upstairs. I knew she wanted to tell me something, she was bursting with it when I came home earlier for a drink of tea. I can always tell with her. I remember standing in the doorway and seeing her lying there, waiting for me. It was me who went up the stairs, but it was the shaman who took her. I knew afterwards that I'd hurt her – it took me a long time to calm her down and bring her back to me. I told her that I'd just got over excited, but she didn't believe me.

I could never begin to explain it to her.

The difference between the way that the shaman has sex and the way I do is that I never lose the woman, I try to give them as much pleasure as I can. There are some lazy pigs of men around who don't bother – Abbey's husband was one of them. He didn't use his fists on her but he hit her with words instead. Just as bad in a way, she really believed that she was nothing but an ugly old cow. But she's beautiful, round and gentle and loving. Olivia was even sadder. She'd never so much as had an orgasm, all the years she was married. Her husband should never have married her. Or anyone else either. He told her over and over that she was disgusting, that all women's bodies are disgusting, until she believed him. Sex with me isn't the God-given answer, but at least it makes the women feel better about themselves.

With the shaman it's not like that. He uses sex as magic, just to bring him to another state of consciousness. The woman is only there as an instrument for him to do this. Sex is part of his rites. There's no pleasure in it for him, not like there is for me, it's a sort of spiritual experience with him, a doorway through to somewhere else.

It was ages before Sally would let me touch her again. I held her for a long time when she did, just cuddling her. In the end she blurted out what she'd so much wanted to tell me. That she'd heard Cat and Fen through the wall in the bath together. Did I already know that they were lovers? I knew how close they are, you've only got to see them together to realize that. And Fen had given me enough clues when she talked about them at school together, though she never came right out with it.

Fen is still asleep somewhere inside herself. An emotional virgin. She doesn't make any effort to reach out to other people, she has a tight hold on herself. The first few days she was here I couldn't get much response at all from her. She was friendly, but she looked at me with those blue eyes and she might as well have been wrapped in barbed wire. All the signs said keep well back, no entrance. So I did, and she trusts me now, she knows I won't try anything with her. It's strange for me, working with a woman and not having her. I want her friend though. Oh yes, I want Cat. She'll come to me when I call.

Chapter Seven

THE weather changed in the night. A thick fog came creeping inland, pouring into the narrow valley. Without the sun, next morning the cottage rooms seemed smaller; there was a faint, mushroomy smell of damp. When Cat got up and dressed, she pulled on a heavy sweater of Fen's over her shirt. There was no sign of her – she must still be over at the stables. Cat went down the garden path to watch for her, and leant on the gate. Everywhere was changed and different in the clinging mist. Fox Hall and the stable buildings seemed distorted, all out of proportion. There was a warm, green smell of bracken and the grass bank by the gate was pearled with moisture. In the stone wall a spider's web was threaded with white beads. Cat knelt down to look more closely at it, seeing the intricate pattern of fine, wet threads, and wondered if it was worth going back into the cottage for her sketch book. She was startled to hear what sounded like a crowd of small children coming running along the road. She got to her feet and watched as, out of the mist, a flock of black-faced sheep came bounding, their woolly bodies bouncing and swaying as they rushed past the gate. The sound of the bleating came drifting back to her, strangely loud through the mist. As she stood, wondering what had startled them, something moved in the mist and came towards her.

It was her angel, coming down from the moor towards her. He looked much less angelic now with a heavy black sweater above his faded jeans. 'Hello there!' called Cat brightly. He swung his head to stare at her, standing in the middle of the road looking as startled as one of the sheep. Cat tried to remember his name, but all she could think of was something to do with trees. Looking at those tight jeans, trunk was the word which sprang to mind. 'Nasty morning, isn't it? Have you been up to the Bridestone?'

He flung back his head in a great spray of fair hair, curling tighter than ever in the damp air, and stared at her without a word. He was holding something. She leant over the gate to see what it was. It looked like a child's toy – an animal of some kind. But what animal had red on its back, like this one? He saw her staring at it and scowled, pushing it up out of sight under his sweater. Then still without saying a word, he turned and walked away. He went through the archway into the stable yard and vanished into the mist without a backward glance.

Cat wondered why he hadn't answered her. He didn't seem the shy sort, the way he stared at her. She turned to go back inside and, glancing up at the cottage next door, saw the curtains at one of the bedroom windows drop silently back into place. The witch was keeping an eye on her. Cat shivered and went inside, out of the clinging mist.

When Fen came in a little later, she was apologizing for the weather almost as soon as she was through the door. 'We can still ride down to the village if you like, but we'll keep off the moor. It's not safe up there when the mist comes down. Something smells good – what is it?'

'Sausages. We need some more food when we're in the village; we're nearly out of coffee. Is there a shop that sells food?'

'Our post office sells everything.' Fen picked up a slice of toast and buttered it. 'It's the local answer to Harrods.

We don't need to cook a meal tonight. We've been invited out.'

'Out?' Cat put down the two plates of food on the table. 'Who's asked us out? Mrs Barton?'

'No. Sally's asked us next door for a meal.'

'Mrs Evil Eye?' Cat sat down and stared at Fen. 'Does she often invite you round for a dip in her cauldron?'

'She doesn't, actually. This is the first time. Michael said she was very keen on us going. About seven, he said.'

'I wonder why?'

'She's probably glad of some company. She doesn't drive, so she's on her own next door a lot. She doesn't seem to have any friends in the village who come here to see her.'

Cat said gloomily that she wasn't at all surprised.

'Don't be nasty. She must get a bit lonely.'

'She could nip out on her broomstick,' said Cat. She poured herself a mug of tea. 'I suppose we have to go, do we?'

'Yes, of course we do. I've told Michael we'd be pleased to go. I don't know what you've got against the poor woman. You like to go out, you know you do.'

'Normally, yes. This doesn't feel much like a social event. It feels more like being invited into the Ginger-bread House. What d'you suppose she'll give us to eat? Probably a quick dish of eye of newt. You haven't got a couple of crucifixes we can wear, have you?'

'Is that likely? It's all in your head anyway. I don't know why you insist on calling her a witch.'

'Double, double, toil and trouble,' wailed Cat, waving her fork in the air.

'Oh, come on you, eat your sausage. Then I'm going to take you out for some nice healthy exercise on Lucy.'

'Aren't you forgetting something? There's a dirty great

fog out there. It's hardly healthy. I'm going to need a hard hat with a miner's lamp on the front.'

Bel stood with his head high and his ears pricked up, watching as Fen saddled up the two mares. Cat held the bridle of the smaller one, Lucy, and shivered as the stallion screamed out suddenly, rearing and lashing out at the half-door. There was something about Bel which frightened her; she didn't envy Fen her job. She swung into the saddle and clattered out of the yard behind the bigger mare. In front of her, Fen sat on Meg as if she'd grown there. Cat had forgotten how right she looked on horseback, straight backed and comfortable. She settled down uneasily to Lucy's short stride, feeling strangely insecure, as if the little mare might dissolve between her legs at any minute.

'Don't go too fast!' she called out nervously after Fen as the big mare ahead of her lengthened her stride on the grass at the roadside. Fen laughed and shouted something back at Cat which she missed. Lucy had broken into a fast trot to catch up with Meg and, until she picked up the rhythm, Cat was bouncing about like the proverbial pea. She groaned and muttered to herself at the idea of Fen calling this healthy, then suddenly she found Lucy's stride and her confidence came back to her in a rush. She urged the little mare on and followed Meg's disappearing hindquarters along the narrow road. They clattered through a farmyard with a duck pond at one side, where a flock of white ducks quacked discordantly and waddled off the road with a flurry of wings on to the brackish water of the pond. Lucy tossed her head and spooked at them, but Meg didn't break her stride for Fen.

They passed the pub and a long row of cottages to the post office at the far end. Fen dismounted and tied the mares to the white fence round the garden. Cat slid off

Lucy as if she were coming down a rock face, scrabbling and awkward. She held on to the stirrup for a moment until she got her legs under control again, patting Lucy's neck before she followed Fen unsteadily into the shop. She could see herself needing a mounting block if she was ever going to get back up in the saddle again. There was a rack of postcards just inside the doorway. Cat stopped to pick out one of Raven's Bay, with bright red roofs tumbling down to an unbelievably blue sea. Taking it over to the counter, she picked up the pen there and began to write on the card quickly, without thinking: 'Having a lovely time, been sunbathing on the beach. Out now on the horses. Been invited out for a meal tonight. Fen sends her love with mine, C.'

Scrawling her address, she added W1 with a flourish, asked for a stamp and pushed the card towards the woman behind the counter. It wouldn't satisfy her mother, but it made Cat feel less guilty. She stood and looked round the shop. It was the strangest post office she'd ever seen. It sold stamps, certainly, but it also sold heather honey, cooked ham, wellingtons, tins of paint and dog biscuits. It reminded Cat of the shop in *Through the Looking Glass* – the one with a sheep for a shopkeeper. The postmistress studied Cat through her round glasses, and Cat wouldn't have been at all surprised to hear her bleat. Picking up Cat's card, the woman glanced at the address, sniffed and, turning, flicked it into the sack behind her. She stared at Cat, eyeing her up and down until she felt her skin crawling. What was it with this place that everyone stared at her as if she had two heads? She stared back at the woman. 'Nasty day,' she volunteered with a big smile. Be nice to the natives.

No answer. It was as if she didn't exist. The woman turned her head and took the list of food Fen handed her. She was looking at Fen quite differently, with a sort of excitement in her. In her late forties, she was round and neat with short curling brown hair. Cat had the feeling she'd seen her before, but where? Unless she was one of those three women who'd been standing by the fence watching the stallion. Cat wasn't sure. She hadn't taken in anything about them except that the tallest one had long red hair. She'd never asked Fen about them – they hadn't seemed that important compared with witches and angels.

If Cat stayed here in this place for too long she was going to end up invisible. First Ash and now this woman. Maybe it was her southern accent. Perhaps she should try the 'Sithee by heck!' approach. She turned and walked out of the shop, going to stand by the mares.

Fen followed her out in a few minutes and came to stand beside her. 'You okay?'

'Less than impressed with your local customs. Is she always that rude?'

'Olivia Watson? Yes, usually. She does stare, doesn't she? She doesn't mean anything by it. It's just the way she is.'

'Where's the food then? Wouldn't she let you have any?'

'Don't panic. She delivers it. She'll bring it after the shop shuts this evening.' Fen untied Meg's reins and climbed into the saddle. Creaking like an old woman, Cat crawled up on to Lucy, only the fact that the post office female would be watching giving her the energy to do it. She turned in the saddle and through the window of the shop saw the woman lift the phone and begin to speak animatedly into it, nodding her head and swinging round to look out of the window. Cat had the feeling she was talking about them, and shrugged crossly as she moved the mare forward after Fen. She was getting paranoid as well as invisible. This was a nice, quiet country holiday. And she was enjoying it, she added through gritted teeth.

The fog swirled damply about them as they moved off down the street, seeming thicker than ever. The mares pricked up their ears uneasily, tucking in their noses to inspect it more carefully. All Cat could see now was the dark shape of Meg prancing along the grass verge ahead of her. It seemed a very long time until the stable yard loomed up ahead of them. She slid painfully out of the saddle and moaned.

'You look like the Tin Man out of *The Wizard of Oz*,' said Fen cheerfully. 'You'll be okay after a hot bath. If you can stagger that far, take the saddles into the tack room for me. It's that door there. I'll put the mares in.'

Cat heard the whispering as she swung the saddles on to the rack. She stood and listened, at first thinking it was something she could hear outside in the fog, then she heard it again more clearly. The thin chanting sound came hissing and curling round her from somewhere above her head. There was a ladder in the far corner, leading to a hay loft. The sound was coming from up there.

It frightened Cat. It was nothing she could make any sense of until one word came falling clearly to her. Epona. And then came the sounds of a woman climbing to a climax, orgasmic and out of control. Above the dying fall of her cry the whisper came again, old and strange. In the silence which followed, Cat stood holding her breath, her hand still on the warm leather of the saddle, listening. Now there were footsteps hurrying across the floor above and down the ladder came the woman with long red hair. She turned when she stood safely on the floor looking up at someone out of sight from Cat, and smiling. She bent her head and began to pick pieces of hay from the front of her dress. The bodice

71

was all undone: Cat could see the woman's full round breasts glimmering in the half-light. There was something hanging on a thong between them. The woman held this for a moment then, tucking it down into the deep cleft of her breasts, she fastened the row of small pearl buttons, smoothed down the long crumpled skirt and crossed over to the door without seeing Cat in the shadows.

Cat recognized the look she'd seen on the woman's face. She'd seen it in the mirror when she'd been with Harry. Someone had just made love very successfully with the red-haired woman.

She waited. Nothing. Whoever was up there in the hay loft was keeping very quiet. It was nothing to do with her; she should go now, quickly, before whoever was up there came down and saw her. But she found herself walking towards the ladder without any conscious decision. She stood and stared up at the small square hole at the top of the ladder, and it seemed to be getting darker and darker as she looked.

Then the sound began again. This time, it was her name that she could hear. 'Puss cat,' came the voice, coaxing and wheedling at her. 'Pretty little pussy. Come up the ladder to me. Here, pussy, pussy.'

She knew that she shouldn't go up to him, that there was something wrong about this, but her feet were on the bottom rungs and her upturned face was as white as milk in the dim light as she began to climb. 'Puss, puss, puss,' came the tempting whisper and all she wanted was to be fucked as the red-haired woman had been. And now he was singing oh so softly and gently to her and up and up went her feet.

> 'I love little pussy,
> Her coat is so warm,
> And if I don't hurt her

She'll do me no harm.
So I'll not pull her tail,
Nor drive her away,
But pussy and I
Very gently will play.'

He was purring softly in the dark above her and up went her feet and now her head was almost at the top of the ladder and she would be able to see him soon and she was all ready for him, wanting what would happen to her when she gave herself to him, when she played the pretty pussy for him.

'Cat? Come on, I'm ready!' Fen's voice came smashing into her from the doorway behind her like a blow and she hated her for being there, for stopping her. She felt the power pulling her up the ladder to him drain away and wailed her loss up into the dark.

'What *are* you doing singing to yourself up there? There's only hay in the loft. Come on love, I'm starving.' Fen turned and set off across the yard.

Cat slithered boneless down to the floor, the rough sides of the ladder scraping her hands and stared up helplessly. She couldn't go and she couldn't stay. Fen was her friend, how could she have hated her so bitterly just now? Very faintly she could hear him laughing at her. 'Off you go then,' he said. 'Come to play with me another time, little pussy.'

And she was free to go. 'No,' she said. 'No, I won't.' And, turning, she ran as fast as she could after Fen, after normality and safety. She remembered then that in a few hours she would be seeing Michael and having dinner with him. For of course it had been Michael. Who else could it have been?

Extract from Michael's Stallion Book

I went up to the Bridestone at dusk. It haunts me, that place. It's never the same twice over. I sat down in front of it and looked at the long valley and wondered what it must have been like when the woods covered it. I leant back against the stone and rested my head against it. It felt cold as ice through my thin shirt. I closed my eyes and the shock went through me in a white flash. When I opened my eyes the moor was gone. It wasn't my eyes I was looking through any more, it wasn't my thoughts running through my head.

There was a fire flickering redly in front of him. A smell of meat roasting, of flesh and bone. The shaman had drawn in a deer from the winter dark for his people and they would eat well for a while. They were sitting opposite him in the firelight, watching him. Always watching him, afraid. They thought with their bellies, they didn't see the patterns in the water. Something moved in the shadows next to him. It was a young girl, coming to crouch at his feet on all fours. The people were giving him their thanks for the food. He reached out and touched the curve of her offered white haunches, then stood and held his arms high in the smoking air.

And out of my mouth, Michael's mouth, came the voice of the shaman, the shaman's words.

'I am. I am. I am the one who walks on hilltops. I have eaten the snake with the bird. I sing with the running water; I am the earth, out of the earth and above it. I speak with the sky dweller, with the water spirits, with the beasts. I speak with those who are already dead, with those who will come after us. For I have been deep into the Underworld. I have seen the tree whose roots grow deep in the heart of the earth. I am the shaman. I am. I.'

He knelt behind the crouching girl and thrust himself into her, falling across her back as he came quickly in her.

Then there was a crackling and a smell of smoke and a terrible wrenching as I came back into my own body, became only Michael again. He had left me for a time, and all I felt was empty. I'd been knocked forward sprawling from the Bridestone and the light was almost gone. I could still feel the girl's body under mine and smell the wood smoke. The pain in my head was terrible. I came back across the moor dragging one foot after another. Sick as a dog.

Chapter Eight

THE smell of damp in the cottage next door was very strong. In the narrow passage moisture gleamed and sweated on the pale walls. There was a line like a high-tide mark round the yellow flowered paper in the living-room, and the black and red quarry tiles showing at the edge of the carpet had a fine, white bloom. Cat sat uneasily looking round her. She didn't want to be here; she didn't want to see Michael. When he came into the room and sat down at the table with them she wouldn't look at him. He began to talk to Fen and sounded so ordinary, so normal, that Cat began to wonder if she'd imagined the whole scene in the tack room.

Sally came bustling in from the kitchen with a steaming brown tureen to where they sat waiting – Michael with Patsy next to him, Cat and Fen facing them. Patsy sat and stared with round owl eyes.

'Come on, our Patsy, stir yourself.' Sally sounded flustered. 'Bring the spuds in while I dish this lot up.' She plonked down the tureen in front of Cat and beamed at her. 'By, it is nice of you to come. It's not often we get visitors. Now, I hope you're both good and hungry, because there's plenty.' And she whipped off the heavy lid.

A warm smell of flesh rose up and, glancing at the food, a bitter sickness rose acid at the back of Cat's throat. It was a baby. In the pot, surrounded by carrots and onion rings was the pale, curved back of a baby. A thin blackness began to creep in on Cat from the edges of the room. She looked despairingly at Fen next to her, but she was watching Michael, engrossed in some talk of Bel's feet.

Patsy came back into the room carrying a tray with two more dishes on it, which she lifted on to the table. She stood the tray against the sideboard and slid into her seat. She stared at Cat. Cat looked from her to Sally and felt pinned by her dark eyes above the gently steaming baby.

Bending forward, Sally picked up a long, thin knife and eased it slyly into the pale, warm flesh. 'Nice, fresh rabbit,' she crooned faintly down the thick-walled tunnel which was closing in on Cat. Knocking her fork to the floor, Cat bent down in her chair to pick it up, closing her eyes and forcing back the waves of nausea. Rabbit. Yes, of course it was rabbit. How could it possibly have been a baby? Cat opened her eyes and saw Patsy's face hanging like a suspended moon under the table, watching her. Clutching her fork she sat up and tried to bring her face under control again. She risked another glance at the food. A rabbit. Why had she thought it was a baby? She'd convinced herself too well that this was the witch's house. That and the fact that somewhere she was still disturbed by what had happened — or had nearly happened — at the stables. Something, though. Something in the way that the rabbit had been so carefully arranged with only the curve of the back showing. Something in the expression on Sally's face as she laid a round, white leg in front of Cat. A heap of potatoes followed, then brown gravy with fat globules swimming in it. The spoonful of mashed turnip which followed filled any space left on the plate. Sally obviously didn't believe in self-service.

Fen nodded her thanks as her heaped plate was put in front of her, still engrossed in the discussion on Bel. Sally served Patsy, then Michael, and took what was left for herself. 'There you are then. Get started – you could do with a bit of fat on you Cat, you need feeding up.'

'This looks grand,' said Michael cheerfully. 'Tuck in, ladies.'

Everyone else began to eat with enthusiasm. Cat took a deep breath, picked up her knife and fork and cut off a small sliver of the meat. She put it very carefully into her mouth. It seemed to her that the more she chewed, the more soft flesh there was. It swelled and thickened in her throat. The taste of it grew more animal, more cloying with each bite. There was nothing to drink on the table, only a row of blue and white teacups set out on the sideboard. Cat swallowed with difficulty and said faintly, 'Could I have a glass of water, please?'

'Water? We can do better than that for you, lass.' Getting up, Michael brought a bottle and some glasses over to the table. 'You try this. Sally makes it from one of her old gran's recipes.'

Cat wondered briefly what she made it from but she would have swallowed bat broth happily at that point. She took a gulp and her mouth filled with the taste of flowers and honey. The heavy liquid slid sweetly into the tight knot at the back of Cat's throat and eased it. 'It's very nice,' she said with relief. Seeing the look of pleasure on her face Fen asked for a glass. Oiled with the mead, Cat managed to eat most of the congealed food. She hid the rest under her knife and fork. Sally took the plate from her with a disapproving sniff, and Patsy at once replaced it with a slice of apple pie. On the plate next to it was a thick wedge of white cheese. As Sally poured her a cup of tea so strong it looked as if it could have supported the spoon, Cat wondered at the strange mixture – apple pie and cheese.

Michael saw her looking down at her plate and

grinned. 'You know what they say up here: "Apple pie without the cheese is like a kiss without the squeeze."'

Patsy giggled at him. 'Who're you going to kiss then, Dad?'

Cat remembered the coaxing hiss of her name and crossed her legs quickly. Michael was putting on a very good act of husband–father, but he hadn't been that with the red-haired woman.

'How's school, Patsy?' asked Fen.

'Okay. We're having a jumble sale soon, for the end of term. Stalls and that. Will you both come?'

'It's to raise funds for the school. All in a good cause,' said Sally. 'You'd enjoy it. The kids will be writing out notices about it soon to bring home; Patsy will make sure you get one.'

'Thanks. I was telling Cat how good at art Patsy is. Cat's an artist as well – doing art at college in London. You'll have to show her some of your work, Patsy.'

The child's face changed, became as hidden for an instant as if a shutter had dropped. She stared at Cat intently, then said, 'Now. I'll get some.'

She slid from her chair and ran off upstairs, coming back with a drawing pad, which she brought round the table to Cat. She stood next to her and opened the pad at the first page.

Cat stared in astonishment. She'd expected the drawings to be good from what Fen had said, but nothing like this. They were done with bright, sharp-coloured felt-tip pens, and were a mass of fine lines of faces peering out of webs of colour – distorted, evil faces. And over and over again, horses galloping, with masses of writhing manes and tails. The child stood watching as Cat turned the pages.

'She's good, isn't she?' said Michael. 'She's got a line of her own already. She's always been able to draw, ever since she was a bairn. Drew before she could talk. What d'you think then, Cat?'

'I think you have a very gifted daughter,' said Cat slowly.

'Really?' Sally beamed at her.

'These are exceptional. Brilliant. Could I take a couple to show my art tutor, Patsy? I'll let you have them back when he's seen them. I'd like to hear what he thinks of them.'

Patsy let out a long sigh. 'I thought they were good, only nobody else does owt like them at school. Miss never puts any of my stuff up on the walls, only pictures of flowers and stuff. I'll do you some new drawings. One for each of you, if you want.'

'Do one of Bel for me please, I'd love that,' said Fen.

'Aye. And one of a cat for you.' Patsy looked sideways at Cat and giggled.

'Bed time for you now.' Sally got briskly to her feet. 'Just help me side these dishes away into the kitchen, then you be off upstairs for your bath. Take the girls into the other room, Michael.'

They followed Michael through into what was obviously Sally's best room. Cat perched uneasily next to Fen on the slippery, black vinyl sofa and stared at the assortment of animals crammed on to the mantelpiece. There was a big photo of Bel hanging above it. Michael switched on the small TV next to the electric fire and turned down the sound. It seemed to be showing a film of a bad snowstorm. Its white, monitoring eye crackled faintly in the heavy silence, which Michael broke by asking Cat how she was enjoying her holiday.

'I like Raven's Bay and that cove next to it. I've been doing some sketching there. Thanks for giving Fen so much free time to be with me. I do appreciate it.'

He cut in on her quickly. 'There's not much for her to do at the stables these next couple of weeks. You two make the most of your stay up here. I can always get Ash to give me a hand if I need one. He's a grand help with Bel. You met Ash yet?'

Fen laughed at Cat's expression. 'She thought he was an angel.'

'He's very beautiful . . .' began Cat defensively.

'He's a lonely lad. You'd be doing him a favour if you made friends with him. He's shy though – you'd have to work hard at it.'

'Michael,' said Fen looking puzzled. 'Ash is –' She broke off in mid-sentence as Sally came through carrying fresh glasses and the bottle of mead. She sank down heavily into one of the armchairs as Michael poured them all a drink.

'Best part of the day is this. Mrs Barton has got it into her daft old head to clean out the kitchen this week. I'm glad of a chance to put my feet up.'

'Is it very old, the Hall?' Cat sipped her mead and wished they could go. What had Fen been going to say about Ash? That he was what? Gay? Celibate? Married? She thought of the way he moved, of his long mouth in the perfect face and hoped he was none of them. Ash, she thought, and something stirred in her, some recognition of how much she was attracted to him. It wasn't the way she felt the pull of Michael's sexuality, but there was something. What was the matter with her? She'd be running about the place with no knickers on begging for it soon. Sex was usually something in the bedroom for her, not the way she'd felt since she came here. It hadn't turned Fen into a sex maniac, why was it doing it to her? She glanced at Fen and wondered if she was used to drinking so much mead – it was going down like water. It was strong stuff, for all its sweet taste; she could feel herself going soft round the edges. She concentrated harder on what Sally was saying.

'. . . built about 1790, the Hall. That's when some of the dust dates from, an' all. By, they're mucky places are these auld houses; it seems to come out of the walls at you.' She paused and stared at Cat, then spoke sharply to her, as if accusing her. 'I don't know whatever you wanted to come here for. Leaving London for this. You'd have been better off staying down there. You've come to a right queer place up here, you know.'

Michael was sprawled long-legged in his chair. He lifted his head slowly and frowned at Sally.

'What d'you mean?' said Fen.

'What I said. It's a queer place where queer things happen. It's always been bad in these cottages, they're too close here to the Bridestone. Too close for comfort. But it's got worse these last few months – much worse.'

'The Bridestone won't hurt you. How can it?' Michael's voice was gentle enough but there was an undertone to it which startled Cat. 'What d'you think it's going to do to you, woman? Come marching down from the moor top to get you?'

Sally shrugged and looked sulky. 'Happen not. I don't know what it can do. I wouldn't go near the thing. You'd never get me up there with that. Things have got worse since that daft lot in the village got all excited over the stone.'

Fen looked as confused as Cat felt. 'Who are you talking about?'

Sally emptied her glass crossly and banged it down on the small table next to her chair. 'Those three women in the village – they call themselves a Writers' Group and they're doing something about the Bridestone. They asked our Michael to take them up and show them it. He never should have done that. All this talking about it

– it was best left alone and quiet. They're always up there now, poking about.'

'Is the woman in the post office one of them?' Cat asked suddenly.

'Aye. Her and Abbey Carter and Amy Martin. All old enough to have more sense. They don't know what they're stirring up. It's bad enough as it is, living here. Noises. Voices outside the window and no one there when you go to look. When we first moved in here, years ago, it felt wrong to me then. One night when our Patsy was about three I was tidying her toys away after I'd put the bairn to bed. She had this lovely big doll Mam had given her. Big blue eyes and long curls, it had. It was in the middle of the floor there, face down and when I picked it up and turned it over, its face had changed. It had like a mask on it, evil, wicked, grinning up at me from under those curls. I screamed for Michael and I threw it, as far as I could in that corner. By the time he came in from the garden, its face had changed back again. It was lying there all pink and smiling at me again. He's never believed me, not from that day to this, but I tell you it happened. The doll's face changed.'

'You imagined it,' said Michael shortly. He filled up Fen's glass again.

'No I bloody well didn't. And that was the summer Patsy started to do those queer drawings. The ones with all those faces in them. All those strange people – where had she seen them when she was just a little bairn? I asked her once who had faces like that, but she wouldn't answer me. She looked at me as if I'd gone daft. It was after that she started to see things, as well. That light in her bedroom, like a big, green ball floating across the room, going through the wall.'

'Which way?' said Cat, knowing the answer before she asked.

Sally looked at her maliciously. 'Which way d'you think? Into your cottage, of course. And it's no better in there, either. Why d'you think it was empty at Easter, just waiting for your ladyship to walk into?' She glared at Fen.

'Why was it empty?' said Fen palely. 'I don't know. I never thought about it. I just thought that whoever was in it before me moved out . . .'

Sally snorted. 'Oh aye, he moved out all right. He moved out in his coffin, after he'd blown his brains out with a shotgun first. I'm surprised Michael hasn't told you all this, him being so keen on local history. Very local all this is. He was the gardener at the Hall, that's why Michael's doing the garden now, why he needed that Ash to help him here. They never found out why he killed himself but I was the one who found him. I saw the look on his face. What was left of it. He was frightened of something.

'And the night that he did it, I was asleep on my own. Michael was over at the stables with one of the old mares who had colic. I woke up and heard this hissing noise. I sat up and looked across the room and in the mirror on the dressing table there was a face looking back at me. It had red slanting eyes and a sort of bone mask thing on its head, on the top of it. Something came in that night, I saw it. It was that night Michael had that terrible dream when he woke up choking and all of a sweat. Something changed that night, in Michael as well. I tell you, it's a queer place you've come to.'

Only the crackling of the TV broke the silence. Then Michael got to his feet and stretched. 'So you had a bad dream. And so did I. That was all it was, Sally. You hung it on Jim killing himself next door yourself, but it had nothing to do with it. You'll be frightening these two off down to London with your daft talk. And we don't want that now, do we?' Threat prickled in his voice as spikily as barbed wire. Sally stared at him and muttered something under her breath, slumping back in her chair and closing up completely. Michael smiled tightly at her and nodded.

Her short skirt had rucked up over her plump legs as she leant back, showing the top of a stocking and a black suspender. On the white strip of exposed flesh Cat saw there was a dark bruise, lying like a flower on the pale skin. Sally saw where Cat was looking and crossed her legs, scowling.

'Well, we musn't keep you two up too late, we've an early start in the morning, haven't we Fen?'

It was their cue for an exit. Cat took it gratefully. She and Fen got to their feet, thanking Sally for the meal. Next time Cat fancied a bite of dead baby, followed by being frightened out of her skin, she knew where to come.

Standing, Fen didn't look too well. She swayed slightly and Cat put her arm round her as they went down the passage to the door. Fen was still clutching a sticky glass, half full of mead. She looked round helplessly for somewhere to put it. Cat prised it out of her fingers and put it on a table by the door. Michael opened the door into the night, blocking their way for a moment. 'Goodnight then,' he said. 'Take no notice of Sally. This is a good place for both of you to be, believe me. And I'm here for you if you need me – for anything.' The door closed behind them.

Darkness fell soft and heavy. Cat didn't know that nights could be as black as this one. She felt as if they'd been put out like a couple of she-cats turned out for the night. Michael had certainly put a stop to any more of Sally's talk. The mist billowed and swirled damply round them as she set off down the garden path, hauling an unsteady Fen after her. She kept hold of the garden wall with one hand and followed it along to their gate. She steered Fen up the path and into the sanctuary of their porch. The thought of that pair of red eyes and the bone mask Sally had seen was all too clear to her as she stood waiting for Fen to find the key. Fen knelt and looked carefully under the door mat, then rose unsteadily and began to look through each pocket in her jeans and jacket. 'Oh be quick, be quick!' wailed Cat. The key was in the last pocket Fen looked in. Cat snatched it from her and fumbled for the keyhole, her fingers brushing something wet as she turned the doorknob. She pushed open the door and switched on the light. Blinking at the sudden brightness, she looked at the door and saw what she'd touched.

Tied to the doorknob was a dead blackbird, hanging by its feet. Someone had pulled off its head. A thick clot of blood fell from it as she stared and on her fingers was a scarlet, sticky stain.

Fen blinked and looked from the dead bird to Cat's bloody fingers and groaned. 'I'm going to be sick,' she moaned and only just made it to the door of the porch.

Cat stood and looked at the bird and listened to the sound of Fen retching and thinly in her head there came the echo of Sally's voice.

'It's a queer place you've come to, a queer place.'

Chapter Nine

'They didn't stop long, your precious guests.' Sally stood in the middle of her living-room and glared at Michael. 'All that fuss I made over the meal and then they rushed off home. I suppose we're not good enough for them.'

'It was nothing to do with the meal,' said Michael mildly. 'The meal was fine. It was time they went when you started talking rubbish.'

'I said nowt but the truth!' she burst out.

'You couldn't have done more to scare them off if you tried. Daft bitch. Why don't you wrap yourself up in an old sheet and go next door and finish off the job?'

'I don't care if they do go.'

'But I care. I care very much. I need them both here until Lammas Day.' He hadn't known that until he said it. The name went roaring through his head, and it was right.

She looked at his white face and saw how angry he was getting with her. 'I don't see why. What d'you need them for? What are you up to, Michael? Something's coming – I can feel it.'

'Never you mind. You keep out of it. Just you keep that big mouth shut of yours, that's all.' He sat down in a chair and picked up the book he had been reading earlier.

'Oh go on, bury your nose in a bloody book like you always do. You'll do owt to avoid talking to me. You've plenty to say to everyone else though. You'll end up blind as a bat, see if you don't.'

He didn't lift his head from the page, cutting her off deliberately and making her only a part of the background. She gathered up the dirty glasses and paused in the doorway. 'I'm off to bed. Don't sit there half the night stuck in that thing and then wake me up expecting anything.' He ignored her and she flounced out into the kitchen.

Lammas. The first of August. Now he had a date to work to and another piece had fallen into place. He sighed happily and let himself sink down into what he was reading. Michael had come late to books; it hadn't been until he was seventeen and living on his own for the first time that he had found the power in them. Before that the children's homes and then the hostel they'd put him in for a year had left him little privacy for reading. Then he got a live-in job on a farm with a room to himself, and the first thing he did was to join a library. At first, he read anything and everything but after that first glut of words he moved slowly towards a more selective reading. The past had reached out and touched him, and now the history of this valley had somehow become his own history.

He was reading an account of Celtic shape-shifting, from the time of the worship of the horse goddess, Epona. As clearly as if he were there, he could see the tribe gathered in the clearing and the great white mare being led in. The king-elect came crawling on his hands and knees into the clearing, calling out that he was a beast, pretending to cover the white mare. Then the mare was killed and put into a great pot and cooked, and the king-elect sat in the pot and ate the flesh and drank the broth of the mare. And so he became the king. The mare died so that the king could rise up from the blood and bones of her. Death and renewal, giving fertility to the crops, the stock and the tribe.

Michael closed the book and sighed. He was trying to make sense of what the shaman showed him but he knew so little. It frustrated him that so much of the old knowledge had gone, passed on only from mouth to mouth with no written form, dying with the last old man who knew the truth. Horse worship had lingered a long time in these parts. There was a tale that even some of the Roman soldiers worshipped Epona. There was a stretch of Roman road a few miles away over the moor. Did the Romans who built it follow Epona? There was no way of knowing, Michael thought sadly.

Last summer, when the soil had been very dry, one of Sally's hens had scratched up an old coin. Sally had run in with it to show him. When he washed off the soil caked on it, there was a woman on one side – not Britannia – all flowery lines and queer looking. He'd looked it up in a library book and the coin was Roman. Sally had been disappointed because it was only worth a few pounds, but just to hold it in his hand was magical for Michael – thinking back to the Roman who'd lost it.

His head full of white mares, of sacrifice, of times long past, Michael dropped the book to the floor, stood and stretched and went slowly upstairs to Sally.

In the bedroom of the cottage next door, Cat was dreaming. It had been a long time before she slept, for Fen had been very restless, muttering and flinging her arms about. Now she had fallen into a heavy sleep, and Cat had slipped down into the dream.

She wasn't Cat now but a much younger self. It was Catherine sitting on the edge of the fragile, straight-backed chair. She smoothed down the pleats of her short grey kilt, for she was wearing her school uniform – white blouse, a scarlet tie, white knee socks and shining black shoes. She looked round the room. Where was she? It wasn't a room she recognized. It was an old room, high ceilinged, with a ring of plaster flowers above her head. There was a low fire burning in the mottled marble fireplace, and a clock ticked on the mantelpiece, its gilt pendulum swinging to and fro among pink enamelled flowers. Outside on the long, paved terrace a peacock screamed, fanning his blue tail as he strutted past his reflection in the long window.

The clock ticked, the peacock strutted and Catherine waited. For whom? Then the shining panelled door at the far side of the room opened very slowly. For a moment the dark square it revealed was empty, then Michael stepped into the room and closed the door gently behind him. He stood watching her and the clock struck four urgently through the room. As the sound died away into a soft ticking, he crossed the faded, rose-coloured carpet towards her and dropped on to her lap a small, beautifully wrapped box. 'A present for you.'

She picked at the stiff silver paper, at the tissue paper lining that, letting it fall to the pale carpet in flakes of white. Finally she held in her hands a small silver box. On the lid of it was an engraving of a swan and Leda. He was thrusting into Leda, his great wings beating over her where she lay with curving, outspread legs. Catherine ran a finger over the sharply cut feathers, over the round swell of the woman's breasts, and clicked open the lid.

Inside the box lay the blackbird without a head. Its dark feathers lay stiffly on the white satin lining, and a dried splash of blood clotted like gouache beneath it. Catherine sat and looked. Stepping forward, Michael lifted the bird delicately from the box and brushed the bloodied stump down the pale skin of Catherine's cheek. As the stiff feathers fluttered across her face, she moaned and woke.

Cat lay in the pressing dark, feeling her heart banging against her flesh, rubbing her hand down her cheek where the bird had touched it. She needed to use the loo; she needed a drink. The light in the bathroom when she got there was too hard, too bright, and the white tiles glistened at her. She sat on the loo and leant her head back against the cold whiteness of the wall, and listened to the voices.

At first she thought these voices were inside her head, were still part of the dream. Only gradually did it come to her that they were on the other side of the wall. First there was a man's voice, complaining of something. Michael. And more faintly, further away from the wall, the thin sound of Sally, on and on. Michael's voice rose suddenly and Cat caught the words 'have to stay'. Then both voices dimmed and faded away from her. Still she sat with her head against the wall, listening. When the sound began, she heard it for a moment before it began to make any sense to her, before an image came into her head of what it was. Then she knew that what she was hearing was the sound of something hitting flesh.

On the other side of the wall, Sally knelt naked on her hands and knees. Michael leant against the wall, admiring the curve of her back, the white haunches of her dimpled bottom and the heavy breasts. He thought of Bel making the great dance, the ceremony which was all important to Michael. He'd been angry with Sally for what she'd done earlier. He needed to use that anger. He moved across to her and slid the jointed bit of the stallion's bridle into her mouth, carefully straightening the leather straps flat against her cheeks. He fastened the girth straps round the soft curve of her stomach and attached the short reins to it. He stood back to admire her.

She was his mare, his to ride. He knew how to pleasure her, to bring her eager and whinnying to him. She wasn't a thoroughbred mare, not like the pair of high-stepping fillies next door. Sally was a Dales pony, round and dark and shaggy. He imagined Cat and Fen kneeling side by side, yoked together for him, bridled as Sally was, and felt himself stiffen at the idea. Picking up his riding crop he stood astride her and caught hold of a tangled handful of long hair. He brought the crop stinging down across her haunches, raising a pattern on the white softness. Between his legs she jerked restlessly and he tightened his grip on the reins. He thought of the stallion, of him rearing and crashing down on his mare and taking her. He thought of Bel's dark strength and felt the shaman's power begin to gather about him in the little room. Throwing aside the crop he dropped the reins and knelt behind her and stroked her. She was ready for him and he went into her in one long thrust. He came at once and as he did so the shaman took him.

The shaman was sitting inside his hut. His eyes were open but he saw nothing of what was round him. He was seeing a man sitting at the top of a tree. He had a bird on his left shoulder and food in his right hand. In his left hand was a drinking vessel with a fish swimming in it. There was a white horse standing at the foot of the tree. The pale-haired man sat cracking nuts, half for himself and half for the bird on his shoulder, sipping the water where the fish swam, breaking the food in half and dropping half to the white horse below him. So they were all one complete whole, all one – bird, fish, horse and man. Then the pale-haired man lifted his head and stared straight at the shaman and the shaman knew him for the one to give his seed to the goddess. This was the chosen mate for Epona.

Michael let out a long sigh as he recognized the man in the tree. It was Ash. He came back into himself and quickly took the bridle from Sally. Turning her on to her back, he began to kiss her breasts slowly, giving her back what he had taken from her. She gave a long moan of pleasure, which rose to a high yelp of delight as his mouth moved down between her legs.

Cat heard her cry as clearly as if she were in the room with them. She recognized the sounds Sally was making now: whatever Michael had been doing to her before, she was enjoying what he was doing now. She imagined Michael as he must look now with a swollen erection and touched her nipples gently, imagining his mouth on them and his tongue sliding wetly across her skin. She began to rub herself, softly at first and then more roughly and her fingers on herself were Michael's, and she whimpered for the want of him. Sally let out a long, wailing scream of pleasure and at the sound Cat tensed and, bending forward, came quickly and silently with her. Michael's power was stronger than he knew that night.

Afterwards, curled up against the deeply sleeping Fen, Cat lay thinking of what she'd heard, of the strange evening next door. And the dead bird. The pattern of soil, the dead rabbit, the scrawling of the word Epona and now a dead bird. She couldn't understand why Fen wasn't doing anything about it – she didn't seem to have even mentioned it to Michael yet. Now she'd met Patsy, Cat didn't think it was her that was doing it. She yawned and thought that tomorrow she really must have a talk with Fen and get it sorted out. She let Sally and Michael and the dead bird all fall away from her, and her last clear thought was of a drop of blood, falling brightly from a yellow beak.

Extract from Michael's Stallion Book

So it's Ash then. I couldn't sleep, all I could think of was that it's Ash. I left Sally sleeping and came downstairs to write here – it always helps me to write in this book, I can see what I'm thinking. For all the rubbish Sally was talking earlier tonight, I begin to understand something which has puzzled me since the night the shaman chose me. Why me? I've no education to speak of, I'm not clever. I know so little it depresses me. So why me? And I think it's this: I'm the man in the right place at the right time, that's why. Like Sally said, next door's cottage was made empty by Jim's death. So Fen came. Then Cat. And there were already those three in the village.

And this cottage is near the Bridestone. Then there is the one thing I have got that other men don't. Women will do what I want them to. And being the way he is, so will Ash. There is a lot to do with him before Lammas. He is a virgin still and it isn't safe to leave him so. I have to be sure he knows how to perform the ceremony. He mustn't fail at the one chance he'll have. I don't see it all yet, but the place is the Bridestone, the time is Lammas. And the man is Ash.

Chapter Ten

CAT woke next morning to the sound of Fen groaning. 'What time is it?'

'Late,' said Cat, getting out of bed and pulling back the curtains. 'Gone nine. How d'you feel, Fen?'

Fen had buried her head in the sheet as daylight attacked her through the window. There was a thoughtful pause, then a pale face appeared over the edge of the sheet. 'Ill,' she said feebly. 'Why do I feel so ill?'

'Because last night you let Michael fill you up with enough mead to keep a Valkyrie happy for a fortnight. That's why you feel ill.'

Fen thought about it. 'Did I dream it, or did a cat leave a dead bird at the door last night?'

Cat pulled a face and sat down on the edge of the bed. 'Some cat. Clever enough to tie the bird to the door handle with a piece of red ribbon.'

Fen sat up and focused on her with difficulty. 'It had no head. Someone had pulled off its head.'

Cat nodded slowly. 'Someone had.'

The two looked at each other, then Fen whimpered and went back under the sheets. Cat opened her mouth to tell her about what she'd heard in the night, through the wall, then thought better of it. Fen had enough to cope with. She'd have to talk to her later. She patted the hump of Fen's bottom and went to get her a couple of painkillers.

'Here. Take these. It's too late now for you to go over to the stables. You sleep it off and go in this afternoon.

Michael will realize what's happened. It's his fault anyway for giving you all that mead.'

'What will you do?' Fen squinted at the tablets fizzing loudly in the glass of water.

'I'll be okay.' Cat drew the curtains closed and left Fen to sleep. The morning stretched endlessly before her. Cat wasn't used to quiet days in the country. She settled herself in the kitchen and did a pastel drawing of the old brown sink and the rack of blue and white plates next to it. For once, it came right from the first line: she was pleased with it. The curve of the plates, the colour of the old shelves satisfied her. She was sitting looking down at it when the phone rang, startling her. Her mother, she thought with a sinking feeling. She went into the other room to pick it up reluctantly. 'Hello?' There was no reply, only the faint sound of breathing. 'Hello?' she said again, more loudly. 'Who did you want to speak to?'

'Come up now to the Bridestone,' said a voice faintly in her ear. 'We need you there . . . at the Bridestone . . .' The deep voice trailed off into the sound of breathing again, then there was a soft purring as the phone went down at the other end.

Cat put down the receiver and stood bewildered. Why would someone want her up at the Bridestone? And who had it been? She wasn't even sure whether it was a man or a woman; it had been a sexless sort of voice. Whoever it was must have thought she was Fen, surely? It must have been a message for Fen. But how could poor Fen go up there, the state she was in? She would go instead of her, Cat decided suddenly. She'd nothing else to do, she could explain about Fen not being well and bring back a message for her. She'd be glad of an excuse to get out of the cottage. It was depressing without the sunshine. The fog looked less thick today but everywhere was grey and damp. And this was the room where, according to Sally, the man had shot himself. Cat shuddered and went quickly into the porch. There was an old anorak of Fen's hanging on a hook there, with some wellingtons lying on the floor. She pulled on the coat and pushed a small notebook and pencil into one of the big pockets. She'd go and see what this stone looked like – it should look good in this light. A pair of the boots fitted her. The moor would be wet and she'd need them. She went out into the mist.

The track up to the moor went alongside the cottage – it was the one she'd seen her angel coming down that day. It seemed to go up along the side of the field, beside the stone wall, but it was knee-high in wet bracken. Cat decided it would be easier if she went across the field – there was a gate at the far side leading into the larch wood. The stone must be on the ridge of moor above it. She climbed over the rickety gate into the field and set off for the far side. There were big clumps of purple spiked thistles patterning the grass and, as she came towards one, she was startled to see a huge sheep get up from behind it, almost under her feet.

The woolly creature stamped a forefoot at her crossly, then pulled back its top lip to sniff at her with outstretched neck before straddling its back legs and urinating on the grass. It swung its big, heavy head to scratch at an itchy flank, its head seeming out of proportion to its closely sheared body. As it did so, Cat saw the great hanging bag of him between his back legs; this was obviously the flock's sperm bank. And he had a nasty gleam in those yellow eyes.

The ram began to back away from Cat with his head lowered, legs stiff as rods, his upper lip flaring again. Even to a London girl, this looked like trouble. Cat ran. He ran as well. She could hear his feet pounding along the short-cropped turf behind her. There was an old tree just ahead of her. Cat got to it just before the ram.

Dodging behind it, she peered round to see him backing off for another run at her. Picking up a dead branch Cat stepped out and, as he charged at her, she shut her eyes and hit him with it.

The branch broke into pieces and Cat opened her eyes, horrified in case she'd killed him. He was standing in front of her, looking thoughtful. She ran before he'd worked it out and was over the gate in the far corner before resentment dawned and he was after her. He stood with his front legs up on the gate, watching her; Cat pulled out her pad and pencil, catching the thick, curving horns and the broad forehead in heavy black strokes. His eyes were very strange. Cat had never looked at a sheep's eyes before and the yellow slits intrigued her. The pupils seemed to be slanting the opposite way to other animals. Satanic. The ram lost interest. Swinging down to the ground he began to crop at the sparse grass. Cat turned and went into the wood.

The moor wind had bent and blasted the larches, stripping them bone white at the far side, high on the crest of the hill. From the top of one of the tallest swung three dead rooks, turning slowly as the mist shifted about them. Why had someone shot them to hang there? Did they attack the lambs? There was an old, dead feeling about this place. Cat was glad to be out of it on the flat ridge of moor on the other side. She shivered at the crawl of the damp anorak on her shoulders and pulled up the hood. It was much colder up here. She jumped as a gorse bush loomed up out of the grey air and snagged at her with prickling fingers. The mist was thinning slightly, rolling back away from her, and she saw how the ground fell away into a narrow valley at either side of the broad ridge she was walking along. Straight ahead of her, thrusting black and phallic into the sky, was the Bridestone.

Nobody had told her. Nobody had warned her how big it was, how threatening. Somehow, because it was called the Bridestone, she had thought of it as something more female, more rounded. This was no bride: this was something you gave a bride to. As she looked, the stone moved towards her. The mist swirled round her where she stood, stupid with fright. The skin at the back of her neck prickled as she remembered Sally talking about the stone coming down the hillside. She felt it come lurching towards her, crushing her under it, splitting her open. She wanted to turn and run, but her legs were dissolving under her and she couldn't force herself to move. She stood with held breath, but there was no sound except for the noise of sheep bleating, faint and far away down the valley.

Cat had been afraid in London; once she'd been threatened by a man with a knife as she came late out of Baker Street tube station. She'd walked the night streets with the prickle of fear which is always there for a woman after dark in London. What she was feeling now was something much more primitive, much deeper. Now she understood how Sally felt about the Bridestone.

There was another movement through the mist, then a flash of pale colour. Cat's heart leapt and banged before she realized what it was. It was Ash. It was his fair hair she'd seen. She forced herself to breathe properly and found she was able to move again. She walked along the narrow path to the stone. 'Ash?' she called, and he came out from behind the grey mass slowly. He leant against the stone and watched her come towards him, his face as blank and beautiful as ever. 'Hello. Do you remember me? I'm Fen's friend, Cat. Was it you who rang her earlier?'

He said nothing, only turned away his head. Michael had said that he was shy, that she'd find it difficult making friends with him. It was going to be impossible if he wouldn't even speak to her. And why had she told him who she was? Of course he knew her. A new sheep round here must cause a lot of excitement, never mind a new woman.

He turned and looked at her and she thought again how perfect his mouth was, the dreaming mouth of a sleep-walker. He bent his head as if he were listening to something, then he pulled her to him, unzipped her anorak and dropped it to the ground. For some reason she thought that he was going to kiss her, and leant in towards him. He caught hold of her T-shirt and pulled it up until it lay rucked and folded above her breasts. He did it all so calmly, with so little emotion, that she didn't fully realize what he'd done until the cold air touched wetly at her breasts. He caught her arms and held them at her sides, turning her to face the stone. He pushed her gently towards it.

'Bless the Bridestone.'

She didn't understand what was happening, what he wanted. She half-turned and tried to pull down her shirt and she saw that out of the mist, out of the heather, there were three figures moving. They came up silently from the pools of greyness in the hollows, three tall figures dressed in long black robes, their eyes blanked out by masks of animals' faces. A crow, a wolf, a hare. In her left hand each of them held a toy horse, decorated with small bones, with feathers and with flower heads. Cat pulled away from Ash and clutched her arms across her breasts as the women came to stand beside her. He caught hold of her again more roughly.

'Bless the Bridestone for us.'

One of the women reached out and touched Cat's breast. Her fingers stroked and smoothed round Cat's nipple and to her horror she felt herself begin to respond to the touch. The woman nodded and suddenly there were three sets of hands on her, smoothing her skin, easing her forward gently until she was almost touching the rough surface of the grey stone.

'Bless the Bridestone,' whispered the women. 'Give your breasts to the stone.' The whispering grew louder, more insistent. 'Bless the stone, bless the stone.' Their hands on her back were pushing her hard against it. She felt the cold surface of it graze against her nipples. The hands were stronger now, she was being held and crushed against the stone and she screamed at the pain. The women's voices rose to a great howl of joy and fell away into silence.

Cat felt Ash touch her shoulder and turn her round. He was smiling at her, pulling down her shirt. Picking up the anorak he put it round her shoulders. 'Cat,' he said gently. 'You go now.' He nodded to the path away from the Bridestone. Cat walked a few paces and looked back, not believing that they were going to let her go so easily. Ash was standing in front of the stone with his arms lifted, and behind him the women were kneeling. They were waiting for something. Faintly across the heather came the knock of a drum beat, pattering like a living heart, out of the mist.

Cat turned and ran in a terror of what she might see. She fled from their silent watching and the mist billowed behind her, blotting out the stone. Her legs were trembling so much that they didn't seem to belong to her. She stumbled over a loose stone and fell to her knees in a patch of bright green grass. Bog water seeped through her jeans and she felt herself sinking into the spongy earth. She clawed at the heather in front of her and hauled herself back on to the path, crouching there, whimpering with fear, with the brackish water trickling wet and uncomfortable down her legs. There was a sudden long call from behind her at the Bridestone, orgasmic and frenzied. Not daring to look back, Cat went racing down the track, slowing down only when the red roofs of the cottages came into sight below her.

Chapter Eleven

'D'YOU want to go home?' said Fen. She was sitting on the battered sofa next to Cat. It was pulled up close to the fire and they were drinking coffee, well laced with brandy. Fen was almost as pale and shaken as Cat. She'd woken up to find Cat in tears beside her bed and still hadn't taken it all in.

'No of course I don't! I'm not leaving you here with all these queer things happening.'

'But there weren't any before you came,' burst out Fen.

Cat thought about it. 'You mean my coming here has set something off?'

'I don't know what I mean. There was that queer pattern in the porch the day you came, then the rabbit and the dead bird and all those strange stories Sally told us. Now this. It doesn't make sense Cat. I don't understand what Ash and these women were doing up there on the moor or what this "Bless the stone" is all about. I feel terrible about it, you should have woken me up if you wanted to go for a walk.'

'Someone phoned here. I thought the message was for you. But maybe it wasn't. Maybe it was me they wanted up there.' Cat shivered at the thought of the women's hands on her.

'What d'you want to do about it?'

'Forget it, as soon as possible. What d'you want me to do?'

'What they did to you was a form of assault. Nobody should get away with doing that.'

'I'm not telling anyone, if that's what you mean. They'd think I was mad. Let's just forget it, like I said. Maybe I just walked in on some play-acting which went wrong. Ash knew what was happening. Why does he go up to such a lonely place every day?'

'I don't know – it's difficult to tell with him.' Fen uncurled herself to put some more wood on the fire.

'Because he's shy, you mean?'

'No. Because he's not . . .'

'Not? Go on, Fen.'

'Normal, I suppose. He's not like other people. He was in a very bad crash on his motor bike a few years ago and he hurt his head. He was thrown against a wall. His memory's gone. Some days he can't even remember his own name. And he doesn't respond to things like other people, most of the time he lives in a world of his own. He'll never be any better.'

'Oh God,' said Cat. She closed her eyes and saw a big black motor bike and Ash smashing against a wall and falling over and over to the green grass.

Fen came to sit next to her. 'I thought you knew.'

'No. I didn't realize. I was trying to make friends with him up at the stone. Like Michael said. I thought I could be his friend.' She broke off and looked at Fen. 'Why did Michael say that then, about me getting to know him?'

'He does need friends.'

'Poor Ash,' said Cat sadly. 'He's so beautiful.'

'Poor Cat.' Fen hugged her tightly. 'Don't go up on the moor again without me.'

Cat looked out of the window to the moor top where the mist trailed like a thick scarf. 'No. And stop worrying about me. I'm okay now. But you've got to find out from Michael if it's Patsy bringing us all these weird offerings – I don't think it is. Promise you'll ask him?'

'Yes,' said Fen uneasily. 'I will. When I get the chance.'

Cat stared at her and said nothing.

In the cottage next door Patsy was doing something which she knew very well she shouldn't. She was crouching on the floor of the living-room, searching through the bottom drawer of the cupboard. She was looking for the book her dad was always writing in, the one she wasn't allowed to go anywhere near. He wouldn't be back home until lunch-time and her mam was out in the garden cleaning out the hen-house. She'd come back inside in a bad temper. She always did after that smelly job. Patsy was supposed to be tidying up her bedroom, but first she wanted to see this book.

She found it under a pile of old horse magazines. She laid it carefully on the floor and opening it read the first entry aloud. 'This is a recipe from an old book. To catch a frisky horse or a nervous youngster running out at grass, make this mixture and spread it on yourself. Oil of origanum, oil of rosemary, oil of cinnamon, oil of fennel. Stand so that the wind carries the scent of this to the horse. If you smear a few drops of it on your forehead on sunny days, he will smell it and come running. Or you can bake little cakes scented with this and coax him.' Patsy was disappointed. She'd expected something a lot more exciting than old recipes. She flicked through the first pages, reading a line, a paragraph, here and there. Enough to see that it was mainly about Bel and his visiting mares. She might have known. Not bothering with any of the later entries she slammed the book shut crossly. As she did so the corner of a photo slid from the pages. Patsy pulled it out and looked.

It was a Polaroid of a woman with red hair. One of those three from the village who were always hanging round her dad. Not as Patsy had ever seen her, though.

She was naked, standing up on the moor in front of the Bridestone. Her red hair was loose and rippling round her face and shoulders. It had daisy chains threaded in it. Round her waist there was a belt of plaited grass, and both of her pink nipples had a knot of grass tied tightly to them. And down between her legs there was a great bush of red hair and it was woven with pink-tipped daisies and buttercups, and a thin plait of what looked like hairs from Bel's tail hung from it. She had something hanging on a string round her neck, like a little bag, and in one hand she was holding a little horse. Patsy had one like that, upstairs in her bedroom. She didn't play with it any more – they were for kids. It was queer to see a grown-up holding one all wrapped round and round with daisy chains. And something round its neck. Patsy looked more closely at the photo. Little bits of white things threaded round its neck. They were bones of something, she thought, and shivered.

She sat and stared at the photo, holding it tightly between her hands and it sang to her. She wasn't interested in how her dad came to have such a thing, she'd known for a long time that he liked other women as well as her mam. She'd heard her mam having a go at him about it for as long as she could remember. The photo was making another picture inside her head and she wanted to draw it. She concentrated on it and the feeling in the room began to change.

The air grew thick and heavy where she knelt and full of an old, musky smell. She narrowed her eyes and stared, and the colour began to drain from the photo, leaving it brown and sepia, like a very old one. The red hair and pink flesh, the yellow buttercups and pink-tipped daisies paled and faded. Only the woman's blue eyes looked up for a moment longer at Patsy, then they too dimmed and were gone. Patsy was staring down at a blank piece of glossy white paper. Still she sat and stared and it seemed to her that another picture was coming out.

There was another pair of eyes beginning to form, glaring up at her, red and slitty and she wanted to put down the photo but she couldn't move, none of her would move. And a mouth was coming round and opening under the red eyes. It was going to say something and Patsy didn't want to hear, didn't want to know what the big round mouth was going to tell her to do. She could hear the first faint hiss of the coming voice and there was the sudden sharp crack of the back door closing as her mother came in from the garden. Patsy blinked and shuddered and the photo went blank again. Then very slowly colour began to seep back into it, first the red hair and the pink flesh, then the flowers and the grey mass of the Bridestone. She pushed the photo back into the book and hid it again under a pile of magazines. Her head felt funny, as if she'd been somewhere without knowing about it. It often felt like that nowadays, as if it were too tight somewhere. She made for the stairs in a rush, closing her bedroom door quietly behind her.

A drawer was out of the chest under the window and was standing on end in the middle of the floor. Patsy scowled at it. How did things move themselves when she wasn't even there? She hadn't left a drawer in the middle of the floor. She pushed it back into place crossly and began to tidy the room by piling most of her things under her bed. She couldn't be bothered to put everything away in the proper place; she needed some paper and her felt-tip pens to get out the picture of the woman which was hurting the inside of her head. She wasn't even going to think about those red eyes and that big round mouth; she'd made them up. She must have made them up. The pain in her head was very bad. She snatched up a sketch pad and her pens and lay face down on the bed. She shut her eyes and out of the darkness there came the picture, waiting to be drawn. A big, wriggling tangle of hair, thin as red wire, fat nipples with grass tied round them and daisies down there. Daisies in a curling mass of red hair, down there.

Patsy opened the box and picked out a red-tipped pen. She pulled off the top just as the voice came floating up the stairs.

'Patsy!' shouted her mother. 'Get yourself down here. I want you to do summat for me. And I hope that bedroom's tidied up when I come up to check.'

'Yes, Mother,' said Patsy crossly. She looked round the room. It seemed okay to her. What did her mother want now? She wanted to start the drawing.

'Patsy!' came the voice again, more urgently. 'Down here, I said. Now!'

She dragged her unwilling feet down the stairs. 'What?' she said sulkily. There was a strong smell of chicken shit in the kitchen, but Patsy decided not to mention it.

'There's a basket of eggs on the table. Take them next door, will you? Your dad asked me to let them have some.'

'Why can't you take them yourself?'

'Because I'm busy, that's why, and because I asked you to.'

Patsy leant against the kitchen table and stared at the brown eggs. She'd thrown one at Cat, that first time she'd seen her, leaning out of the window all bare. She wished she hadn't, now. Cat had been nice about her drawings and she was going to show some of them to a real artist, in London. But it had been funny, seeing the egg go up in the air and crack on Cat like it did.

'Don't stand there with a daft grin on your face,' said

her mother staring at her. 'Get on with it before they all go bad, will you?'

She had no right to be so nasty. Patsy was going to take the stupid eggs for her, wasn't she? Just because she didn't want to go next door herself. Lazy cow. Patsy felt all the badness coming back inside her again and scowled at her mother. Sally shrugged and turned her back on her, busying herself at the sink. Patsy sighed heavily and reached out a hand for the basket, hating her. The eggs came up out of it one after the other, hurtling up to crack hard against the ceiling. Sally put a hand to the back of her neck and spun round. Yolk and egg-white dripped slowly down on to her and a piece of eggshell landed on her cheek.

She had her hand out to hit Patsy when she saw how the eggs were coming out of the basket like bullets, firing themselves up at the ceiling, coming out all on their own. Patsy was standing at the end of the table, white-faced and shivering. The last egg smacked against the ceiling and spattered down to the floor.

'I didn't,' stammered Patsy. 'I didn't – not this time.'

Her mother's hand fell to her side. 'No,' she said. 'It's okay, love. I saw them. You didn't touch them.'

'How? How did they?' whispered Patsy.

'Don't fret. It was maybe you in a queer way – you're at a funny age. No, I don't mean you did it on purpose. It happened to me once, when I was your age. Frightened me to death. Come here, give us a cuddle, there's a good lass.'

Patsy crunched over the broken shells to the safety of her mother's arms. 'I'll clear it all up,' she said in a muffled voice.

'Good lass. Let's have a cup of tea before we start on it. I'll put the kettle on.'

'What happened to you?' asked Patsy timidly, kneeling

109

down and beginning to gather up the broken shells. 'When you were as old as me?'

Her mother stared out of the window as the water filled the kettle and began to laugh. 'My old gran was still alive, living with Mam and me. That would be your great-gran. She was having a baking day and she wanted me to help her. I didn't feel like it, I wanted to be outside playing with my mates. She went on and on at me until I got so angry I could hardly breathe.'

Patsy crouched, listening, as her mother put down the full kettle and switched it on.

'She had this big bag of flour on the table and I suddenly thought how funny she'd look, covered in flour. And up went the bag, sailing through the air just like your eggs did and it emptied itself over her head. She was covered in the stuff, coughing and wheezing and screaming her head off at me. She was as white with it as a ghost. My mam came in through the door at the noise, took one look and clouted me over the ear. She never did believe that I hadn't thrown the bag at gran. Gran saw what happened but I don't think she would let herself believe her own eyes.'

Patsy's head was filling with cartoon strips of her mother and the bag of flour flying through the air, the flour settling like dust everywhere.

'Come on love, sit down and have a hot drink and a piece of cake. You look like a little ghost yourself. Then you can start on the floor while I give the ceiling a wipe. We'll not mention what happened to your dad, shall we?'

'No, let's not. What will they have next door for their tea now, Mam?'

Sally shrugged. 'Who cares? Bacon butties. Whatever they fancy.'

'That sounds nice, bacon butties.' The hot tea crept into the ache in Patsy's stomach.

'You want one for yours? I'll do you one. Just don't ask me for an omelette, that's all.' Sally's dark eyes met Patsy's and the pair began to giggle as the last drops of yolk dripped from the ceiling to splash stickily to the floor next to them.

Chapter Twelve

THE organ died away into silence and the congregation rustled and sank on to the uncomfortable wooden pews. It was years since Cat had been in a church. There was an old smell in this one, of years passing, of dust and mice. She had woken to the sound of church bells ringing faintly to find Fen standing by the bed saying urgently that the car would be there in fifteen minutes. 'What car?' she muttered and groaned as she saw the mist pressing thickly against the window again.

'Mrs Barton's. Did I forget to tell you? She takes me to church every Sunday morning then back to the Hall for coffee.'

Cat reached out for the mug of tea on the bedside table. 'I don't feel very keen to meet any more villagers. I had enough yesterday.'

'You can't stop in here for the rest of your holidays. And nobody is going to do anything to you in church. Not when I'm with you.'

She looked so fierce that Cat laughed and drank her tea quickly.

Next to her now, Mrs Barton's suit smelled of mothballs. Cat turned her head to find the other few members of the congregation watching her with interest. There was a stained glass window set into the side wall and the sun suddenly broke through the mist to send a spray of purple and blue light on to the man sitting below it. Cat caught her breath at the splendour of him and the feelings she had when she first saw Ash at the kitchen window came back stronger than ever. He looked strange; unearthly. He turned his carved head and saw her watching him, eyeing her gravely for a moment before he smiled at her. It was a long, sweet smile and it wiped out the fear Cat still felt. He was her angel again, glorious, holy.

Cat smiled back at him, then the expression on her face changed to one of anguish as Fen dug her sharply in the ribs. She realized that everyone else was getting ready to lift up their voices to the Lord.

'He who would valiant be,' sang all the people, ''Gainst all disaster.' Fen was carolling away in a high, pure voice at one side whilst Mrs Barton boomed strongly down in the region of her sensible black shoes. Ash's smile had been one of recognition and pleasure. He must have meant her no harm in that scene at the Bridestone yesterday; Cat had got caught up in something she didn't understand. It was unfair that he was always going to be on his own, never to know the love of a good woman. Or the body of a bad one. But if he liked her, if she could, after all, make friends with him, help him somehow, draw him back into normal life and fill in some of those black spaces in his memory. She imagined making love to him, saw him rising from the grave of his hurt mind with his memory restored. She thought of him standing naked and triumphant – her pilgrimage, her cockle-shell of valour. She glanced back at him again and saw him standing with uplifted face, singing in the glory of the purple and the blue.

Cat turned her head and began to sing and in her head Ash unfolded his feathered, purple-stained wings and, as magnificent as the angel Gabriel, soared to the highest point of the roof, shining against the arches there. He moth-winged softly down through the still air, handing out miracles wrapped like chocolates in silver and gold paper to the kneeling open-mouthed congregation. She felt the air stir as the great wings beat softly above her. His long glittering hair brushed her face as he gathered her to him. She lay against his chest lamb-innocent, sin-free, and rose with him to the highest point of the altar where he rested in a pool of golden light. Her clothes fell from her like dead leaves to the forest floor of the church, far below them. His feathers brushed her naked breasts and she parted her long legs for him. Leda and the swan, she clung to him; his broad wings were round her back and she was safe. Between her legs she felt the first faint blessing of him then, like a holy sword, he pierced her, in and in until she was purified and changed by him. And he was hard as a white bone inside her.

The vicar looked up from his hymn book and caught sight of Cat's uplifted face with astonishment. He looked at her parted mouth, at the ecstasy beaming from her shining eyes and hope landed on him like a white bird. Here was the glory of the Lord shining from this young stranger's face. He decided to add on another section to his sermon on the power of God to move, even today. As the hymn came to an end, the people lifted up their voices on a final note, the hills rejoiced and so did Cat.

She sank back down into her seat and swallowed hard. She wanted to put down on paper that image of herself with the angel. She passed the rest of the service in working out the best angle for the angel's wings, the best way to catch the splintered mosaic of coloured glass. As the congregation filed out at the end of the service, the vicar took her hand in his dry one and shook it firmly. 'I do hope we shall see you again,' he said. She'd been an inspiration to him somehow, Cat thought, seeing the way he stared at her. She smiled politely and nodded.

Mrs Barton hurried them along the path to the little car park and urged the pair of them into the back of her car. She pulled out jerkily on to the lane. 'How d'you like living here then, young woman?' she asked Cat over her shoulder, narrowly missing a couple of sheep as she did so. 'A bit more peaceful than that dreadful place where you live. I can't think how you stand the pace. Not like living here.'

Cat and Fen looked at one another, then Fen grinned and stared out of the window, leaving Cat to answer. 'Yes, it's very peaceful here,' said Cat politely, thinking of the dead rabbit in the porch and of the feel of the Bridestone against her bare skin.

Fen groaned and turned it into a cough. 'I'm taking Cat to the jumble sale at the school next week.'

'Ah, yes. Thursday. Sally's having some kind of stall. Good job you reminded me, I promised young Patsy I'd sort out some old books for her. Coffee for us now, and some of Sally's home-made bickies. I must say I thought we were never going to get away today – never known the vicar to preach for so long. Can't think what set the man off like that.'

They drove the rest of the way to the Hall in silence.

The three women in Abbey's cottage were sitting round the table, concentrating on decorating the little horse which stood in the middle of it. Abbey was sticking feathers on the haunches and legs whilst Olivia threaded a necklace of small silver and blue beads. Amy was intent on cutting out a saddlecloth of black and white fur from a larger piece on her knees.

'Is that cat skin?' said Abbey suddenly, pausing with a black feather between her fingers.

'Yes.' Amy measured the piece of fur carefully against the horse, then threaded her needle. 'And don't ask me where I got it from because you don't want to know.'

Abbey said nothing. She stuck the last feather in place

and pushed the horse across to Amy. She folded her arms and watched her as she began to stitch the fur together below the horse's stomach. Amy looked like one of her own cats, she thought. She had a pointed little face with big green eyes. And a couple of odd whiskers on her chin. 'Why didn't you ever get married, Amy?' she asked her curiously.

The needle didn't pause, sliding silver in and out of the soft fur. 'Never wanted to. Look at you two anyway – neither of you could keep your husbands.'

'Oh, you could have had mine any time, Amy. You only had to ask. I didn't want him.' Olivia tied a knot and slipped the necklace over the pricked-up ears and head of the horse. 'All those years he never touched me, made me live with him as if I was his sister. All my best years that will never come back. I feel cheated now, when I know what's it's like being really wanted by a man.'

'And such a young one,' said Abbey.

Olivia grinned. 'He never seems to get tired, does he? There must still be plenty over for Sally or else she'd be complaining. I'll tell you both something. That time when Michael fucked all three of us, that was the first time in my life that I'd ever come. I didn't know that's how it felt.'

'He's a very good lover. I'd have left my old man any time for him. You could have had my husband with a free packet of tea, Amy love. Not that you'd have wanted to keep the bugger. You can get up in a morning and feel ugly and useless easy enough without needing a man to keep on telling you that you are. The sex was no good, either. He let himself get fat and he was that heavy. It was like being under a mattress when he got on top of me. He couldn't get it up very often and he would lie there pumping away and getting nowhere while I was making out grocery lists in my head for something to do. And it was always my fault he couldn't do it, it was because I was old.'

'Michael doesn't think you're old,' said Amy. 'You like sex with him all right.'

'So do you.' Olivia began to put the small beads back into the pansy-patterned box on the table next to her.

'I didn't know what I was missing.' Amy glanced quickly at the other two. 'I never did get you two thanked for helping me the way you did that first time. I don't think I could have done it if I'd been on my own with Michael.'

Abbey shrugged. 'Don't be daft. It was harder for you with not being married.'

'I enjoyed it,' said Olivia and the other two stared at her in surprise. 'And don't look at me like a couple of owls. That was something else I didn't know, how nice another woman's skin feels. And you have lovely soft skin Amy, and such nice little tits –'

'Watch her Amy, she'll have us doing a replay in a minute.' Abbey's laugh fell into the silence in the room as Olivia stretched out a hand and stroked Amy's long silver hair.

'No!' said Abbey sharply and the coldness of her voice made Olivia snap her hand back. 'Michael wouldn't like it if we did it without him. We have to save it and share it with him. Use it properly for the power. So don't you two go sneaking off behind the bike sheds like a pair of naughty kids. Buy yourself a good vibrator, Olivia, and try a few experiments with that.'

Olivia looked intrigued. 'Have you got one?'

'I got one the week that my husband walked out on me for his bimbo. It never tells me that I'm old and ugly, I can come when I want to and all it ever needs from me is new batteries now and again. It's not the same as the way a young man tastes and feels, I admit that. Let's face it though, not many men of Michael's age fancy older women the way that he does.'

'He fancies younger ones as well,' said Amy. 'Do you suppose he's fucking Cat and Fen?' Two cross faces glared at her. 'Sorry. I was just thinking, that's all.'

'Well don't! We don't want to know, even if he is, thank you. We've done the horse for Cat as Michael asked us to, so let's leave it at that.'

Olivia scowled. 'I don't see why she should have a horse anyway. Why should she need one like ours? She's nothing, she's only here as a teaser. Michael said so. What's she going to do with it?'

'Same as she did with the rabbit and the bird, probably. If Michael says she has to have one, then we make her one. Don't be daft, Olivia. Who's taking it? I took the rabbit. Olivia took the bird. Your turn, Amy.'

'I do my share – I was the one who made the phone call to get her up to the stone,' said Amy. 'But I'll take it. They'll be in church like good little dears. It'll be a nice surprise sitting on the door step for them. Seeing as it's Sunday, I'll copy out a bit of the Bible to put with it.'

'A bit out of the Bible? That seems the wrong place for you to look for a quotation. I didn't know you knew any of the Bible.' Abbey laughed. 'Something out of the Song of Solomon?'

'A bit about the horse of course. "Hast thou clothed his neck with thunder? The glory of his nostrils is terrible."'

'That sounds just like Bel,' said Olivia. Abbey nodded and the three women got to their feet and crossed the room to a low table standing below the window. Their faces were close together as they knelt beside it and stared at the model they'd been working on.

One of the decorated toy horses was standing on top of a shallow box painted green. Behind it, there was a long, narrow piece of rock upright in a block of modelling clay, with a flat piece laid in front of it. There were some figures made out of the same clay arranged in a row before the stones. On their round heads were tufts of hair: one had long red hair, one a mane of silver grey and the third had a wisp of dark curls. In front of these and a little apart was a heavy-breasted one with a tuft of dark hair. She was facing the horse's head where a man stood at each side, one with long fair hair and the other dark. None of the figures had faces: only the hair showed who they were. The men were obviously so from their jutting erections, as thick as one of their arms. The horse had been added to as well, so that he was an erect and entire stallion. There were offerings spread in front of him; a blood-stained feather, a scrap of white-stained cloth, a shell shaped like a finger nail.

Abbey leant forward and placed the last figure at the horse's head. It was much taller than the other women, with a long hank of yellow hair hanging down its back. Pressed into her body were tiny, coloured glass beads, patterning round her curving stomach and snaking down her back. Round her waist there was a thick silver ring. Abbey pushed down the little figure, bending its legs so that it squatted below the horse's head. It had a slit between its legs, leering up at the stallion. It was a *sheelah-na-gig*, grotesque and exaggerated.

'The goddess,' said Abbey softly and the other two repeated it after her. All three faces took on the same expression – fearful but expectant.

Cat closed the small, white gate behind them and hurried up the path behind Fen. 'Mrs Barton seems very keen on me drawing Bel. She was very nice about me going over there whenever I want, wasn't she? Fen? Fen? What's the matter?'

Fen bent and picked up something from the doorstep. Cat groaned. 'Oh God, not again!'

'No, it's nothing nasty. Look.' Fen turned and held it out to Cat. 'It's something nice this time.'

Cat stared at the little horse and thought she'd seen one like this before. Ash had been holding one that time he'd passed the gate, coming off the moor. But his had a red, sticky-looking patch on its back. There was a piece of tightly folded paper tucked under the horse's fur saddlecloth. Fen pulled it out and read it. 'Hast thou given the horse strength? hast thou clothed his neck with thunder? . . . the glory of his nostrils is terrible. He paweth in the valley, and rejoiceth in his strength . . . He swalloweth the ground with fierceness and rage . . . he smelleth the battle afar off.'

Cat stared at her. She wasn't sure that this was nice at all, even if Fen was. She was getting very fed up with coming back here and finding these scary things. 'Show me that paper,' she said suddenly to Fen. Fen passed it over to her and stood admiring the decorations on the horse. 'It's typed,' said Cat in surprise. 'That proves it wasn't Patsy. What did Michael say, by the way, this morning when you asked him about her?'

Fen went red and wouldn't look at Cat.

'You haven't asked him about it. Fen, you promised. Right. You stay here and admire that thing. I'm going to sort this out with Michael. I have had just about enough!' She stormed out of the porch and banged the door behind her. Fen winced and watched her run across the road and under the arch.

There was no sign of Michael anywhere in the yard. Cat marched across to the gate in the corner leading into the walled garden behind the Hall as if she knew where he was. He was right down at the far end, in among the canes, picking raspberries into an old basket. It was already half full and he was humming happily to himself. Cat stood behind him and watched, wondering where to start.

'You're all dressed up in your Sunday best,' he said suddenly without turning his head. 'Pretty as a picture.' He turned to her and brushed her mouth with a fat raspberry. She opened her lips automatically and he slid the soft fruit between them, leaning forward to kiss her lightly. She tasted the fruit and him together and jerked back her head.

'I didn't come here for that.'

'No?' He bent back to the fruit. 'What did you come for, then?'

'Because I'm getting frightened. Because there's things happening here that I don't understand. And I won't have anything happening to Fen. I want you to put a stop to it.'

'What things?' he said, pulling the soft fruit from its white cores and dropping it into the basket beside him.

'A disgusting dead rabbit in the porch. A dead bird hanging on the doorknob with its head pulled off. And now when we've got back from church, someone's left a toy horse with nasty fur and bits stuck all over it on the doorstep.'

His fingers stilled. 'Have they now? And is this what frightened you?'

It sounded stupid now she'd told him. She began to understand how Fen had found it impossible to tell him at all. But she had been frightened. She wasn't going to tell him what had happened to her up at the Bridestone. 'Yes,' she snapped defiantly.

'This is the country. Nature red in tooth and claw. We live nearer to death than you do in the city. It's not chocolate-box pretty here and it never was. But I'll see it stops if you're frightened.'

'I thought maybe it was Patsy.' She stopped, realizing how rude that sounded.

'No. It's not Patsy, I'm pretty sure of that. She knows better than to get up to mischief like that.'

He hadn't seen his daughter hurling eggs through the air at me, she thought crossly. Her anger was leaving her and she shifted from foot to foot uneasily. She'd no right to be here in Mrs Barton's garden. He picked up the basket and moved deeper into the canes, out of sight. What was she supposed to do now?

'Give me a hand,' he called back to her. 'There's a lot of fruit in here.'

She pushed her way into the brittle canes but there was no sign of him. Only the leaves rustled at the far side and were still again. 'Stop playing silly games!' she called crossly. The sound of a car door slamming in the yard and an engine starting up startled her. Mrs Barton was going out. Fen had told her that she went over to Scarborough every Sunday afternoon to visit a friend. So she wasn't going to discover Cat trekking through her raspberry patch, which was a relief. Cat listened until the sound of the car died away into silence. Nothing stirred in the garden; not a bird sang. She scrambled through the canes until she found herself standing on an old, flagstone path. Which way had he gone? One way seemed to lead to the house, the other deeper into the heart of the sleeping garden.

Cat hesitated, then at the far end of the path she saw a pale scrap lying there. It was a raspberry leaf with three fat raspberries on it. This way, then. She picked up the fruit and slid it into her mouth, walking towards the small, white door. It swung gently on its hinges and was still again. Through there? Was she supposed to go into the house after him? Mrs Barton had gone out, but even so. She shrugged and went inside. The house closed itself round her, hot and silent. She was in some sort of garden-room with bunches of onions hanging from hooks in the ceiling. There was a long shelf of vases under the window and the room smelled of flowers. She went through the door at the far side.

Now where? In front of her was a long, narrow corridor with doors off one side. And in front of the door at the far end there was another silvery raspberry leaf of fruit for her. She ate the berries delicately, sliding them into a mouth dry now with fear. She shouldn't be doing this. And something nasty was going to jump out at her and shout, 'Boo!' any minute now. She was walking in a fairy tale. She didn't know which one yet, but something here was waiting for her. She opened the door and went through. In front of her there was only a flight of stairs, narrow and uncarpeted. She went up them one by one, listening and twitching.

At the top, another long corridor with doors off it. And again, at the far end, another flight of stairs with the red fruit waiting for her on the bottom step. These stairs were narrower than ever; she could touch the walls at either side of her as she climbed. They were thick with dust and there were footmarks, going up ahead of her. Up and up to the very top of the house where the air was hotter than ever. She pushed the half-open door at the top of the stairs and walked through into the attics. This first room was full of furniture, of broken chairs, pictures with splintered glass and a three-legged table where a dead bird lay. It must have flown in somehow and not been able to get out. Cat turned in a panic back to the door she'd just come through, but it was still half open. She could go back through it whenever she wanted. She hesitated, then went slowly through into the second attic room.

It was smaller, packed full of chests and boxes, of old newspapers, yellowed and brittle. And still there was no sign of Michael. She had almost lost sight of what she was doing here by this time. The house had swallowed her, wrapped her up in its old memories, its dried butterflies of past years. She crossed the room and turned the handle of the door to the third and last attic. She saw herself three times over, walking to meet herself, reflected three times over in the long mirrors of the row of wardrobes against the wall. In front of the dusty window was an old Victorian rocking horse, very slowly moving backwards and forwards on its long rockers. But still there was no sign of Michael; only the basket of fruit stood on the broad window-seat with a dead butterfly lying next to it. She crossed the dusty floor and leant against the grey dappled horse, stroking his red, flaring nostrils. On the red leather saddle of the horse lay the last leaf full of raspberries for her. She crammed them into her mouth, let the leaf fall to the floor and climbed up on to the horse, pulling up her skirt to slide her leg over him. She began to rock slowly backwards and forwards and the middle wardrobe began to creak.

The mirror on the door began to move; the door swung open very slowly, inch by inch opening on to a black pit of darkness; out of it a brown paw slid. It touched the floor with a sharp click of yellow claws. And still the dappled horse moved slowly backwards and forwards, backwards and forwards, as Cat held her breath and stared. And another paw and then all in a roll of shaggy fur the great brown bear came out of the wardrobe and the room was full of the smell of it. And then Cat knew which fairy tale this was. This was 'Beauty and the Beast' and the beast was going to eat her all up. The bear swung his heavy head and stared with little red eyes at her. She could hear his heavy breathing filling up the room.

The horse rocked faster and faster but there was nowhere it could take her. She tried to scream but no sound came out of her. Then the bear padded across the floor and reared up on his hind legs, his long claws drawing red lines down her bare thigh and his bulk was on her, dragging her from the horse with a clink of silver stirrups. His weight carried her to the dusty floor with a thud which took the breath out of her, then he was on her, his huge paws wrapped round her and his long fur brushing against her skin. Then very softly he said in her ear, 'And Pussy and I together will play. Take off your clothes for me.'

And then it was Michael and the bear at the same time and all in one and as he crouched in front of her she saw how the skin was split down from the chest and there was his white skin and his thickly swollen prick. Her hands shook as she pulled off her clothes and let them fall to the floor, standing with bent head submissively before him. He stroked across her breasts lightly with his claws and she shivered, crossing her arms instinctively. The bear began to growl menacingly from the back of his throat, swinging his head at her and raising his claws to threaten her. He crouched on all fours with a low rumble as she let her arms fall to her sides and his hard, cold nose thrust itself between her legs, snuffling at the pale, shaved skin. He stroked the smooth cleft with the back of a paw and at the touch of his fur on her she groaned, reaching out to touch the top of his head.

He grunted in satisfaction and stretched up to his full height. Picking her up he shambled across to the rocking horse, where he sat her sideways on the saddle, facing him. He set the horse gently swinging with a blow of his paw and shuffled across to pick up the basket of fruit. He carried it across to where she sat and dropped it on her lap. Then he sat back on his haunches in front of her and waited. Side to side she rocked, barely moving, liking the friction of the red leather seat against her bare skin. She knew what he was waiting for. Bears are great lovers of juicy berries and the beast was growing hungry. She balanced the basket next to her on the broad haunches of the horse and picked out the first handful. She crammed the fruit greedily into her mouth, licking with a red tongue at the juice which ran from the corners to run down her chin and mark the full column of her throat.

Side to side the horse rocked and the bear hunched closer to her. She picked up another handful and crushed the sweet fruit against her nipple, holding the heavy breast in one hand to rub the red mass of pulp round and round its fullness, over the hard, stiff little nipple, where the juice beaded and hung like blood. And again on the other full breast. Then a pause. Side to side the horse rocked, gently swinging. Another handful of fruit. Down the valley between the stained breasts to the flat plane of her stomach. She eased her legs a little way apart and sat herself back in the saddle. She stroked the red fruit along the soft skin, bending her dark head to watch her fingers on herself. The flesh of the raspberries was sun-warm against her slit, slippery and erotic. There was a movement in front of her and she looked up, startled. The bear was on his feet and he was taking off his head. Underneath it he was wearing Michael's head. Now he was a bear wearing Michael's head. He came to her and laid a massive paw at each side of her, holding her by the hips to keep her still.

With a long red tongue he began to lap at her, lightly at first and then harder, his smooth tongue eating her and the fruit together. He nibbled and sucked at her until she felt herself begin to come and wriggled forward, catching hold of his dark head and pulling it tighter in towards herself. A paw cuffed at her angrily and he growled, biting her so that she cried out at the sudden pain. She sat frozen into stillness and he nodded and lowered his head to feast on her again. When she thought that she could stand it no longer, when she was so uncomfortable she was clawing at the saddle to be set free of this, he lifted his head and grinned at her, a red-mouthed grin dripping with juice. He stepped back from the horse and peeled off his skin, stepped away from the bear and now was only Michael. The bearskin lay in a patch of sunlight with its dead head watching them.

He lifted her round to face the horse's long tail and climbed into the saddle next to her. The horse creaked protestingly but it took their double weight and began to rock slowly backwards and forwards again. Michael held her head between his hands and kissed her small ears, licked the pink folds of them, came to her mouth and slid his tongue between her parted lips. She could feel him filling the dark cave of it. He kissed her throat, holding it between his two hands as if he could pick it like a flower stalk. Backwards and forwards they rocked as he bent his dark head to her breasts, holding their weight cupped in his hands, rolling his tongue round the nipples, scratching at them, pulling them roughly between his finger and thumb. She was melting for him, pooling away into nothing but the touch of his hands and his mouth on hers.

She reached down and felt how ready for her he was, springing hard and erect from the bush of dark curls. He lifted her on to his lap and she slid down on to his prick with a long moan of delight, locking herself on to him, pushing herself hard down on him to take him as deep as she could inside herself. She wrapped her arms round his neck and pulled his mouth down on to hers, snaking her tongue wetly into his open mouth and thrusting it quickly in and out. He reached round her for the narrow red reins and began to move the horse faster. Quicker and quicker it moved on its long rockers, creaking and groaning on the old floorboards. When it could safely rock no faster he caught her by the hips and came silently into her. He took her with him into orgasm and she arched back from him and came with a sigh of release. She felt as if she had been coming since she took the first step through the little white door.

'Beauty and the beast,' she murmured and he smiled and kissed her. Slower and slower the horse moved now, coming at last to a gentle stillness. Michael and Cat sat face to face on the dappled horse with their arms round one another. She felt safe here at the top of the house with him. She belonged to him now. She was Michael's.

Chapter Thirteen

THE sun came up over the sea and burnt out the last patches of fog. It was low tide and the abandoned rock pools lay silver on the sand. Inland, the sun marked off the folded hills and thrust long fingers into the narrow valley. Already, the day smelt hot.

A shaft of sunlight touched Bel's nose where he stood dozing by his empty hay net. Much of his time was passed in sleeping, some seven hours, perhaps, out of twenty-four. He'd slept through the warm night in short stretches, for most of the time standing, but towards dawn lying down flat in the straw. Horses dream only when they are lying down like this; they show the pattern of their dreams by their rapidly moving eyes. Bel had dreamed. Perhaps of coupling with an endless stream of ready mares, of running with his own herd down a long, green field. Or perhaps of nothing more than a series of broken images thrown up by the frustration of his days.

Bel was a perfect foal-machine. He was a fine Cleveland Bay with a wide, deep body and powerful long quarters; his mane, tail and legs were a shining jet black and his body bay. He belonged to this region as a native born, for since medieval days his ancestors had travelled the Dales as pack horses, broad backed and sure. The sunlight dappling his head widened into a growing patch of light as the top half of his door opened. Michael fastened it back against the wall and spoke briefly to Bel, identifying himself. The stallion whickered deep in his throat at the smell of fresh water as Michael came into the loose box with a full hay net and bucket. He pushed his mouth greedily at the water, sucking with closed lips.

'Give up, hoss,' said Michael affectionately, trying to put down the full bucket in place of the empty one. Water splashed over his feet as he took down the empty net and hung up the full one in its place. Lifting his head Bel shook it from side to side, then moved to the net where he lipped it delicately before pulling out a wisp and beginning to chew. Michael watched him for a moment to see if he was happy, checking all was well with him. Bel was his 'brother' as in the old days horsemen were brothers to their horses and his relationship with Bel was a strong one, almost psychic. Almost a marriage, he thought ruefully, if you listened to Sally grumbling about Bel. He had a dream once of Bel with Sally, her under the great belly of the horse, coupling with him. Women and horses were an old and magical combination. Look at the Arabs: they gave their foals for the first three years to the women to rear. And it was the North American Indian women who reared the war horses. It still remained in this country, that old veneration for horses left over from the time of horse worship — few British people would sit down even now to a nice plate of horse meat. 'Sacrilege, my beauty,' he said, running a hand down Bel's shining flanks.

The sun was already stronger as Michael shut the door behind him. He was early this morning; there was no sign of Fen. He grinned to himself at the thought of the two of them curled up like a pair of puppies. Fair head against dark. Nipple to nipple. Smelling of night-warm flesh. Opening the doors of the loose boxes Michael led out the mares by their rope halters and took them through to the field. He watched them move slowly away, sniffing the grass before dropping down their heads to graze. They had a good life, these two. He found them dull compared to Bel, lacking his spirit. He checked the water in the stone trough by the gate and came back into the yard to find Ash leaning on Bel's door.

'Now then, Ash,' called Michael. 'You can go in, he's having his breakfast.'

Ash nodded and swung open the door. He stood and waited for the stallion to come over to greet him with a soft grunt. Bel had lost most of his interest in his food as soon as Michael left him. Ash latched the half-door carefully behind him as the horse blew gently at the front of his shirt. He began to smooth the thick neck, scratching him roughly – Bel liked that. The horse swung his head round and in turn began to bite lightly at Ash's back. Then he moved past him to the door and looked out. He picked up the faint smell of the mares and, as their scent reached him, the erection which was never very far from him began to rise. The Victorian niceties of acceptable behaviour were nothing to him. The last time that Michael had ridden him through the village he'd scandalized the entire population by seeing himself in the post office window, where he had at once fallen in love with himself. Developing a magnificent erection he'd hurled himself joyfully at his reflection. Only the fact that Michael was such a fine horseman had prevented Bel from making a very painful covering of himself in a shower of glass.

Bel was restless now, shifting from foot to foot. Ash stood and admired the magical growth which appeared so often. His own erection was a poor and worthless thing compared to this. Ash remembered then that Michael had said it was time for Ash to do it with a woman, to do what Bel did to his mares with a woman. Ash loved Michael, he would do anything for him, but he wasn't at all sure about this. Last night on the TV he'd seen a man and a woman together on a bed. If that was what Michael wanted him to do then it was very dangerous. It looked to him as if the woman was eating up the man. She swallowed him up inside her body, and held him fast. Once, in the village, Ash had seen a dog with a bitch and it had seemed to him then that the bitch ate up the dog, caught him with her red mouth down there. All Ash knew was how Bel mounted his mares. Whether he'd ever known anything else he couldn't remember. His head hurt with trying to remember what he knew and what he didn't. What he did know was that he didn't want to put parts of himself inside a woman unless he was sure that he could get them out again.

He stood and whispered this to Bel and, between his own legs, felt his prick start to grow. He stroked himself dreamily through his jeans and leant against Bel's warm side. Passing the stable door, Michael automatically glanced in to see what the horse was doing. He saw how it was with Ash and knew by the look on his face that he was miles away.

Going into the loose box Michael spoke to Ash who smiled vaguely at him but made no reply. Michael knelt down and unzipped Ash's jeans, reaching in to stroke him. His eyes widened at the size of what he found tucked away in there. Ash gazed down sleepily at him as if all this had nothing to do with him at all. Michael lifted out the heavy weight of the boy's penis and held it in his hands. It felt so odd, to hold a man's prick like this for the first time. It was so powerful a part of a man, there should be a better name for it, a name with a bit of dignity, not something you saw scrawled on the dirty walls of urinals. It shouldn't be an insult to call somebody a prick. Or a cunt either, come to that. Ash's prick was beautiful, white skinned and blue veined and as solid as a piece of sculptured art. Michael felt himself begin to harden as he stroked Ash. He got to his feet and pulled the boy close to him and cuddled him, kissing the high cheek-bone, stroking a hand along the line of the jaw. Ash looked at him from somewhere a long way away and smiled. He reached for Michael's hand and pulled it back down to himself. 'I like you touching me there,' he said to Michael's surprise. 'Do it some more.'

Michael felt as if he'd just been handed a precious piece of porcelain and was terrified of breaking it. He began to stroke Ash's penis then caught hold of his prick tightly as he felt him begin to orgasm. Ash came quickly into the straw at Michael's feet and Michael hugged him, telling him he had done well, telling him that he was nearly ready now for his first woman.

Ash was still a bit doubtful, but now Michael had touched him down there and held him and it felt nice, it was all right. Nothing had got trapped or broken. He put his prick away and patted it comfortingly. All safe again. The stallion was bored with being ignored. He pushed his nose in between the two men and snorted. There was no quick release for him. His erection died back slowly. Michael left him to Ash, and in a little while Bel let himself be led back to his food, where he began once more to pick at the dried, scented flowers of the hay.

It was even hotter in London than it was in Yorkshire. Coming in with an armful of books from Marylebone Library, Alice Denby stepped into the house with a sigh of relief. London was full of noise and fumes in this weather, especially along Marylebone Road. She could smell disinfectant. The surgeon must be in his rooms on the ground floor. The receptionist came out of the waiting room and smiled at her. 'Good afternoon, Mrs Denby. There was a postcard came for you by second post.' She walked over and, picking it up from the neatly sorted heaps on the hall table, handed it to Alice.

Holding it very carefully, hoping it was from Cat but not yet allowing herself to look at it, she opened the ornate gates of the old lift and stepped in. The lift creaked into movement and took her slowly to the third floor. Alice got out and closed the gates, unlocked the door of the flat and, going into the living-room, dropped the books on to the sofa and crossed the room to sit on the window-seat overlooking the gardens. And only then did she allow herself to look at the card.

Blue sea, red roofs. She studied it as carefully as if it were in code, as if it could tell her what Cat was doing, then turned it over to read the message on the back. 'Having a lovely time, been sunbathing on the beach. Out now on the horses. Been invited out for a meal tonight. Fen sends her love with mine, C.'

Invited out to supper. But who with? And where? The card told her nothing. Nice as it was, it told her nothing. What Alice needed was a fifteen-page letter with foot-notes and index, accompanied by photos. She turned over the card to the view again. She could see how it was possible to have a lovely holiday in a place where the sea was so blue and the cottages clung to the cliff like an artist's dream. Maybe Cat was working very hard, filling page after page of her sketch-book so cleverly. As Alice sat holding the card, she felt increasingly uneasy. She was still worrying about that phone call, about that bruise on Cat's face. And who put it there. But she hadn't given Cat's number to that nasty, angry young man. Or her address. So Cat was quite safe where she was. Wasn't she? Alice sighed and let the card fall to the seat beside her. She leaned back into the corner of the window and stared down into the gardens.

There was a long, narrow row of them, secret gardens

leading down to the row of mews cottages, and, beyond them again, across a higher row of rooftops was the Telecom tower. Alice liked the tower. It was a lighthouse, keeping her safe at night when it was jewelled with red and orange lights. She looked back at the gardens. Already there was a greyness, a dustiness, as though the summer was wearing itself thin with so much heat. Alice thought of summer, of winter. The days appeared before her like a ribbon unrolling, all of them the same.

There was no air in this flat, no weather in the city streets. No seasons in bricks and mortar. She wished she were with Cat, breathing the air of those wild valleys. Cat came before her eyes, on the moors, running through the heather, Catherine and Heathcliff. Had she met him yet, that dark stranger Alice had waited for all her life? She saw in slow motion Cat in a long, sprigged muslin dress, silhouetted on a high crest of moor in the arms of a dark and passionate Heathcliff. She saw her standing in the wine-dark heather with her lover, saw his hands unfasten the buttons on her bodice. She saw Catherine naked to the waist as she had seen her in the garden, Heathcliff's mouth moving down to the small tips of the full white breasts. Alice blinked, stopped the film in her head with a jerk, froze it as his lips closed about the pink bud.

Crossing the room with quick, hard footsteps so that, in the room below, her husband winced and looked up at the ceiling, fearing for the old plaster, Alice placed the card on the mantelpiece of the Georgian fireplace. It leant there between the silver clock and the framed photo of Cat as a child. It lay there like an amulet. Alice stood and stared at it and shivered. There was something wrong with Cat, she thought again. Turning away unhappily she went across to the sofa and picked out from her library books a volume of Virginia Woolf's diaries. Taking it to the window-seat, she began to read.

Cat and Fen, coming back from a peaceful day in the sun at Raven's Bay, paused apprehensively at the porch door. There was nothing waiting for them this time, no signs or omens, only some papers lying on the door mat.

'I told you Michael said it would be all right now,' said cat as Fen bent to pick them up. 'He promised to sort it out.' She hesitated as if she were going to say something else, then changed her mind.

Fen began to read out one of the papers to her as they went into the cottage. 'This one's a notice about the jumble sale. Thursday from two o'clock. Then there's a list of stall holders – cakes, books, second-hand clothes and Mrs Sally Anderson, bottle stall.'

'Bottle stall? As in home-brewed poisons? Arsenic to dilute. Add your own water. Tincture of foxglove. Nice selection of newts' eyes.'

Fen ignored her. 'Look at these. Patsy's done the drawings for us. The ones she promised us when we had supper there the other night.'

Cat stretched herself out on the sofa and yawned. A combination of sun, sea-air and drawing all afternoon had made her sleepy. 'Can I see? She's really talented, you know . . .' Her voice died away as she saw the look on Fen's face. She sat up and held out a hand. 'Show me.'

'Look. It's you.'

It was Cat and a black cat at one and the same time. It was a cat's body, curved and taut the way a cat is when it plays with a mouse. Its ears and long whiskers were a cat's but the eyes and mouth were not. One of the front paws was resting on the tiny body of a man, and from the cat's half-open mouth there hung a tuft of curling, yellow hair. And the little man under the cat's paw had only a bloody stump where his head should have been.

Cat looked at it and shuddered. 'Oh my God. Now d'you believe that Patsy's mother is a witch? That's Ash. I've bitten off Ash's head.'

'This one's not much better.' Fen sat down next to Cat and passed her the second drawing.

'The stallion? It's Bel, isn't it?'

'Oh yes, it's Bel. But take a look at the woman standing next to him.'

The stallion was magnificent, strong and muscled with his head up and his mane and tail in a wild, tangled cloud round him. Next to him stood Abbey as Patsy had seen her in the Polaroid in her father's book. Cat sat and stared at the grasses round the woman's nipples, at the daisies plaited into the red mass of pubic hair. 'But where would Patsy get the idea from to draw someone like that?'

Fen shook her head and had no answer for her.

They stuck the pictures up next to their bed and when Cat woke very early next morning, before Fen for once, she was still thinking about them. She lay looking at them until Fen stirred in her sleep and flung an arm over her. Cat turned her head to look at her and ran a hand down Fen's bare brown back. A pair of startled blue eyes opened in front of her, then Fen smiled and touched Cat's face gently. Their mouths came together, warm and soft, and Fen's long hair fell across Cat. She pushed a knee hard between Fen's parted legs and she groaned and rubbed herself against it. They made love gently and slowly and it was Fen who came to Cat's fingers with a long groan of pleasure. Cat watched her face as she came and thought how strange an orgasm is in a woman, how self-contained women become and how far away they seem to go. Fen opened her eyes and sighed happily, then touched Cat between her legs. 'You haven't come yet,' she said lazily.

'No, don't.' Cat moved Fen's hand and held it in her own. 'I have to tell you something.'

Fen blinked at her then grinned. 'You're pregnant? I'll make an honest woman of you my love, never fear.' She looked at Cat's face. 'Cat? What's wrong?'

'When I went to see Michael yesterday. He ... we ...'

Fen stared at her and a grin of delight spread across her face. 'Are you trying to tell me that you and Michael had a romp in the hay?'

Cat sat up on her elbow. 'You don't mind?'

'Don't be daft. I do mind that you didn't tell me all about it as soon as you came back from the stables though. I did think you had a rosy glow to you at the time, but I thought it was because you were still angry with me for not tackling him about Patsy.'

Cat bent and kissed her. 'No. I know you don't like scenes. He said it wasn't Patsy, he was pretty sure, but he'd make sure it stopped.'

'And it seems to have done. So, he knows who it was?' said Fen thoughtfully. 'Oh, never mind that now. As long as there's no more carcasses. I want to hear about Michael. It must be strange, doing it with a man. Knowing what to do with such a different body from ours. So go on then – is he how we thought, and hung like Bel?'

Cat grinned. 'Yes, he is actually. You are sure you don't mind, Fen?'

'As long as you're happy that's fine by me. You know that. And as long as you still want me, of course.'

'Yes please,' said Cat. 'Now what was that offer you made me before?' Fen's fingers slid into her urgently. 'That's nice,' said Cat softly. 'I followed Michael up to

the attics in Fox Hall. There's a rocking horse there . . .'
And somehow it seemed to Cat then that he was there
with them both, and she wanted Fen to fill her as he
had.

Extract from Michael's Stallion Book

Cat came over to the stables this afternoon with Fen to start on some drawings of Bel. She's good – she let me look at her sketchbook before she started. Some lovely ones of Fen. I have the feeling that she's told her about what happened in the garden yesterday when Cat came looking for me. All to the good if she has: Fen's looking at me differently, noticing me more. She's beginning to wake up. I left Cat in with Bel and sent Ash in to keep an eye on her in the loose box whilst Fen and I got on. Bel wouldn't hurt her, but she's nervous of him and he picks that up so quickly. Makes him edgy. I sat her on a bale of straw in the corner and she was fine.

I was curious to see her drawings. I went back in half an hour to check on her and looked in over the half-door. She was working away, talking to Ash. He was leaning against Bel and listening, watching her with a lot of interest for Ash. So I left them to it.

It must be a good feeling, being able to draw like that. Being able to put Bel down on a piece of paper as real as life. I know every inch of that horse and the name of every joint and bone. She knows nothing: only how he covers his mares and she likes that. But she can look at him and see how he is formed. So real you look to see him breathing. And if I try to draw him he looks like something designed in the dark. Patsy has it, I don't know where from. It's a great gift.

The drawing Cat's done for Mrs Barton is grand but it's the second one she did that pleased me more. When we'd finished seeing to the mares, Fen and I went back to the loose box and Ash came hurtling out of it with a great grin on his face.

'Look!' he said. 'Ash with Bel.' And she'd drawn one of him with the stallion, the way they stand with Bel resting his head on Ash's shoulder. She'd made Ash so beautiful – I

hadn't realized that women saw him like that. Very, very sexy but needing protection at the same time. He turned to hand it back to Cat as she came out of the loose box behind him and she shook her head.

'*No,*' *she said.* '*The one of Bel on his own is for Mrs Barton. This one is for you.*' *I was very pleased with her, saying that. Nothing to what Ash was. I've often heard the expression* '*his face lit up*', *but it really did for once – it was like a light had switched on inside him. He put his arms round her and hugged her and she kissed his cheek. And he liked it! I've never seen Ash touch a woman before; it was a long time even before he'd let me put my arms round him and give him a hug.*

I asked him what he wanted to do with the picture. I had this sudden horrible feeling of what it would do to Ash if his father found it and ripped it up. Knowing Dave, he'd do just that. Ash stared at me with his face going blank.

'*I've brought some card with me. I'll mount it up for you, Ash. Then you can pin it up somewhere.*'

'*In the tack room would be nice,*' *said Fen. She was obviously thinking along the same lines as I was.* '*It would be quite safe there and we could all see it. Share it with you.*'

Ash liked that idea. He gave the drawing back to Cat. '*You'll give it to me again?*'

'*Promise. Come and have a coffee with us and we'll do it now – if that's okay with you, Michael?*'

It was more than all right with me. It was perfect, Ash getting more friendly with Cat. I couldn't believe it. There was Ash marching out of the yard with Cat at one side and Fen on the other, with never so much as a backward glance at me. That must be what it feels like when your kid leaves home. Then Cat turned and winked at me and gave a wriggle of her little bum. And Bel stuck his head over the door and whickered as if to say it was high time somebody gave him a bit of attention.

Chapter Fourteen

THE weather grew hotter and more brooding than ever. On the Wednesday afternoon Ash leaned against the wall of the loose box, watching Bel. The heat in there was thick enough to touch. Ash had been there for some time while the stallion paced backwards and forwards in a path from his hay net to the door, breaking the pattern from time to time to lean out hopefully. But nothing happened. No-one brought him a bride.

Ash licked his dry lips. He was thirsty. As Bel swung round and paced away from him Ash pushed open the door. There was a trough outside, with a tap. Ash turned it on and watched the clear spring water come bubbling out, then bent and put his mouth to it. He rolled the coldness round his tongue and let it ease down his dry throat. As he leaned over the trough he saw reflected beside him for a moment the long head of the stallion, elongated and distorted by the water. It lay fractured on the thin skin of the surface as Ash swung round in surprise. The horse stood beside him, blowing into the trough, lipping delicately at the water. Then he lifted his head and gave a loud cry and was off across the yard, thundering under the arch and away out of Ash's sight.

Ash stood and watched him go then bent and carefully turned off the tap. He looked at the stable door. Open. His fault. Not bolted it properly. Michael would be angry. Ash was glad that Bel was out – it was too hot in there for him. But still. Bubbling up a long way from the surface of Ash's mind came the awareness of how angry Michael was going to be. Angry with Ash for letting Bel out. Wiping the water from his mouth with the back of his hand, Ash looked carefully round the yard. Michael wasn't there. He closed the half-door and looked thoughtfully at it, then closed the top half as well, bolting it securely. There. Now no one would know what had happened. He ran across the yard and under the arch, out on to the road. 'Wait for me Bel,' he called. 'Wait for me.' If he could catch the stallion and bring him home, then Michael could not be angry with him.

Bel raced along the grass in front of the cottage and, at the sound of a car in the distance, swung sharply off the road on to the sheep track threading through the bracken up on to the moor. The bracken broke green under his feet as he pushed through it, his head tucked nervously into his chest, looking for tigers in the green shade. Sweat broke dark on his flanks as he pushed through the last of the thick fronds and out on to the heather. He turned and began to run along the ridge top. On either side of him the valleys lay in a pool of light, golden on scattered farms and cottages far below. Bel ran in a frenzy of being free, gulping in the sweet moor air as the wind, which is always blowing on these hills, whip-cracked at his flying mane and made a banner of his streaming tail. He lengthened his stride and settled himself into an easy lope. There seemed no reason why he shouldn't run to the very edge of the world.

Far below, Ash toiled up the sheep track. Looking up, he caught a glimpse of the stallion briefly for a moment, silhouetted black against the skyline, then he was gone. 'Wait, wait for me,' he cried again hopefully. Michael and the empty stable had dropped like a pebble to the bottom of his mind. 'Bel, Bel,' he crooned to himself and pushed on through the bracken.

Coming into the yard, Michael was horrified to see Bel's top door fastened. 'Christ, in this heat . . .' he muttered and ran across, flinging back the top half and bolting it securely to the wall. 'Bel? Come up, lad,' he said, peering in. Then again, in dismay, 'Bel?'

The stallion was gone. He opened the bottom half of the door and walked in slowly to stand in the heat of the empty loose box. How could Bel have got out and bolted the bloody door behind him? Maybe he was in the field with the mares . . . Michael was running before he finished the thought, knowing that it was hopeless before he got to the field gate. The mares were there all right, stuffing themselves as usual, but there was no sign of Bel. Michael ran back into the yard and stood helplessly wondering where to start. He took a deep breath, made himself begin to steady, to draw up calm from inside. Mrs Barton's car was out. Thank God for that. No need to tell her what had happened until he'd got Bel back. If then. But for the stallion to go missing now, when the days were running through so fast to Lammas, with only a few left for him to draw all the threads together.

He must have gone some time in the last hour. Michael had been working in the Hall garden – he'd have heard if someone had taken the horse and boxed him up, heard the horsebox drive off. So he'd gone on his own feet then. If he'd got out on the road, he could have gone any of three ways. Out on the coast road, down to the village or up on to the moor. Michael knew he was going to need help. Fen drove, she had her car. Patsy should be home by now. He ran across the yard to get them organized.

Cat opened the door to his urgent knocking. He pushed straight past her to find Fen.

'Have you seen Bel? He's gone missing. We've got to get him back. I can't lose him now, not when it's so close. Can you take your car, go along the coast road? I'll take Patsy and go to the village in the Land Rover.'

'Can I help?' said Cat.

'Aye, if you could go up the moor path to the top, you'll have a good view of the valley from up there.'

'Where's Ash? He'll help . . .'

'It must have been Ash who let him out. The door was bolted shut behind him. I'll kill the bugger when I find him.'

'Ash, presumably,' said Cat as the door banged behind Michael. Fen muttered something desperate and, grabbing her car keys, ran after him.

This time, Cat kept to the path at the side of the wall. She wasn't going to risk crossing the field and being chased by the ram again. She came scrambling out of the larch wood and, turning to get her breath, caught a glimpse of Fen's car below her, moving along the road like a metal insect. Around her, the folded hills seemed to stretch empty for mile after mile to the faint blue smudge of sea on the horizon. There was no sign of the stallion, no sound but that of sheep bleating in the distance. She set off towards the Bridestone.

She didn't want to be up here on her own at all. She stood well back from the stone: she wasn't going any nearer to it than she had to. There was a sound, wailing faintly over the moor to her. She held her breath and listened. It was someone singing. It was Ash coming towards the Bridestone across the moor, leading Bel by the halter and singing as he came.

The stallion came slowly, for he was tired now. Ash had caught up with him at the end of the long ridge where he was standing, nervous at going down the steep cliff which fell away at his feet. He'd been cropping jerkily at the short turf which grew at the rock edge and Ash took him by the halter and whispered to him. Bel followed him back from the steep edge and across the moor. He twitched an ear now at the sound of Ash singing and blew down his nose, a long 'hrrrmph' of breath.

Cat could make nothing of the song Ash was singing. It seemed to her to be dredged from some ancient past, to come out of the bitter land itself. She hesitated, wondering whether to speak or just to let Ash pass her where she stood, half hidden by the stone. But Bel knew she was there. He swung round his head and dug in his forelegs. Ash's song died away and he turned to look at Cat. 'I'm taking Bel home,' he said happily and led on the stallion. Bel seemed larger and more powerful than ever, seen this close as he swung past Cat with sweat-darkened flanks. She followed them down from the moor.

Halfway to the village, Michael suddenly slammed on the brakes and brought the Land Rover to a halt. Patsy jerked forward in her seat belt and yelped. 'Dad, what are you doing? Dad?'

He sat motionless, his hands clutching at the wheel, staring ahead out of the windscreen. He turned his head very slowly to look at her and she screamed in terror because it wasn't her dad looking at her, not any more, it was something else looking at her like that thing with red eyes had looked at her in the Polaroid. She tugged uselessly at the seat belt, whimpering and desperate to be out of the Land Rover and away from the thing next to her. She could smell it, like an animal, like the horse smelled and its eyes were all red and starey . . .

'It's okay Patsy,' said her dad. And it was him again. She wiped her wet face with her hands and took a shuddering breath. 'It's okay love. Bel's safe. Ash is bringing him home now. Come on, we'll go back and meet them.'

He swung round the Land Rover and set off back to the stables. But how could he know that, thought Patsy. And what if he changed into that other thing again when she was with him, and this time he didn't come back?

Much later that night, Michael leant against the stable door and watched the bats flittering in the dim light. An owl was calling along the lane. He hooted back to it, repeating its round, smoke-rings of sound until the bird, confused, took flight and feathered softly past him. Mrs Barton's car had come in half an hour ago. There was nothing he need tell her now. It had been bad, losing Bel like that. The shaman had shown him that the horse was safe, shown him Ash leading him across the moor. And the horse was fine; Michael had given him a good rub down and later a warm bran mash. Ash had led him into the yard all smiles. Pleased with himself for bringing Bel back, forgetting by then that he'd let him out. There was no use getting angry with him; Michael didn't want to frighten him away from the place. Not now.

He yawned, listening to the sound of the horse in the loose box. He'd stay here for most of the night with Bel, just to make sure. Then he'd take him out on the long rein for a couple of hours after breakfast – the horse would be stiff, better to put him on the rein rather than ride him. Not that Bel minded Michael riding him, he was good like that. Most stallions wouldn't let a man up on them. He yawned again, thinking that tomorrow would be fine again, from the feel of the air. Something was happening tomorrow. What was it? It was the jumble sale at the school, that was it. They'd have a fine day for it. He yawned again and went back inside to Bel to check on him.

Michael sat at the table with his stallion book in front of him. He wondered whether to write down that Bel had been missing but there was no need. From the library book he'd just finished he pulled out a piece of paper with some notes on it and flattened it next to the book. It was still very early in the morning, only just gone five. He was satisfied now that Bel had come to no harm and could be left. He could smell honeysuckle where he sat. He'd brought in a big bunch for Sally and put it in a white jug on the table, where the heavy scent was filling the room. He knew it was thought of as an aphrodisiac in the old days, this strong scent. He hoped it was. He'd left a bunch of it in the porch next door, and he'd three more posies left. Then all their naughty, ruttish dreams would rise together as his women rode the night-horse for him. Sweet honeysuckle, sacred rowan and spiking bramble were all plants which held strong magic.

Michael jerked and dropped his pen as in the room above him Patsy screamed out wildly in her sleep, then was still again. Most nights lately she was doing this, saying she couldn't remember anything about it next morning. Sally never stirred. It would take more than that to rouse her.

What had he been thinking about? Plants. Sally's mother knew a lot about herbs and the way to use them. The trouble was, she'd never write any of it down, any of the old recipes. It was all in her head, bits she remembered from her mother Moll and her old gran. It was a queer old cottage, that, four generations of women living there, right back to Great-Gran Hepsy who must have been born about 1880. And never much sight of a pair of trousers between them, not staying longer than to hang overnight on the end of the brass bed.

Michael had been born in 1960, the same year as Sally, but he'd nothing further back than himself. It was different now that the laws had changed, now there was access to records for adopted children. He imagined himself knocking on some strange woman's door. 'Hello mother, I'm your long-lost son.' No way. He didn't want to know, thank you. He'd married Sally and taken her family as his own. Now he had Patsy. He'd been pleased the baby had been a girl. Another woman – sons were nothing to him. It was in the daughters the earth power lay. He stared down at the notes he'd made, trying to make sense of them. He'd been reading about the Society of Horsemen, how they had a ritualized bond between man and horse, how they won over the horse by the five points of feeling. And scent was the most important. The word was given to a new man at his initiation as a symbol of identity between him and his horse. Like he was with Bel. Bonded. But then the book had gone on to tell him something new. The toadmen.

These were horsemen with a very special talisman: the bone from a frog or toad. Michael began to copy his notes carefully on to the next clean page in his book: 'Keep the bone safely about you, or grind it up and mix it into an ointment. When you rub this on your horse, you are the master of him. But to get this bone, you must make a pact with the devil. Catch your toad and hang him on a blackthorn to die. Let the small birds come to pick his bones. Take the skeleton to a stream and throw it in. One bone will float upstream against the flow. It will be a forked one, like the shape of the part of a horse's hoof called the frog.'

Totems and talismans. Michael thought of his own powered-up small horses, of the talisman bags round his women's necks. All to gather power he could tap into, a source of magic for him to use.

The women rubbing their breasts on the stone were powering it the same way. Not so long ago in these valleys the farmers would put up smaller versions of the Bridestone in their fields which they called rubbing stones. Just as the people then believed touching the Bridestone increased human fertility, so they thought these smaller stones brought fertility to their cattle, by rubbing against them. When Michael touched the Bride-stone now, he could feel the power crackling through him like an electric shock. It was almost ready to be used. Michael pushed the book away from himself and yawned. He was very tired now. He must remember to make sure that Sally took that bottle of mead to the jumble sale. And that the right person got it. He yawned again and, getting wearily to his feet, went over to the armchair. He would have a couple of hours' sleep before he went back to Bel.

At two o'clock Fen pushed open the door of the classroom and a roar of noise hit her. She stepped back on Cat's foot and Cat yelped. 'What's this jumble sale in aid of?' she said, peering round Fen. The room was full of mothers and children all surging and pushing round the desks set out as stalls round the walls. It looked as if the entire female population of the village was crammed in here.

'It's to raise money towards a TV for the school.'

Anything to link this place to the outside world seemed like a good idea to Cat. She looked round the walls at the children's art pinned up there. Patsy was right – there was nothing of hers there, only pretty pictures of cottages and flowers. Fen reared up her head above the crowd at the door and, with Cat in tow like a smaller tug, sailed off across the room. She was making for a stall piled high with old clothes at the back. A selection of the better ones had been promoted to coat-hangers and were gathering a thin film of chalk dust where they hung from the top of the blackboard.

Fen began to sort through the sweaters. Cat lifted up a hairy, custard-coloured cardigan which would have fitted round her twice and put it down hastily. Who would buy these cardigans with no buttons, these pink bras with sagging elastic? And who could have given them in the first place? Cat felt something hard under the bras and pulled it out. It was an old powder compact, a silvery one with a blue enamelled flower on the lid. She opened it carefully. There was still a trace of powder left in it, smelling faintly of flowers. She held it up to look in the cracked mirror and there was a face behind hers, malignant and staring. It was the red-haired woman who'd been in the hay loft with Michael that day. Cat snapped shut the compact and turned, but there was no sign of that red hair in the woman pushing against her. The woman behind the desk said something in an accent so strong it could have been in a foreign language. Cat turned back to her. 'Sorry?'

The woman said it again, more loudly. Cat looked at Fen to translate. 'It's a pound if you want it.'

A 1940s compact for a pound. Cat got out the money and handed it across. 'Hello,' said a voice at her elbow. 'Mam says to come over to her stall, over here.' Patsy took hold of Cat's hand and burrowed her way into the crowd, with Fen following. Spells for all, thought Cat. Walk up, walk up, get your spell here to turn your neighbour's sheep bald. But Sally's stall was full of bottles – Cat wondered what possible connection there could be between a jar of pickles, a bottle of sherry and a bottle of shampoo. Patsy held out a jam jar full of straws to them. 'Pick one,' she said to Cat. Cat did as she was told and looked at Fen. 'Now what do I do?'

'I'll show you,' said Patsy. 'Fen, can I pick your straw for you?'

'If you'd like to.' Fen handed over the money for the two of them. Patsy picked out a straw from the back of the jar and pulled a rolled-up scrap of paper from the top of it. Sally watched her with a curious concentration.

'Number thirteen,' said Patsy. 'Mam, Fen's got

number thirteen.' She sighed, and Cat caught her looking at her mother in a relieved way, as if she'd passed some sort of test.

'Unlucky number,' said Fen.

Cat pulled out her number and unrolled it. 'Mine's number nine.'

'This is yours, then,' said Sally and handed her a fat jar of yellow honey with the number nine fastened on the side.

'What about Fen's prize?' Patsy looked anxious. Her mother lifted a bottle from the back of the desk.

'Here you are, number thirteen. You've gone and won yourself a bottle of my mead. I know how much you like it. You keep that for a special occasion.'

'Is it a special sort of mead?' Patsy stopped with a gulp as her mother turned on her a look which would have stripped paint.

'Did you give Miss that box of books and magazines that Mrs Barton sorted out for you?'

''Course I did, as soon as I got to school. Come on, you two, come and look at the book stall.'

When Cat looked up from sorting through a pile of old magazines, Fen seemed to have disappeared. Cat was surrounded by strangers, shoving and pushing and staring at her. Especially the one standing next to her; she was scowling fiercely at Cat from behind her round glasses in a way that Cat recognized. It was the woman from the post office, Olivia somebody. She was clutching a big carrier bag to herself with a froth of white lace spilling out from the top of it. Whyever had she bought what looked exactly like a wedding dress, wondered Cat. The woman saw where she was looking and hurriedly pushed the lace back into the bag. Cat didn't care that much what she'd been buying, she could buy herself a wedding dress as long as she didn't want Cat for a bridesmaid. She turned away from her only to find herself pressed tightly on the other side against a woman with long silver hair and a face like a cat.

'Miaow!' said this one softly. 'Who's a pretty pussy, then?'

Cat swung round, anxious to find Fen and get out of here. The red-haired woman was standing just behind her, smiling sweetly at her. The edge of the desk was cutting into the back of Cat's legs, as the women edged closer and closer to her, their moon-like faces pushing threateningly towards her. She was back at the Bride-stone, she could feel the three pairs of hands on her back, feel the women pushing her on to the rough stone and 'No, no,' she croaked, flailing out her arms wildly and sending a pile of glossy magazines slithering to the floor.

She crouched down among them as if that would save her, trying to gather them up with shaking hands as the three pairs of feet inched in with their high heels stabbing closer and closer. Then they were gone and it was Fen's shabby sandals beside her, Fen's face looking amused as she knelt beside Cat. 'What are you doing down here? Funny place to read.' She started to pick up the magazines.

'I'm not reading them, I knocked them off the desk when I saw the women . . .'

'Which ones? There's a lot of them here.'

When Cat stood up with her arms full of magazines, the women had gone. But there was a child with a parrot's head standing next to her. It turned its bright red and blue feathers sideways at her and squawked. There was a brown furry mouse behind it, stroking its whiskers. Cat stared round her in a panic, convinced that she was going mad, or that the women had put some kind of weird spell on her. In between the women, the children came pushing and they were all wearing animals' and birds' heads – lizard-green scales, black and white fur, feathered and beaked. There was a red fox snapping at a crowing cockerel, a tiny elephant curling its trunk round the neck of a pink pig. There were more and more of them crowding into the room, filling it with the noise of their bleating, their barking and cackling.

The magazines slid to the floor again as Cat clutched at Fen as the only sane and solid thing left in her world any more. Fen was saying something to her, but she couldn't make out a word in all the uproar of noise. Then there was the sharp sound of authority. A small, grey-haired woman stood up on a chair and clapped her hands and the creatures fell silent one by one, turning their masks to look at her.

'Children! Children! That's quite enough.' And not a feather stirred, not a beak clattered. 'Now, mothers, we have a little surprise for you all this afternoon. This past term the children have been lucky enough to have been given the chance of working with our local Writers' Group, who've been coming into school once a week and, with the children, have produced a play. It's called "The Rainbow-Coloured Ark", and gives us a strong message about how we need to save our environment . . .' At the back of the room a mother stirred restlessly and dropped one of her carrier bags. She blushed and picked it up under the frozen stare of the head-teacher. 'I won't keep you any longer in here, we'll all move out into the playground as there's more room out there.' Squashed and uncomfortable, the mothers nodded and smiled in relief. 'So, if the children will go first, then you all follow me into the yard, we'll start in a couple of minutes.'

She climbed down from her chair and went through a door at the back of the classroom. Hopping, stamping, skipping and frisking, the creatures followed her. Picking up their loaded bags, the mothers followed, anxious to get a good view of their children.

'You look as if you need some fresh air,' said Fen. She gathered up the scattered magazines again and threw them on to the desk. 'You're so white, are you okay?'

'Yes. Yes, it was just . . .' Cat stopped. This wasn't the right place. 'Let's go out and watch the play. D'you suppose Patsy's in it?'

'I imagine they'll all be in it. Didn't you see Patsy? She was the one with a mane, wearing a bridle.'

They followed the last of the mothers out into the yard where the three women stood together at the side of a big cardboard Ark, and round their feet the masked children were kneeling.

Chapter Fifteen

It was the first day of the school holidays and Patsy was already bored. She stood in the middle of her bedroom and wondered why she felt so strange. She was prickly somehow, uneasy inside her own skin. She'd woken herself up screaming in the night but she couldn't remember why. Something had frightened her though, so that somehow she didn't want to leave her mam this morning. She could hear her now in the kitchen, doing Mrs Barton's baking for the week. Patsy wanted to draw but she couldn't see any pictures inside her head, it ached too much. She wanted to do some more pictures for Fen and Cat – they'd said they had pinned up the others she'd done on their bedroom wall and that made Patsy feel good. It had been one of her best pictures, the one of that Abbey woman with daisies between her legs. Patsy frowned and wondered now why her dad had that picture stuck in his book about Bel? She imagined her mam's face if she ever got to see it and giggled.

She stood and listened. There was a lot of clattering in the kitchen and Patsy could smell chocolate cake. It was a nice warm, comfortable smell and it made Patsy feel better. She got out her folder of drawings and spread them out on the bed. She stood and stared at the top one. Someone had been writing on it. She snatched it up angrily. It was her dad's handwriting. Bloody nerve, him looking in her folder, never mind writing in it as well. She read out the words.

'The most lustful of all females is the mare.'

'So what?' said Patsy. She still didn't want it written

on her drawing. She looked at it and thought it wasn't that good anyway. The stallion was all right but the mare he was with was wrong somehow. But that still didn't give anyone the right to scribble on it. She narrowed her eyes and concentrated on the piece of paper in her hand, bringing all her anger to a sharp point in the middle of it. A small eye of blackness winked up at her, spreading across the paper like a slow stain, turning the drawing to ash as it crept. Patsy moved like a sleepwalker over to her waste paper bin and the dead flakes dropped into it softly, rustling into nothing.

Patsy blinked and shook her head. What had she been going to do? Her head ached worse than ever, like someone was sliding a knife in it, and it felt all of a muddle. She had stomach ache as well, now. The smell of the chocolate cake was stronger and browner than ever. Leaving the rest of the drawings scattered across the bed, she went slowly down the stairs to the kitchen, needing her mother, hoping that she'd be in time to scrape the bowl clean of cake mix.

Over at the stables, Ash was standing next to Bel's head, as close as he could get to him for protection, with his eyes shut. On the other side of the loose box Michael was in the straw with Abbey. She was on her hands and knees with Michael behind her. Ash could hear him talking to her. He was using his stallion voice, different from his other one. He was calling Abbey his good little mare. Ash was keeping his eyes shut so that he couldn't see what Michael was doing but the voice coaxed at him, made him feel a little safer.

He risked a quick glance then screwed up his eyes again in horror and hid his face in Bel's mane. Abbey, she was all bare. Pink and fat and bare. She was arching her back and swinging her head from side to side so that all her red hair was flying. Michael was pushing himself inside her, just like Bel did with his mares. She was eating him up and he would never get out again; he could hear her making happy noises as she ate him.

Ash shifted uncomfortably. His bits were all swollen up again like they did sometimes with Bel. The woman was putting a magic on him the same as she'd done to Michael. She screamed out, high and scary; Bel stamped his foot. Then there was silence. Ash heard his name. Maybe it was safe now. He risked another look through slitted eyes to see what they were doing, and it was all right, Michael was free from the woman and she hadn't hurt him, he was standing behind her smiling. He looked pleased; he was saying nice things to Abbey. She stayed on all fours and turned her head to look at Ash.

'Now you Ash,' she said. 'Now it's your turn.' She wriggled her round pink bottom and her red hair fell across her smiling face. Ash grabbed a handful of Bel's mane in horror and clutched it tightly, burying his face against Bel's neck. Michael's hand was on Ash now, stroking his back, telling him to go to Abbey as she wanted.

Ash's feet took him over to her. He stood behind her and reached out a hand to touch her warm flesh. She shivered at his fingers on her and Ash knew that she was ready for him, the way the mares were for Bel. Michael was behind Ash now, unzipping his jeans, stroking him there until he couldn't bear the nice feeling of it any longer. Crying out he knelt behind Abbey and went into her in one hard thrust, pushing into the warm valley of her. He held himself there until he came with an astonished pride, then opened his eyes to pull hastily back, turning to Michael to see if he'd done anything wrong. Michael pulled him to his feet and hugged him and, scrambling to her feet, Abbey kissed him and flung her arms round him. Ash stood cradled and safe in their arms, his face beautiful with pride at having pleased them both so much.

'I did it for you,' he said to Michael. 'I did it like Bel.'

Hearing his name the stallion snorted and stepped forward to them, thrusting his head between them to nuzzle at Ash's shining, transfigured face.

'He's telling you that you're as good as he is now, lad,' teased Michael.

Ash stroked the stallion's nose. 'As good as Bel,' he whispered.

The letter from Cat's mother lay face upward on the mat in the porch, where the postman had dropped it earlier.

Dear Cat,

It began very neatly and carefully.

Thank you for the postcard of Raven's Bay. It looks a lovely place, all those little cottages are very pretty. I'm so glad you're doing some riding with Fen, the fresh air will do you good after so many late nights here. You said on the card that you were going out to supper, was it to one of Fen's friends? What did you wear? What did you eat? I hope you are meeting some nice people. It's very hot here in London. I would love a breath of moor air. Does the wind come wuthering round your cottage?

(Here there was a break in the controlled writing and, when it began again, lower down the page, there was an urgency in the black, sprawling words which wasn't there before.)

This has been a dreadful summer for the children. So much violence – is it always worse in hot weather? Every time I pick up a paper or turn on the TV there is more harm being done to the children. So many little girls. The child in a white

159

cardigan found murdered in a ditch. There was a photo of her in the paper with flowers in her hair. Children are all victims. How are they to understand it's not their fault? We live forwards and understand backwards. I am so afraid for you, far away in Yorkshire. But it's not my fault, I didn't give that angry man your number when he rang me or your address. I did as you asked me, Cat. But why did he say that about the bruise on your face? What did he mean? I am afraid that I'll pick up a paper and you'll be the harmed child. I'll be so glad when you're safe home again with me and this bright, bloated summer is over. It is peeling too many layers off us. I am afraid.

(And here again, another break in the letter. A gap at the bottom of the page and a new beginning overleaf. Controlled, careful again.)

Nice as your card was Cat, it didn't tell me a lot. I'd love to have a proper long letter from you, or at least a phone call. I kept ringing you yesterday but you were out. I don't know how much money you took with you, but I'll put some in this letter for you. You and Fen treat yourselves to a nice meal somewhere. You are sure you're eating properly? Give our love to Fen and lots of love to you darling from Mummy and Daddy.

(And at the very bottom of the paper, scrawled in a hasty afterthought, the words: 'Be careful. Be very careful.')

Coming in from the stables, Fen picked up the letter. Going into the kitchen she filled the kettle and switched it on. Cat must still be in bed. Fen leaned on the window-sill while she waited for the kettle to boil and hoped Cat would want to go out with the mares when she surfaced. It was going to be hot again. A long ride would do the mares good.

As Fen yawned and gazed out of the window, two figures came hurrying down from the moor, staring in at her as they passed. Fen looked at the two women in surprise. She was starting to feel haunted by this lot. Olivia Watson from the post office and that queer Amy Martin from that old falling down bungalow. Where was Abbey this morning? Strange not to see her with these two. And how strange they'd both looked, excited somehow. Carrying toy horses, like the one she'd found on the doorstep. What could they have been doing up at the Bridestone so early in the morning? She thought of what had happened to Cat up there, and of how she'd been so frightened at the jumble sale by the three women. Had it been them? Whatever had been going on up there that day, it wasn't finished yet. Fen didn't want to think about it. As long as she didn't let Cat go off on her own, as long as they kept well away from the Bridestone, then nothing else would hurt Cat. The kettle boiled and after making two mugs of tea, she carried them up to Cat.

She was still asleep, flat on her back with her arms flung wide. Fen set the mugs on the bedside table and bent and kissed her. Cat sat bolt upright with a cry. 'Oh God,' she said in relief when she saw it was Fen. 'It's you. I was dreaming I was back up at the Bridestone.'

'Funny you should say that.'

'What?' Cat yawned and stretched.

'It doesn't matter.' Fen pulled the letter from her jeans and dropped it on the bed.

'What's that?' Cat gulped eagerly at her tea.

'Letter from your mother by the look of it.'

Cat groaned and put down the mug. 'I don't actually have to read it, do I? It'll depress me for the rest of the day.'

'Oh come on, she is your mother after all. Of course you have to read it.' Fen drank her tea and watched Cat's face with amusement. She ripped open the envelope and tugged out the letter crossly. A fifty-pound note fell out on to the bed. 'Very nice!' said Fen. 'I wish my mother would send me letters like that. All I get from mine is letters telling me her latest plot-line. What does she say, then?'

'Rabbit, rabbit, rabbit,' said Cat crossly, skipping through it. 'She wants me safely back home and am I wearing clean knickers.'

'Cat, she doesn't say that . . .'

'Practically. She gets madder.' Cat tossed the letter on to the floor. Its message of warning lay unread. It was too late, anyway.

'D'you fancy some exercise?' said Fen.

'Not if it involves horses again. How's Bel today?'

'He's fine. Michael's a bit odd. Chased me back home this morning as if he couldn't wait to be rid of me. And I couldn't get a word out of Ash. Would you like to take the mares to Bay this afternoon? The tide should be right about three.'

'Am I going to ache again?'

'No, you'll be fine this time. Promise.'

'I might be up by then,' agreed Cat, curling up under the bedclothes again. Fen grinned and finished her tea.

They came off the cobbled causeway on to a sweep of yellow sand. Fen had been right about the tide. It was well out. A few families of holiday-makers were sitting in neat groups below the cliffs, but apart from some children, splashing at the water's edge, the sea was empty. The mares moved off along the creaming edge of the flat water over the corrugated sand, their hooves spraying up a fine, silver shower. Fen opened up Meg into a gallop and Lucy happily followed her. A flock of gulls rose screaming from the ridged sand ahead and wheeled above them and, between Cat's legs, the pattern of Lucy's stride beat into her like a drum. She moved to the music in mindless delight, tasting the salt air sharp in her mouth.

She glanced over her shoulder and saw, far behind them at the other end of the bay, dark-boned ridges of rock, exposed by the falling tide, green-fringed with weed. A group of fossil collectors was picking its way slowly out along the bony fingers, small and dark against the pale horizon. Cat felt that she was part of the machinery of the mare pumping beneath her, part of the space and the light of the sunlit afternoon. Everything was heightened for her: she was held in a bubble-bright awareness that now, in this place, she was happy.

They reached the far curve of the bay where the towering headland thrust out to bar their way. 'What's on the other side?' called Cat, pulling in her mare next to Fen. The mares danced and cavorted, wild with the joy of the run.

'It's that bay where we sunbathe. We can't go round the point. The tide will be on the turn soon. Come on.'

They swung round the mares' heads and began an easy walk back across the wet sands. 'How high is it?' Cat stared up at the cliff above them.

'About six hundred feet.'

'Why is it Raven's Bay? I don't see any ravens.'

'The Danes invaded this coast and planted their colours up there on the cliff top, so they say. They had a raven for their emblem. Supposedly the local dialect has strong links with the Danish language.'

'That explains it,' said Cat. 'I knew that woman at the jumble sale wasn't talking English to me. It was pure Danish.'

'It could well have been, from the look on your face,' agreed Fen.

Cat leaned forward and patted Lucy's neck. 'I did

enjoy that. It reached parts of me that other forms of exercise never do. Makes me all of a tingle.'

'Makes me hungry. I could just eat some fish and chips.'

Cat groaned. 'Everything makes you hungry. It's very erotic, is all this bouncing up and down with all that power between your legs. Like the seat of a bike only better. That's why so many little girls like riding ponies when boys lose interest. It's all this bouncing on your bum. Have you ever read any of Anaïs Nin's books?'

'Can't say I have.'

'I should have known – all you ever read is ancient copies of *Horse and Hound*. Anaïs Nin wrote the most marvellous, delicate erotica. I read one of her diaries and riding had that effect on her, too. I remembered a bit of what she wrote, I liked it so much. Something about "the smell of the horse between my legs, the turmoil of smell and heat and motion so that I wanted to lie on the grass and be made love to." There you are. It's not just me. Wouldn't you like to lie on the sands and be made love to?'

Fen turned to her and grinned and, as she opened her mouth to answer, Cat sighed. 'No, don't tell me. You'd rather have your fish and chips. Come on then, where's the shop?'

Fen laughed and kicked Meg into a gallop, back through the lacy edge of the waves to the causeway. As they came off the sands, Cat turned in the saddle and looked back. Already the sea was moving in again, beginning to erase the scribbled pattern of the long line of their hoof prints. The fossil hunters were slowly making their way back along the ridge, and the holiday-makers collecting up their assorted children and buckets and spades. Far off, down by the water's edge, the gulls had settled again, their wings flickering silver in the late afternoon light. The mares snorted and, cresting the causeway, clattered up the narrow street.

Michael stood by the sink in the kitchen washing his hands, letting the cool water run over them and thinking of unicorns. Of how only a maiden could catch one, sitting in a glade where the unicorn could see her, and him coming milky and dim through the trees towards her, laying his heavy head in her soft lap, losing his wildness, lying there sleeping until men came with heavy nets to trap him, to kill him for the bone white horn on his forehead.

It was seeing Ash with Abbey earlier that had made him think of unicorns, realizing that Ash had seen himself as something the woman would destroy, would eat alive. But still he'd done it for Michael and he'd proved himself ready. Hearing the door slam, he looked up dreamily, lost in a green wood where a maiden cradled a sleeping white unicorn between her open legs. Sally put down her basket on the table and flopped into a chair.

'By, I'm hot,' she sighed. 'I've been roasting a chicken over there for her. Roasted myself at the same time, I think.' She unbuttoned the top of her dress and, pulling it away from herself, blew down at her breasts.

Michael turned off the water and dried his hands. 'I'll get you a drink,' he offered and she watched him cautiously as he went over to the fridge and brought a tin of orange over for her with a tray of ice cubes. He poured the fizzy orange into a glass and dropped in a handful of ice. He handed the glass to her and stood watching as she gulped it thirstily. She'd been wary of him lately, since the shaman had taken her instead of him. He wasn't always sure of what he'd done to her now; he knew she was frightened of him in a way she never used to be. There was a time when nothing he did to her in bed could have frightened her. He needed her to trust him again.

She put down the empty glass on the table and nodded at him. 'Thanks. I needed that.' She stirred the melting ice in the glass idly with a finger, then licked it and looked at him slyly, consideringly. Pulling open the front of her dress she tipped the ice into her hand and began to rub it slowly round her breast. The cold ice was smooth on her warm skin and she groaned with pleasure at the feel of it, rubbing it across the soft nipple and watching it harden. Michael tipped out more of the ice cubes from the tray and pushed them across to her. 'Don't stop then,' he said. 'Go on.' He sat down opposite her, watching her closely.

She had his whole attention, his entire body focused on her and she knew it. Lifting her breasts with one hand, she smoothed the ice round and round them with the other. She squeaked and giggled as the ice water ran slowly down between her breasts and trickled on to her stomach. She glanced up at Michael to make sure he was still watching. She knew the look on his face. She had him caught on the hook of her. Slipping an ice cube into her mouth she went to him and knelt between his legs. She picked out his prick like a prize flower, taking the tip of him between her wet, cold lips, sliding him into the ice-cold cavern of her mouth. And still he sat with his arms folded, watching her, knowing that any movement from him would frighten her away.

She began to coax him, rolling him round her tongue like a fine wine, sucking at him from the rooted base to the creaming tip. He looked down at her bent head and clear in his mind there came an image of himself as the caught beast in the glade, his head in the maiden's lap, his strong white horn destroyed.

In the late afternoon, Patsy was sitting down among

the trees at the bottom of the field when she saw Fen and Cat lead the mares through the gate. She wondered where they'd been. She herself had spent most of the afternoon sitting there getting hotter and crosser every minute. She wanted to draw the big oak tree, but the more she tried the worse it got. All the branches kept writhing about and twisting on the paper until she couldn't see what she wanted to draw any more. She felt strange again. As if someone else inside her was trying to get out. There was a funny feeling in the cottage as well, as if it were waiting for something to happen. That was why she'd come out here.

She yawned and stretched. She was tired – the trouble was, she didn't like going to sleep any more because then the dreams came. And the voices. But the voices couldn't be in the dreams because they woke her up when they started whispering. It was all right her dad keeping on at her to listen to them and hear what they said, she kept on telling him it wasn't any words she could understand. He wasn't the one that was frightened half to death anyway. It was all right for him. 'Listen and see what they say.' Ha, ha. She didn't want to know what they said. And she'd seen those red eyes again as well, glaring at her from her mirror this time. She could feel the nastiness filling her up again as she sat hunched in the grass, cuddling herself tightly. She looked uneasily over her shoulder into the trees, but there was nothing, only a little wind stirred the tree tops, rustling the leaves. She sighed and turned to watch the mares again. Having to go to a new school in September was bothering her as well. New teachers after all those years of having just the same two. Having to go all that way into town on the school bus. Horrible. She sat and stared at the pencil she'd been trying to draw with and it made a sharp cracking noise and lay in three pieces on the grass. Patsy felt much better. She rocked herself backwards and forwards and called to the mares inside her head.

They came snuffling up to her to see what she was doing and stood lazily resting beside her, swishing their tails at the flies. Patsy scratched their noses and thought how nice they smelled. Taking Lucy by the halter she led her over to a fallen tree and, climbing on to it, slid across the mare's back. She leant forward along Lucy's neck as the mare stood dozing. Her skin felt nice, made Patsy feel as if she wanted to get closer to her warmth. She took off her shirt and threw it down on the grass. The slight breeze ruffled the leaves again and sent prickles down her back. She wanted all of herself touching Lucy. Wriggling round she pulled off her shorts and dropped them on top of her shirt. She threw her leg back over the little mare and sat still and straight and naked. Sunlight came dappling through on to her skin. She felt magical; she was part of a fairy tale. Tugging up the mare's head she dug in her heels and got Lucy moving along the dip in the field.

As the little mare moved slowly through the long grass there was a cracking of twigs in the trees and a rustling in the grass. Patsy knew who was coming out of the trees behind her: it was her tribe and she was the Horse Goddess. Lost deep down in a spell of her own making she lifted up a hand in regal greeting, never turning her head, her back straighter than ever. The shaggy, ghosting horses moved out of the trees and into the sunlight, pale as shadows. The little mare flickered her ears nervously and began to sweat. Behind them the bigger mare whinnied loudly and Michael heard the frightened cry. Dropping the brush he was sweeping the yard with he ran to the field gate and, clambering over it, ran to the top of the dip. And he saw.

He saw his tribe again, mounted on their rough ponies,

familiar and dear to him. And someone leading them, a young girl he didn't recognize, one who hadn't yet been given to him in ceremony. He frowned and wondered how it was he didn't know her. She rode her mare well. That too was strange to him, that a horse as fine as this one should be ridden by such a young girl. Whoever she was, she was his by right, for he was the holy man and the priest of these people. She needed to be sanctified by him. He stood gazing down on the procession, then moved down the slope to meet the girl.

She looked at him out of her dream and shook with horror. It was her dad standing there staring at her when she had nothing on, but he'd changed again. This wasn't her dad, he was wearing his jeans and shirt but his eyes were wrong again. They were burning red at her and she could smell him again, like that time he'd changed in the Land Rover. Then his hand was on her leg, pulling her roughly off the mare who plunged and bucked, then galloped off among the trees.

Patsy screamed as the ground hit her with a thud and the breath was knocked out of her. She struggled to get away from him but he had a tight hold on her ankle. He was crouching down beside her where she lay sprawled on her back and his hand was touching her breasts, stroking between her legs and he shouldn't, not him, most of all not him. And 'No, no, Daddy!' she howled, kicking and wriggling, scratching her nails down his face so that he shook his head and looked confused, turned as if he was looking for somebody else behind them.

Michael winced at the sudden pain in his face, wondering what had caused it. He couldn't see properly. Something seemed to have slipped sideways. He rubbed at his stinging face and his fingers came away stained with blood. He stared at Patsy crouching on the grass. Why was she out here with no clothes on? He got to his feet and stepped back from her. 'Get up,' he said, 'get your clothes back on. You're too big to play like that now.'

She crawled away from him, not daring to take her eyes off him, not believing that he'd stopped. Then she scrambled to her feet and was off after the mare, desperate to be away from him, her breath coming in sick jerks and a pain cutting into her side. She hated him for frightening her like this: she knew what he had been going to do.

Michael stood and watched as she pulled on her clothes and ran towards the gate. He rubbed his bloody fingers down his jeans and slowly followed her across the field.

Chapter Sixteen

THERE was a distant roll of thunder in the next valley just before midnight. It faded into the distance as the storm moved away for a time, but it left the air heavy and oppressive. Cat woke thinking that she'd heard something. Some sound outside. A car door banging, perhaps, a little way off. She was thirsty. She reached out and picked up the glass from beside the bed but it was empty. Sliding out of bed without disturbing the sleeping Fen she went downstairs and into the kitchen, pausing to look out of the window in the long living-room. Nothing. She'd imagined the noise. She switched on the kitchen light, sending a pool of brightness out on to the grass outside and lighting it as clearly as a stage. She took a carton of milk from the fridge and poured some into a mug and, sipping it, she wandered over to the window, to look out on to the grass.

And in from the thin edge of darkness a figure slipped. And a second and third. Their long, black-hooded robes billowed and flapped as they began to dance round and round in the patch of light. The mug fell from Cat's fingers and smashed in two at her feet as one by one the faces turned to where she stood – hare, crow and wolf. The masks dipped and turned, spun and wheeled as the dance grew faster and the bare feet pattered on the grass. The window was open a slit at the bottom: she could smell the night air, hear the whisper of their dancing feet. The dance grew faster and more frenzied. One of the figures peeled off into the dark leaving two spinning with arms uplifted, then one dancing by itself in a wild circle before it too whirled off into the dark and was gone. Cat had been holding her breath; she let it go now in a long sob of fear. Why were the women here? What did they want this time?

They were coming back into the light, slowly now, pacing gravely across the grass to the centre of light. One was carrying a three-legged stool, one a bundle of what looked like clothes. The last figure to come into the light was walking very carefully. She was swollen in pregnancy, a huge swelling under her black robes. They set down the stool. The pregnant woman eased herself on to it, opening her legs and flinging back her arms, tipping her hare mask to the sky with a long, keening groan. The other two knelt between her legs, pulling and tugging under the robe, holding up something pink and feebly wriggling. They wrapped it in a shawl and tied a bonnet on the bald, round head. They gave the bundle back to hare-face, who sat and crooned to it, rocking to and fro, to and fro as round the stool the wolf and crow danced in joyful celebration. And then they stopped.

Still as stones now they huddled together round the stool where the bundle lay alone. The three came to their feet slowly and heavily, pacing in a ring round the stool. Hare-face lifted up an arm. The sleeve of her robe fell back to show her hand tightly clenched on the bone handle of a knife. It cut a bright glitter through the air as she plunged it down into the bundle lying there so still and silent. It came out painted red in the pale light. She held it up triumphantly and turned to give it to wolf-face. Three times the knife rose and fell; three times it struck into the small shape.

They reached out their hands and lifted the still figure from the stool, gravely and ceremoniously now, carrying it on linked, uplifted hands. Carrying it towards the window. They were bringing it to Cat.

'The Coming One. This is the Coming One,' they sighed. And, 'Dead, dead, dead,' they mourned sadly.

She spread out her hands on the glass of the window, she didn't want to see this, she didn't want . . . and they pressed the bloody face in its pink-frilled bonnet against the window. Then they were gone, leaving a faint, red smear on the glass.

Cat slid down to the floor and everything went black for an instant. She felt a sharp pain in her hand and forced open her eyes. She'd cut herself on the broken mug. She sat and looked stupidly at her bleeding finger. What had she seen? And why had they shown it to her – for they knew someone was in the kitchen because of the light. It couldn't have been a baby. Christ, she couldn't have stood here frozen to the spot and watched them slice a knife three times into a baby? But it had moved. She was sure it had moved.

Nothing was making any sense to her and she felt very sick. Nobody would kill a baby like that in front of a witness. It had been a performance, like the one she'd got mixed up in at the Bridestone. She'd seen them act out something, but what? What was she seeing in this place? And why didn't Fen ever see any of it? It seemed as if for some reason Fen was being kept away from it. Right. So keep it that way. She'd clear up the broken mug and spilt milk, find a plaster for her finger and say not one word of what she'd seen to Fen. Not a baby, oh, don't let it have been a baby! A doll maybe. Dolls don't die. But they don't move either, and they don't bleed. Something in the shape of that head, something that wasn't a baby. A rabbit? It had been a rabbit. Cat put her arms round her knees and rocked herself backwards and forwards as tears spilled from her for the death of some small creature. And 'Not a baby, not a baby,' she grieved over to herself.

In the bedroom of the cottage next door the shaman's eyes glowed redly in the dark. He licked his lips and grunted with satisfaction. The token sacrifice had been made and offered up. The rest would follow now. Michael turned uneasily in his sleep and muttered something incoherent, then sank back down to where the shaman filled the dark cave of his head. There was a thick black mist swirling in front of him and his feet were on a cart track. The pebbles were cutting his bare feet. The mist thinned to a watery yellow sunlight and he saw that he was standing between two green fields, thick with flowers. In the distance, coming towards him, there was a chariot, pulled by a single red stallion.

And it had only one leg, and the chariot pole was driven through his body and held with a silver peg in the middle of his forehead. There was someone walking beside the horse, a dark-haired girl with a forked hazel stick, driving a red and white cow. The cow was heavy with milk so that, as she walked, it spurted white from her on to the dusty track. The woman standing in the chariot, driving the red stallion, was wearing a cloak which left her breasts bare, and a cloud of fair hair crested her proud head.

It was the goddess; it was Epona, and it was Fen.

The high scream from the next room sliced through the dark to bring Michael back into his head with a violent jerk. He lay sweating, aware of the erection he had, puzzling over what he'd seen. The strange red stallion with one leg was like a roundabout horse, but the red horses of the Celts were the death-bringers, as the men with red hair were the bearers of death and disasters. Whose death had Epona been driving? Michael shivered and reached out for Sally, but the bed beside him was empty. He heard voices from the next room and went to

174

find Patsy in tears with Sally sitting holding her in her arms and rocking her.

'Sorry love, didn't mean to wake you,' said Sally. 'She's having a bad night with those dreams again. Something about red eyes. Something about you as well.' She stared at Michael suspiciously, and Patsy whimpered and clutched at her mother.

'Poor little lass. I'll make us all a hot drink – fancy a cup of tea, Sally?'

'Thanks. Give over Patsy, now. It's only your dad. He'll make you some hot chocolate. We're both with you now so you're all right.'

Patsy wasn't convinced. She clutched her mother tightly until Michael had gone out of the room. Sally noticed and wondered why.

It was still hot in the kitchen. Michael opened the door and stood looking out into the dark. The word sacrifice came into his head as clearly as if someone standing beside him had spoken. He frowned out into the night, wondering why he felt as if something was happening which he should know about – he didn't trust the three women not to move things forward on their own. He shrugged and thought that they wouldn't get up to much in the middle of the night. Especially with a storm on the way – he could hear it crackling away over the hilltop.

His head ached and he shook it crossly as he shut the door and crossed to put the milk on to heat. He found drinking chocolate, tea bags, mugs. Sitting down at the table to wait for the milk to heat he opened a magazine lying there. One of a bundle Sally had got for him at the jumble sale. He yawned and looked down blearily at the page in front of him. As he took in what the picture was, the first brilliant flare of lightning ripped up the dark, and a long roll of thunder followed. He jumped and looked blindly out of the black square of window as the light in the kitchen flickered and dimmed, then shone steadily again. He looked back at the page.

He was seeing a photo of the White Horse of Uffington. It was brightly coloured, with a queer look to the light. The horse stood out sharply against the yellow of the field behind it. There was a strong feeling of unease coming off it, as if whoever had taken the photo hadn't been happy to be there. The figure leaped across the curve of the hill. It was strangely modern in its lines, although it was so old that nobody knew when it was made. Or why. It reminded Michael of a cave painting. The same code of passing on information seemed to be held by its taut lines. Chesterton had written a poem about this horse. Michael had the words written in his stallion book. He knew them by heart. He said them now under his breath:

> 'Before the gods that made the gods
> Had seen their sunrise pass,
> The White Horse of the White Horse Vale
> Was cut out of the grass.'

It was celtic art. Michael felt convinced of it. It was a cult figure, some symbol of the tribes in that area, and surely there to be worshipped. It was Epona.

What awe it must have inspired in the tribes, this vast creation. Over 360 feet long. Michael had never seen it. There was so much that he'd never seen, so many journeys he hadn't made, things he hadn't learned. He tore out the page very carefully. Tomorrow he'd stick it into his book. It was another sign. He stirred the hot milk into Patsy's mug and winced as another streak of lightning lit up the valley. In the dead silence before the thunder, he heard the first rain begin to fall lightly on to the dry earth.

Sally stayed with Patsy for the rest of the night, for the thunder and lightning had been the last straw for her. And in the early hours of the morning, as the storm moved reluctantly away from the valley, Patsy began to bleed for the first time. The bad feeling in the cottage was worse than ever now, and somehow the rooms did not seem as empty as before. From this point on, things began to move much faster.

'But it was pink!' said Cat wildly, sitting up in bed. 'Its face was pink!' She'd seen it when it had been pressed against the window and there'd been no fur. So it had been skinned then, and dead all along. She'd seen what the women had wanted her to. It had been them making it twitch and jerk. It had not been alive at all. She groaned at the pain in her aching head and lay back down quickly before it split wide open. She looked up at the ceiling, listening to the silence. The storm had gone rolling round the valley for what seemed like hours last night, as if it had been trapped there by the hills. The first crack of thunder had brought her upright, clutching Fen. She was no help: she didn't like storms either.

Cat could hear the faint sound of church bells. She'd forgotten it was Sunday. After a while, all the days were alike here. Fen was going to have to go without her this time, there was no way she could manage to sing hymns this morning. She lay and waited for Fen to come back from the stables. When she finally arrived, smelling a little too strongly of horse for Cat's fragile state, she was full of sympathy and brought Cat up a tray of tea and toast.

'You don't mind if I go to church with Mrs Barton, do you? You stay here, you look really rough this morning. I'll drop the latch on the door so you needn't worry about anyone coming in.' She hesitated, looking at Cat's pale face. 'Maybe I should stay here with you.'

'No, no you go. I'll sleep it off. I'll be fine by the time you get back. It's only a headache. You must go or else Mrs Barton will think I'm leading you into wicked city ways.' Cat gulped thirstily at the sweet, weak tea.

'There's some pain killers on the tray. Don't open the door to anyone, promise?'

'Promise. Go on, off you go. Say one for me.'

She heard the door shut after Fen and the handle rattle as she checked that it was locked behind her. There was the sound of a car door banging, and the noise of it moving off. Another vehicle pulled away behind it. Michael must be taking his family to church as well. Cat wasn't sure she liked the idea of being the only one left in the two cottages. She took three aspirins and went slowly into the bathroom. She looked as strange as she felt, pale yellow and crumpled. She splashed some cold water on her face and, going back into the bedroom, opened the window wide. It had stopped raining; the air was cooler and smelt fresh. Cat broke up the toast and threw it out of the window for the birds. She yawned and winced as pain jolted through her head. Walking very carefully back to the bed, she drank another cup of tea, then, burrowing down into the warm hollow of the bed, she pulled the covers and oblivion over her head. She sank away into nothing.

She didn't dream of a dead baby. Not this time. She was up on the moor at the Bridestone; she was very much afraid and something was coming after her. Something very old with the head of an animal was coming towards the Bridestone over the moor. There was a terrible smell of something rotting, and the sound of voices, dimly through a mist. Whatever was after her was getting very close. She couldn't run. Somehow she was tied to the stone. She could smell the stinking, sour breath getting nearer, hear the women's voices grow louder and then she woke. The dream flickered past her as she tried to remember it but all that was left was the fear.

She wiped the sweat from between her breasts with a corner of the sheet and told herself that bad dreams were all she could expect now in this place, after what she'd seen in the night. Leaning across the tray, she picked up the glass of water. That was when she realized that she could still hear the women's voices chanting. They were coming from the cottage next door, but it was empty in there. The sound was getting nearer and louder. It wasn't any language she'd ever heard, it was one phrase repeated over and over with a dreadful, slow malice. The glass splintered on the edge of the table.

The voices grew higher and more insistent, seeming now to come from the porch below her. The pain of the high screeching inside her head was blotting out everything else: she couldn't think any more, tears were pouring down her face and she screamed for it to stop, to let her go. Then there was silence, soft and breathless. Waiting. Then the sound began again, a soft crooning that came faintly to her, compelling and hypnotic. She smiled happily and nodded. They wanted her downstairs. The voices were calling her to come to them. Calm-faced now as a young child, she got out of bed and pulled on her dressing-gown. She went to the top of the stairs. She could smell honeysuckle, sweet and strong, and there seemed to be a light shining from the porch. Ah, but the voices were sweet now, Lorelei sweet, and she began to go down the steps, one by one.

She knew where the voices were leading her; they were going to the Bridestone. It needed her. It was calling to her. Sally was wrong, there was nothing to be frightened of at the stone. It needed women. It liked women. That was why it was called the Bridestone – because it called you to it as its bride. She tried to open the door into the porch, but it was locked. Fen had locked it. She'd said not to let anyone in, but she hadn't said Cat couldn't go out. She unlocked it and pulled open the door. There was no-one in the porch but she could still hear the singing, pulling at her faintly in the distance. They were going without her. She ran across the porch and opened the outer door. The white gate at the end of the path was swinging slowly shut, as if someone had just gone through it.

Cat ran down the path and across the grass beside the cottage. Nothing was real to her any more, everything shimmered and was too brightly coloured, like a cartoon, now she was outside. She pushed through the thick bracken and went bare-foot and expectant into the wood. In front of her a branch moved, a twig broke and something was ahead of her in the trees. Then the singing began again, haunting and pure, drawing her along the path. In the gaps between the trees ahead of her a crow flapped from a low branch, a hare twitched her long whiskers, a long-tongued wolf glinted green eyes in the shadows.

Cat ran along the path and it seemed to be growing longer under her feet. She was never going to get to the end of it, she'd been running and running for ever and her bare feet were cut and bleeding with the sharp stones. She'd come into the green wood as a young woman but she'd go out at the other end of it an old, bent crone. She would never get to the Bridestone in time, she wailed sadly. He wouldn't wait for her; he'd take himself another, younger bride. She wanted it to be her. But she should be wearing her wedding dress, she thought anxiously and her feet stumbled and faltered. A stone slipped from under her and she was falling down and down through the bracken, leaving the path high above her. She crashed against the fallen trunk of an old tree and crumpled against it.

On the path above her the three women stood and watched. They saw her lift her head and heard her moan, saw her try to get to her feet and left her, hurrying off through the trees.

Cat's nose was bleeding and her head hurt. She wiped the blood from her scratched face with the sleeve of her dressing-gown and sat down heavily on the tree trunk. She looked down vaguely at the blood-smeared cuff. Why was she wearing her dressing-gown? And where was she? She'd fallen — she could see that by the line of broken bracken she'd drawn down the hillside. She was in the larch wood above the cottages, but she had no idea why. She stared round her in the silent wood. She wanted Fen. Getting painfully to her feet, she began to crawl on her hands and knees up the steep bank back to the path.

Extract from Michael's Stallion Book

I shouldn't have gone to church. I knew that as soon as I sat down and looked at the front pew. Only Mrs Barton and Fen were there, so I knew Cat must be on her own in the cottages. It was too late then. I only go there to please Sally and because Mrs Barton likes us all to go. It's not my god in there and not my religion. What sort of a faith is it that teaches people their bodies are shameful? It was stupid of me to leave the cottage as it was, there was so much power loose in the place with Patsy starting in the night. You could feel it building up thick as smoke in there. I might have known the three women would try some mischief with me out of the way. They picked the right moment and tapped into the force.

We drove home in front of Mrs Barton's car – I came back fast because I was uneasy. Five minutes after we got in, Fen was banging on the door in a state. She'd found the cottage doors open and no sign of Cat inside. She'd gone outside to look for her and seen her coming down from the wood. Poor kid was only wearing a dressing-gown and her bare feet were a right mess. Fen got her inside and ran for Sally. I gave her something to knock Cat right out, best thing, let her sleep and forget everything. I went next door later to check it had worked and she was out like a light and peaceful as a baby. She'd had a bad fright and a nasty fall up there – lucky for all of us it was no worse. What the women imagined they were going to do with Cat once they'd got her to the Bridestone, I can't imagine.

Abbey rang me up to see if she'd got home all right and told me what they'd done. I was too angry with them to talk much and she was frightened – I could tell that by her voice. I don't think they'll try any more tricks of their own. Best say no more about it to them – they got a bit carried away by their own power, I think. They'll be up first thing in the morning at the Bridestone to bless it, as usual.

Chapter Seventeen

ONE by one the three women gave their breasts to the Bridestone; one by one they made the pattern. Wide-eyed in the bracken, Patsy crouched and watched. She couldn't make out too clearly what they were doing but she didn't dare creep any closer for fear they might see her. She could see they were bare to their middles – couldn't very well miss that. They were rubbing their tits on the stone. Why were they doing that? What did it feel like, that rough stone against your nipples? And they had little purses round their necks on a string which they were rubbing on the stone in a big spiral pattern. Patsy shivered and huddled lower into the green bracken.

She'd woken very early this morning and, from the window, had seen the three of them climbing up the moor path. Something was going on and Patsy wanted to know what it was. Their cottage felt queer. Worse than ever after that storm last night. Her dad was as jumpy as a cat. She was keeping well out of his way; he scared her, the way he looked at her. It wasn't her fault, what he'd tried to do to her the other day, but it felt as if it was. She was making sure she wasn't on her own with him, sticking close to her mam.

She flattened herself hurriedly as the women pulled on their shirts and began to come slowly away from the stone, laughing and talking as if they'd enjoyed what they'd been doing. She risked a glance at their faces: they were shining with that look some people got from going to church. And each of them was carrying a little toy horse, all decorated with flowers and ribbons, like the big heavy horses at the village show were always done up.

Patsy watched their backs disappear down the path and waited until they were out of sight in the trees before she got to her feet. The Bridestone loomed black and silent in front of her and she hesitated. Maybe she should just go home now. But she wanted to know how it felt to touch the stone like that. After all, she was as much a woman as they were now, since she'd started in the night. There must be more to it than just giving you a bad stomach ache. There must be things she could share in now. Her body did what other women's bodies did, so she'd try this out for herself.

She stood at arm's length from the mass of it and peeled off her T-shirt, shivering as the cold moor air touched her small breasts. She reached out and touched the stone with the tips of her fingers, brushing it lightly, then took a deep breath and gave herself to it as she'd seen the women do, pressing her nipples hard against it and holding her arms round its roughness.

For a moment nothing happened. She was aware of the roughness of it under her skin and there was a bird calling over in the trees. Then faintly she felt a tingling in her nipples which grew stronger, a buzzing, stinging feeling which shook her convulsively so that she screamed out and wrenched herself back, falling in a heap as her legs gave way under her. She lay for a moment staring up at the stone then grabbed her shirt and was up on her feet and running, not daring to look back, for her mam had been right all along and this was a bad place. She ran for the trees with her mouth a round O of terror and the moor seemed to be an endless lonely place and being a woman a terrible thing to be to Patsy now.

*

'Now,' said Michael to Ash. 'Go to her now for me and do what you did with Abbey. Take her in the trees.'

'She won't hurt me?'

'Abbey didn't. You remember?'

'I remember. You were both pleased with me.' Ash smiled happily. He was having a good day. He could remember lots of things and he was going to do something else to make Michael happy. He set off across the yard then stopped and came back, looking worried. 'What if she doesn't want to?'

'Oh, she'll want to. She likes you, Ash.'

Ash nodded. Michael and Abbey and now this one, all liking him. He set off across the yard.

Michael watched him go, screwing up his eyes. He was seeing a double landscape for much of the time now, his and the shaman's. The shaman was growing stronger. Michael looked at trees now and felt himself to be a part of them. He was one of the birds soaring and flying overhead. He felt the air under his wings. Past and present were becoming one to him and he knew all that was yet to come had long been ordained. He would bring his people together at the Bridestone on Lammas Eve as the shaman wanted. There were not many days left now, and he had a lot to do.

Picking up the scythe he crossed the yard to the mares' field. The thistles were to be cut down before their silver heads blew everywhere. Mrs Barton didn't agree with sprays, it was all the old ways with her. The land was better without all those chemicals on it but it was a tedious job all the same, knocking down the prickly things by hand. He closed the field gate behind him and stood looking about. Not as many as he'd thought. And it put him in the right place at the right time.

Cat had woken strange and dreamy after all the horror of the day before. It seemed to have moved away from her, as if it had happened to someone else. She had a far-off recollection of Fen getting her into bed, of Sally appearing next to her. Sally? How could it have been Sally? Cat had drunk something bitter out of a glass which Sally had given her and then everything had started to hurt less, had got very small and bright, and there had been Fen's anxious face and Sally's watching one spinning round and round, then nothing.

Cat shifted uncomfortably in the bed. Fen had gone to the village on an errand for Mrs Barton, having asked at least three times if Cat would be all right. Her orders had been to stay in bed until she got back, then they would have a nice lazy day in the garden. Cat had meant to stay where she was but she was hot and restless. She got out of bed and ran a bath. Lying there in the scented water she found herself thinking of Ash. She hadn't got much closer to him yet than making a series of drawings of him as an angel, and that wasn't all he was. The image of him in her head grew and swelled and she needed him. She wanted him to take her as he had in her fantasy of him in church. She climbed out of the bath like a dreamer, pulled on shorts and shirt over her damp flesh and went out into the lane. She stood there, waiting. She knew he'd come; she could feel him wanting her and she was ready for him.

And when he came, he took her hand and they climbed over the wall and went across the field to the trees without saying a word to each other. There was no need for that.

Michael knew they were there, among the trees. He propped the scythe carefully out of harm's way on the other side of the gate and padded off down the field, keeping to the shadows of the tall hawthorn hedge. He slipped into the clump of trees like a red fox stalking, leant against the nearest trunk and listened. He heard the greedy whimpers she was making and pricked up his ears and twitched. He knew those sounds from Cat. He crept through the foxgloves; edged nearer in the bracken fronds. He was nothing but a pair of eyes glistening, slitting through the dimness. And then he saw them, and knelt before the ritual, and he was all shaman now.

He caught his breath in awe at the sight of Ash. He stood perfect in a dapple of sunlight breaking through the leaves, innocent, angelic, but from his loins thrust Lucifer, powerful and terrible. The naked woman was very beautiful, but she hadn't the power of this man.

Cat knelt dreamily at Ash's feet and took the wafer of him into the red cave of her mouth. Her flesh closed round him, startling him for it was nothing he knew, and he caught hold of her hair, warning her. She loosened her mouth on him and, leaning back, gentled him with her hands on his long thighs. His fingers began to stroke her hair, and he stood, accepting.

The shaman watched. He sent out his power and his will to Ash to stay calm, to remember Abbey and the good feeling. He saw Cat's tongue begin to flick over the pale skin and, just as he thought Ash must come, must give himself in the sea-cave of her mouth, she drew away from him again; peeled herself wet off the rock of him.

In the bracken the shaman worshipped the phallic image of the man, standing with his prick tight against his stomach, green dappled in light. He was the first man-god; he was one of the ever-living, shining ones. Now, thought the shaman, focusing his power on the woman. Now let her play her part for him and let her play the mare.

Cat shook her head and blinked as the wave of his thoughts hit her then turned and haunched herself on all fours in front of Ash, crooning his name harshly to herself. Her breasts swung round and heavy as she braced her forearms. She arched her back and winked her vulva at him and called him to her. Through the green leaves he danced towards her, brushed against her spread thighs, curled back his top lip and tasted her. He nipped at the soft, round curve of her bottom. Arms uplifted, he stood silent for a long moment and the shaman gathered his will into one last push into him. Taking his prick in his hands, Ash eased himself into her, smooth as silk in the red flesh.

The shaman watched. It was no longer Ash he was watching but man become stallion. He knew the changes in that body now – the rising pulse rate, heightened blood pressure, the rise in heat off him. He felt the blood running to the eyes, the ears, the lips. He knew the message travelling down the spinal cord to the nerves and muscles round the base of the penis. There was a state now in Ash of rigidity, holding the greatest possible tension. He held himself in perfect stillness, then gave a shudder and began to move in her, pistoning into her with long, hard strokes. He came with a scream of triumph, his long fair hair whipping back as he swung his head from side to side.

As the cry died away among the trees the shaman closed his eyes wearily. He was drained, emptied out. Ash had proved himself. He had covered the Teaser. The last pieces were falling into place and the time was now. It was time to gather his people to him and begin.

Extract from Michael's Stallion Book

And then right at the last moment I almost went and ruined everything. I was coming back from Abbey's and all had gone well there, the women are building their own force with their rituals. They are sure of what they are doing. When I came past the pub in the village I saw Fen's car parked outside it, so I pulled the Land Rover up next to it and went in. I should have driven straight on. I was too near the edge. The women's robes and their chanting and the final act of sex with Olivia as the selected one had brought the shaman right to the front of my head. He's always strongest then, when I go into a woman's body. It's like a queer kind of emotional drunkenness being with those three so that I become more than myself, possessed.

There were only a few people in the pub. Cat and Fen were sitting at a table in the corner by the fire, laughing at something together. They're so close, those two, touch one and you hurt the other. They looked up and saw me and waved me over to them. I walked across and saw that Fen was wearing a hat: it was a sort of trilby, it looked good on her. But it came to me as I went towards her that she'd cut off all her long hair. There was no plait down her back, only this bare nape of neck above her jacket collar.

And the shaman took over. I felt a terrible anger come raging through me. She had no right to do this: there is such power in the hair. Cutting it short has always been a terrible form of punishment. The first thing they did when they tested a witch was to take off all her hair. Take away her magic with it. I thought that's what Fen had done. And that long mare's tail of hers was part of what she is. The goddess and the Great Mare. She had no right to desecrate herself like that. I heard my mouth open and the shaman's words spill out, wild and cursing her and I heard them swell and press out against the walls of the room. She was white faced and frozen. I reached out and snatched off the hat.

It was like one of those adverts on TV. Her hair was all tucked up inside the hat and it came falling down like water round her shoulders. Cat was staring wide-eyed at me and everyone in the pub was standing silent, watching. I was back inside my own head again and a very embarrassed man. 'I thought you'd cut off all your hair,' I stuttered.

'She's just washed it, you idiot. It's none of your business anyway.' Cat's claws were well out. 'She can shave her head bald if she wants to.'

I pulled a chair across and sat down with them. It took me half an hour of apologizing and really turning on the charm before they were even speaking to me again. Fen didn't put the hat back on — I think she didn't dare, not whilst I was still there. Too frightened she set me off again. When I left them I stood up and reached out and stroked her hair and I did get a half-smile from her. Cat's fur was still standing up on end. I need to have her on her own with me to put that one right. And I am running out of time.

Chapter Eighteen

IT was Tuesday morning 30 July, and there were two days left. Michael came back from the stables and went into the kitchen, crossing to the sink to wash his hands and vaguely registering that Sally had her coat on. And there was a suitcase standing by the table. Where did she think she was going? He picked up the towel and began to dry his hands, watching her. He said nothing, for he knew that if he left her alone, she'd come out with whatever this was all about.

She flounced across to the oven and, taking out a plate with his breakfast on, slammed it down on the table in his place. 'Get a move on,' she snapped. 'You haven't much time.'

'Oh?' he said mildly, dropping the towel on the draining-board. 'Am I going somewhere, then?'

'I am. Me and Patsy. On the 9.30 bus from the village.'

'Where are you off?' He sat down slowly and began to cut up his food, holding the knife and fork very steady to hide his anger.

'Off to Mam's. I'm having nowt to do with it, our Michael.'

'With what?'

'That's the trouble. I don't know what. But you're up to Something. I can feel it.'

Having worked herself up to the point of telling him she was going, Sally began to calm down. She sat down opposite him and poured herself a cup of tea. 'I keep on thinking about that poor kid next door in such a state on

Sunday when we got back from church, and Fen wasn't much better when she came running to me for help.' She sipped at the tea and watched him.

'Cat had a bad dream, a bad fright, that was all. It wasn't meant to happen, any of that. It spilled over into their cottage from in here. It was all mixed up with Patsy starting for the first time. It won't happen again.'

'That's another thing. Patsy. She's scared of you. What have you said to her to upset her?'

'Nothing. I wouldn't hurt Patsy, you know that.'

'She's got something in her head. I think she'd be better away from here for a few days.' She cradled her mug in her hands and shivered. 'I'm scared. Whatever you're doing it's too big for me. I want nowt to do with it. This place feels bad and I want Patsy out of it. I know it's got summat to do with those two next door. All that fuss over making sure they got that bottle of mead at the jumble sale. What had you put in it? I don't know why you bothered anyway, they'd have licked it straight off your fingers if you'd asked them to.'

Into his head came a picture of Cat and Fen kneeling at his feet, their red tongues sucking at his fingers, and he swallowed hard. He pushed his empty plate away from him and looked at her. Maybe it was best if she took Patsy out of the way. He'd said the truth – he wouldn't hurt her. But the shaman would. He knew he'd done something already to frighten her and he had a nasty idea what. Sally was right.

'Aye. Take the bairn away for a few days. Get your things and we'll be off for that bus.'

Sally jumped up and, going to the bottom of the stairs, shouted for Patsy to come down. She turned back to Michael and stood hesitating. 'Are you angry with me for going?'

He shook his head and held out his arms and she came

into them. He could feel her trembling. 'You go and have a few days with your Mam. I'll get everything back to normal for when you come home.'

'Will you come for us?'

He nodded. 'Monday?' he said at random, for he couldn't see any further than tomorrow. After that it was just a blank.

'Fine. I've cleared it with Mrs Barton already. She's going away herself tomorrow so it all fits in.'

Fits in, fits in, beat Michael's head. He smiled at Patsy standing hesitating in the doorway, picked up the suitcase and went out to start up the Land Rover.

The women were sitting on the grass behind Amy's bungalow. It was hot and still. Spread out on the grass in front of them lay a wedding dress, white lace and virginal.

'We were very lucky, finding this at the jumble sale.' Amy stroked the ginger cat sitting on her lap. There were seven cats playing round them, hunting in and out of the tangle of wild flowers which was Amy's garden.

'Luck had nothing to do with it,' said Abbey tersely. 'It was meant for us. You know very well that everything works to a pattern for Michael.'

'Even supplying a dress for the bride.' Olivia spread the long sleeves out at each side of the bodice and straightened the bell-like skirt. 'Where shall we start?'

'I'll do the bodice. You two start at the hem of the skirt and work up.' She emptied a bag of small snail shells on the grass beside her and began to glue them like beads round the high neckline.

Amy pulled out a piece of fur from her workbag and began to snip it into small pieces.

'Should you be doing that when he's watching?' Olivia nodded at the big ginger tom.

Amy grinned. 'Why not? It was his grandad.'

Olivia shrugged and began to stitch black feathers round the hem of the dress. 'What will the Teaser wear?'

'Oh I found a dress for her as well. We don't need to bother much with that one. It's this one for the bride that needs the talismans.' Abbey opened another bag. 'Look what I've got. Gorse flowers. Flowers of the sun and very magical.' She laid them out in two rings where the bride's breasts would be. The other two nodded and bent to their work. The only sound in the garden was the sharp clicking of scissors, the humming of bees in the flowers and the deep-throated purr of the ginger cat on Amy's knees.

Much later, when they were almost finished, Amy went inside to make them some lunch. It was only then, glancing in the bathroom mirror as she washed her hands, that she realized her own totem bag was missing from round her neck. She stood and stared at her white reflection and tried to remember when she'd last had it. Up at the Bridestone, very early that morning for the blessing. The string must have snapped after that. But how was she going to tell Michael? He would be so angry with her. She could have lost it anywhere up on the moor, walking back down to the road to Olivia's car. She'd never find it, not now. Michael's anger waited like a blow for her as she went heavy-footed, sickly and afraid, back into the garden to tell the other two.

Up on the moor top, Cat was sitting on an outcrop of rock, looking down into the valley below. She was working on one of her 'Landscape with Figures' series. She'd put down the linen-fold hills with hard, sure lines and was pencilling in a flock of sheep bouncing and bleating along a lane, with a man on a bike and a black and white sheepdog following them. On either side of the lane, the patchwork fields were every shade of green, and heat shimmered on the hills. The only sound was the distant clinking of the mares' bits as they moved from foot to foot, half asleep in the heat of the afternoon. The tops of the stunted larches where they were tethered were hardly moving in the faint breeze. There was a rich, mushroomy smell of moor. Cat began to darken in the shadows on the hillside, thinking how bleak this place must be in winter. They'd ridden the mares almost to the place Bel had run the day that Ash let him out. In all the valley below, Cat could see only the one man moving.

'Isn't it empty?' she said.

'It's very beautiful,' said Fen indignantly. She began to gather up the remains of their picnic, finding a squashed biscuit which she happily ate.

'Must you? I didn't mean it isn't beautiful. It is. Very. It's just that I prefer a few more people about. I can see why Emily Brontë couldn't live without her moors though; if you live in a place like this, streets must feel a bit confining. There's just one man in the whole valley, look, down there with the sheep.'

'There's plenty of sheep. And the odd curlew.'

'If that thing that sounds as if it's being strangled is a curlew then it's certainly odd,' said Cat. She closed her sketch book and went over to push it into her back-pack.

'Can I see?' Fen stared at the drawing then sighed.

'It's not that bad, is it?'

'Of course it's not. You've got it all there to take away with you. I just wish I could do something. I can't draw or write or sing or anything. I seem to be waiting for my life to start, somehow.'

'You're brilliant with horses. I'm terrified of Bel and you're not.'

'It's not much though is it?'

Cat hugged her. 'I wouldn't want to change you. You need cheering up. It's been lovely up here, so nice and normal. Why don't we go out tonight and spend that money my mother sent me? D'you know somewhere we can go for a meal? It would do us good to get away from the cottage for a while. Somewhere we can relax.'

'What a good idea! There's a place in Bay called the Lobster Pot. It's very old, right on the sea front and does very good food. You'll love it – I'll phone and book us in when we get back.'

'Great. Let's be off then. The flies must be getting to the mares a bit.'

'You just want streets and people,' said Fen.

'Anything with two legs would make a change,' agreed Cat.

They rode the mares slowly along the narrow sheep-track which cut across the moor to where the Bridestone stood in the distance.

'We're coming to a flat stretch, it's okay to gallop here,' called back Fen. She urged the big mare into a canter, for Meg was already dancing and fretting to be off, and let her lengthen her stride into a gallop. Lucy tossed her head and snorted, then was after her. Dust rose up about the mares' feet, and the wind caught at them again, making their tails stream like banners behind them. A coil of Lucy's mane wrapped itself round Cat's wrist and they came out of the sun towards the Bridestone like ancient ghosts.

The smell reached Meg first. She broke her stride and swung her hind-quarters round, shivering and breaking out into a sweat. Coming up closely behind her, Cat reined in Lucy sharply, only just avoiding crashing into her. 'Christ! What is that smell?' she said in disgust, then looked beyond Meg at the stone. A dead sheep lay on the flat slab in front of it, and a cloud of blue-green flies rose sluggishly from the blackening blood as they came nearer. The ewe lay with the wide mouth of its slit throat grinning redly at them. Its stomach had been cut open and all the entrails pulled out. They lay spread out on the slab next to the ewe, a dreadful mess of pink tubes and fleshy organs, a pattern of oozing, bloody threads. Once Cat had looked at it she couldn't look away. Someone, she thought, must have put their hands inside the body and pulled that lot out. She swallowed hard and tried not to smell the dark smell of blood.

'Look,' said Fen on a dying fall of breath. 'Look on the top of the Bridestone.' In the curving hollow cupping the phallic thrust of the stone's head stood one of the toy horses. It wasn't brown any more; it was a sticky-looking red. A long, thin line was seeping down the stone away from it.

Cat stared in horror from it to the ewe and saw how the Bridestone had become a shrine with its sacrifice, a place of holy magic and power. In a dreadful way, it was complete now as it had never been in living memory. This is how it must have looked, thought Cat. She felt as if she and Fen were held there by the strength the Bridestone was gathering into itself as they watched. Then Meg gave a sudden shrill scream and reared, tearing off down the path towards the larch wood. Cat took Lucy on after them at a fast, nervy trot, not daring to gallop on such a rough path. Once they were into the trees, Fen managed to pull Meg up and waited for Cat, staring back at where the stone was black against the sky. They walked the mares jerkily into the wood, and the footsteps came crackling down to them at an angle from higher up among the trees, so that they could hear the rustle of dead leaves long before they could see him. He leapt out on to the path in front of them and barred their way with outstretched arms.

It was Ash. He was naked to the waist and Fen and Cat stared in sick horror at his chest. It was striped with blood, barred and scribbled with clotted blood. Stuck to the stained skin were feathers, lying in intricate designs of whirls and circles. Where they were not bloody, they shone bright gold. His long hair was twisted up and knotted at the top of his head. Threaded through it was a bunch of curling tail feathers, long and flickering as he moved. And down his cheeks and across his temples, smeared round his mouth, the blood again. Red blood and feathers.

Meg was panic-stricken now. She screamed and lunged for the edge of the path to get past the horror in front of her and slipped, coming down heavily to her knees. Fen felt her going and stepped out of the saddle as she went down. She was at her head, soothing her, as the mare scrambled shakily to her feet. She coaxed the mare back on to the path and stood in front of Ash, hesitantly saying his name.

The dead, blank eyes stared at her out of another place. Fen tried to edge Meg past him but as soon as she moved, he snarled at her, reaching out and wrenching at the reins so that Meg reared and swung her hindquarters into Lucy. For some minutes Cat fought with the little mare to keep her from bolting back along the path. She was terrified of Lucy slipping down as Meg had done – she wasn't a good enough rider to keep as cool as Fen had done. When she coaxed the mare round the right way again, Ash was standing a few steps back from Fen, arms above his head, chanting something Cat could make no sense of, a low humming sound which rose until he threw back his head in a long, drawn-out howl.

Cat sat unsteadily in the saddle, gripping Lucy's mane with one hand and couldn't believe this was Ash. She'd been with this man; she'd opened herself up and taken him inside her and she was shaking at the idea of him penetrating her now. Her Ash, her gentle, lost angel had nothing to do with this bloody savage. She and Fen were trapped here on this path with the Bridestone and its sacrifice behind them and this thing in front of them. He was very dangerous: he wasn't just dressed up in a few feathers for the fun of it. He had come from some dark ceremony. It must be connected with the killing of the sheep, but more than that. He was out of his time and place and Cat hadn't known that she could feel such fear. He was lowering his arms and his howling was dying away into a low crooning. He was tugging at something in the waistband of his jeans.

It must be a weapon, it was a knife, and Cat saw again the neat slit in the sheep's stomach. He was reaching out for Fen and Cat couldn't do anything to stop him: the path was too narrow for her to go anywhere except stay where she was, tucked behind Meg's tail. 'Get back from him!' she yelled. 'Get back up on Meg away from him, Fen!'

But Ash's bloody fingers were closing on Fen's throat and he was pulling her towards him. She screwed up her eyes and wrenched back. Something wet touched her forehead and she waited for the pain. It wasn't a knife. It was something soft he was stroking her face with, wiping down her cheeks. The smell of blood was stronger than ever and she gagged as the bloody cloth stroked across her mouth. She struck out at him, kicking at him in a flurry of Meg's stamping, panicking legs and her own. He fell back away from her, still holding the cloth, crooning to himself, then sank to his knees and touched the ground at her feet with his forehead, making obeisance to her. He crouched without moving there and she stared down at him with the blood striping her face like an open wound. Then he leapt to his feet, let out a blood-curdling triumphant yell and went running off through the trees.

'Oh quick Fen, now,' moaned Cat. 'Get back on Meg and let's get out of here before he comes back.' Fen swung herself into the saddle and set off headlong down the path, slipping and sliding on the loose stones. Lucy bucked and broke into a canter after her, cutting off Cat's wail abruptly as she struggled to stay upright in the saddle. The long bracken at one side of the path stirred as she passed and for an instant she thought she saw eyes watching her. Then faintly down the path after them came the sound of a woman laughing, high-pitched and eerie.

Chapter Nineteen

WHEN Fen came down from her bath, she found Cat sitting at the kitchen table.

'Coffee?' she asked, and poured one for Fen without waiting for an answer.

'Thanks. Is it all off my face?'

'Yes. Don't worry. It's all gone now.' They sat and stared at one another. 'You do believe me now that there's something nasty going on?'

'Yes. Yes, you were right. I think you should go home.'

'Not without you. I'll only go home if you come with me and stay with us in London.'

Fen sighed. 'Mrs Barton's away. I can't just walk out and not be here when she gets back. I'll have to give her a week's notice.'

'When will she be home?'

'Friday morning.'

'Right. So on Friday, as soon as she gets back, you go and see her, tell her you're leaving, tell her to stuff her week's notice. She can keep this week's money instead. Then we head south. Please, Fen? I really can't take any more of this place.' Cat stared at Fen's bent head and thought she must be the perfect example of her star sign, Taurus. April-born and stubborn as a bull, she dug in her heels and snorted if you tried to move her.

Fen looked up and stared at her out of intensely blue eyes. 'Yes. I think that's the best thing to do. But I still feel I should be here, somehow.'

'No, you shouldn't. We've got to get away before one

of us gets badly hurt. Ash could easily have stuck a knife in you, Fen. We couldn't have stopped him. I'm going to phone my mother now, you just stay there and don't change your mind. She'll be really pleased you're coming to stay. Then we're out of this mad place in a few days.'

Alice *was* pleased. Cat heard the sharp intake of her breath as soon as she heard Cat speak. 'It's okay, there's nothing wrong. I just wanted to let you know that I'll be home on Friday and Fen's coming with me ... Yes. Yes. She'd like to stay if that's all right? ... Yes. I knew you'd say that ... No, we're fine, really. Just fancied a change. Fen will drive carefully, yes, she always does. And we'll take our time. We'll see you late on Friday. Love you too. Bye.' Cat put down the phone and went back into the kitchen. 'There. She's delighted you're coming. Told you she would be.'

'Thanks. Cat, I don't know about you but I still feel shaky. D'you still want to go out to eat?'

'No, I don't! I've lost my appetite somehow and you're not driving anywhere. Tell you what, you go and light the fire in the other room and I'll make us some soup and sandwiches.' She poured herself another coffee and thought that in three more days she'd be out of here. She might just manage that.

In the deepest part of the night, they lay side by side in the feather bed, neatly tucked in under the fat quilt. Moonlight shadowed the room, licked in the dark corners and glittered on Fen's unbound hair where she lay sleeping. Cat looked at her and wondered how she could sleep. The shadows on her face were black as blood; she looked like she had done when Ash daubed her face so horribly. Cat felt as if she would never sleep again. If she lay and counted sheep then the last one over the gate every time would have a leering, seeping slash of a throat. She thought of the smell at the Bridestone and swallowed hard.

There'd been so much death since she came here. It was all going round and round in Cat's head in a black circle. She shifted restlessly. Her head hurt, and something was pricking at her bare back. Running a hand over the bottom sheet, she found a feather sticking up through a worn patch in the old linen. Her movement disturbed Fen, who stirred and flung herself on her back. Cat brushed the feather gently across her mouth, and Fen flinched and opened her eyes wide.

'What?' she said. 'What's happening?'

'It's only me; I can't sleep.'

'Oh. I thought it was . . . Did you wake me up just to tell me that?'

'Oh no, ' said Cat. 'Not just for that at all.'

She wanted to blot out this place, to fill herself and Fen with other feelings, happier ones. She wanted to make her own white magic on Fen and heal her, put right the badness of this place. She knelt between her ankles and licked delicately at the small, round bones. She came lapping at the moon-dappled skin, stalking the long body and feeding off her in the dark. She came gnawing on the flat bones of her shins, sucking at the soft flesh on the thighs, nibbling the thin skin of the inner warmth there.

There was only the sound of her tongue licking on flesh in the room, creaming the brown skin. She travelled round the edge of the tangle of fair hair and up the flat plain of the stomach to the perfect well-hole of the navel, where she bent and lapped with the tip of her red tongue. She came purring up the ribcage to the small hills of the breasts, to the valley between them; came licking up the long stalk of the neck to the small ears, over the stained eyelids and down at last to the waiting mouth. It parted for her and she licked over the swollen, soft bottom lip, tasting the soft inner flesh of the cheek, the high arched roof, tasting it scarlet in the dark.

She lowered herself on top of Fen, breast to breast, cunt to cunt, and her fingers edged into Fen. Then Fen's mouth took hers and pleasure came slowly sliding in and out of them until they were done. They lay holding one another in a loving peace, and Cat thought how good it was to know this body as well as she knew her own. She crawled back next to Fen and curled in towards her. 'Now you're safe,' she said. 'I've made you all safe.' Fen smiled and kissed her.

Sitting up, Cat picked up her pillow and shook it, hoping that now she'd be able to get some sleep. Fen yawned. 'What's that thing?'

Cat froze where she sat, clutching the pillow to her.

'What? Where?'

'It was under your pillow. Look.'

Cat turned her head very cautiously. Fen was holding some sort of small bag on a long, broken string. 'That's not mine,' she said. 'I've never seen it before.' She took it from Fen as if it would bite.

Fen sat up and stared at her. 'Then how did it get there? It's not mine either – *I*'ve never seen it before.'

'Someone's been in. Maybe they still are in.' Cat stared round the room in horror.

'The door was locked. Nobody's in here with us.' Fen frowned down at the little bag. 'So if it's not the door then I suppose it must be a window. The kitchen window's always open a bit at the bottom but it's a very small one, you'd have to be little to squeeze through it.'

'And who do we know who's that little?'

'Patsy!' they both exclaimed together, and looked relieved. Patsy didn't seem too much of a threat to either of them.

'Open it then,' said Fen. 'Let's see what she's brought us.' Cat nodded and untied the string fastening the mouth of the bag, tipping it upside down on to the white sheet.

There was a pebble with seven dots painted on it.

A piece of dry tree bark.

The jawbone of some small creature – a rat, perhaps.

A sprig of dried oak leaves.

A lump of red clay with a sheep's tooth embedded in it.

A tawny owl's feather.

And a square of cloth, stiffened and stained with white.

Fen reached out a finger and stirred the strange mixture.

'Don't touch them!' Cat pushed away Fen's hand.

'Why not? It's only stuff Patsy's collected at school for us, isn't it?'

'I don't think this has much to do with Patsy. It's too weird to be something off the Nature Table.'

'Pebbles and feathers aren't weird.'

'And that bit of cloth?'

'What about it?'

'D'you know what's on it?'

Fen pulled herself further away.

'I think it's semen, Fen. And whose is it? And who's been carrying something like that round with them?'

'And given it to us,' whispered Fen.

Cat looked at her frightened face and crammed all the things back in the bag. Getting out of bed she went across the room to the long disused fireplace. There was a yellowed newspaper crumpled in the grate. Cat emptied out the bag on top of it. There were some matches on the mantelpiece. They were damp; it took four before Cat managed to get one into a pale flame. She held it to the paper. It smoked sullenly for a moment, then burst reluctantly into flame. The leaves and feather burnt first, then the white-stained cloth and the bag itself. Cat watched the flames lick at the bark and blacken the frail bone. She knelt until the flames died back into black ash; until all that remained was the pebble and the smoke-stained piece of clay with the sheep's tooth in it.

'Was it really that, on the cloth?' asked Fen unhappily.

'I think so. But it doesn't matter now, it's all gone anyway, whatever it was.' Cat stood up and held out her hands away from herself. 'I'm going to get washed.'

The ash settled with a soft, rustling sound as Cat came back from the bathroom, and the smell of burning was fading from the room. She climbed back into bed and the comfort of Fen's arms and, cuddling up close to her, pushed from her mind bone and twig and feather.

The shaman knelt and on the white cloth in front of him spread bone and twig and feather. Pulling a small jar out of the bag beside him, he dipped his fingers into it and, standing, streaked the red clay and fat mixture down the woman's cheeks. Across her forehead he drew three red lines. She shivered in the cool night air as he tugged her unfastened dress from her shoulders, for she was wearing nothing under it. He touched each nipple lightly with the clay and on each breast drew a tight spiral of red. Kneeling again, he took another handful of the mixture from the jar and drew a thick line from between her breasts, down the curve of her stomach, to the silver bush of hair between her legs.

Down each leg the line again and, on each foot, the spiral. He turned her round. Three lines across her narrow shoulders. A line to follow the backbone. On each curving buttock the spiral again. Down the back of each leg the thick red line; then she was ready. Moonlight slanting into the loose box chequered her back and haunches as he took her by the hand and led her over to the far side of the box, where the stallion was tethered by a short rope to a ring in the wall. The shaman presented the woman to him. She stood by his head offering herself, breasts and shadowed legs in the moonlight.

The stallion grunted, intrigued by the smell of the woman and the strange scent of the mixture smeared on her. He flared his red nostrils delicately, moving back a short step. The shaman waited. Then the stallion lowered his head and, reaching out, touched the woman between her breasts. The shaman let out his held breath in a long sigh of relief. It was a good omen, the stallion accepting her. He stroked Bel's thick neck and led the woman back to the white cloth spread out on the straw. Picking up the things he'd taken from the bag, he spread them in a big circle, and each object he held for a moment in his cupped hand, drawing up power for it from deep inside himself.

Owl feather, and he saw the owl fly black against the night sky, hunting with bloody claws. Bone of a shrew, cunning and fierce to protect itself. Tooth of the ewe which had died by the knife to offer up its entrails for him to read its message. A pebble smooth and round as a breast from the brackish beck water where he'd found it. A sprig of alder, the power of three held fast in it – fire from the red of the tree trunk, water from the green flowers, earth from the brown bark. Now all that was missing to replace the talisman bag which the woman had lost was the scrap of white-stained cloth.

She was standing watching him, outside the circle. He took her hand and led her into the centre of the circle, as naked now as she was. Here she knelt at his feet with bent head. He caught hold of her hair and lifted back her head and she took him into the round hole of her mouth. He raised his arms above his head and waited and strength came pouring through him so that he cried out and swelled between her lips, coming quickly. Kneeling beside her, he wiped her mouth gently with the white cloth then moved from her to place it in the circle at her feet. It was complete.

He laid her down in the centre of the circle and knelt at her feet, kissing them, moving up her body to her breasts and back to her cunt where he worked patiently for a long time, kissing and stroking her until she caught her hands in his hair and arched her back; she came to the very edge and fell back again, waiting for him to come into her. And he used his fingers to let her break under him in a long whimper of fulfilment.

The stallion moved restlessly then, whinnying across her dying cry, stamping his feet and rubbing his head against the ring where he was tied. She lay spread-eagled, long waves of pleasure rippling through her. The shaman knelt at her feet until she lay quiet and still again, then he began to gather up the objects from the circle, one by one, whispering to himself a litany of names as he did so. They lay now in a long line on the spread altar of her body, from her mouth to her ankles. And then he lifted each one again and touched it to her mouth before he placed it, sanctified, inside her new fetish bag. The last piece which he took was the most powerful; he lifted the piece of white-stained cloth which had lain across her cunt. He dropped it into the bag and tightened the string around its mouth.

Then he raised her to her feet and, holding the bag high above his head, slipped the string of it round her neck. He kissed her swollen mouth, her breasts, her cunt, and kneeling before her, kissed her feet. She stood above him, proud on the crest of her orgasm and took the bag in both hands from him, smiling down at him.

He knelt there wearily, with all the energy drained out of him. It seemed to him to be impossible for him to get to his feet again. The stallion blurred in front of him as he stared round the loose box and he realized that it was no longer moonlight but a pale dawn. Already night had slipped over into the next day. It was Lammas Eve. The names of the great festivals sang through his head: Imbolc at the year's beginning when the ewes came into milk, Beltane in May when the cattle went out to grass. And now Lughnasa, the old name for Lammas. The gathering of the harvest. And then to come at the year's ending was Samhain, when the dead rose from the grave. Lammas, Lammas, echoed his head and he felt as if he must kneel here for ever.

'I'm very cold,' said Amy hesitantly and Michael came back into himself with a terrible pain. He groaned and doubled up, retching where he knelt, frightening her. She caught hold of his hands and helped him to his feet. He rocked unsteadily and she pulled him to her, comforting him. He held her close to him and knew that it was the last day. It was Lammas Eve, and there was so much to be done. Already the sun was up. He cuddled Amy and told her she'd done well; the terrible anger he'd felt when she came to tell him that she'd lost her bag was gone now, used up in the ceremony. He'd been desperate when she told him though, when the powering of the stone musn't be broken and she'd been so careless, so stupid. He pushed her towards her clothes and she smiled at him and began to dress herself quickly. He pulled on his own jeans and shirt like an old man, stiffly and slowly. Powering up her new bag had drained him just when he needed his strength to be at its height. He walked slowly across to Bel where he untied him and gave him a handful of pony nuts from his pocket. He leant against the warm bulk and when he turned, the woman had slipped out of the loose box and gone.

He must go home now and try to get a few hours' sleep before he started on all that there was to be done. He left the stallion, closing the door carefully behind him. He couldn't afford any more accidents. This was the shaman's day and it must all go as he'd shown it to Michael.

Chapter Twenty

THE sun woke Cat. She lay wondering why she felt so pleased, as if something nice was going to happen, then remembered. It was Wednesday today and they were leaving on Friday. She got happily out of bed and began to gather up the grubby shorts and T-shirts which she and Fen had scattered all over the room. She carried them all down to the kitchen, dropped them in the middle of the floor and looked hopefully round for the washer. Not a sign of one. She even opened the cupboard doors under the sink, but without success. 'Thank you, Mrs Barton,' she said crossly and fished out a yellow plastic bucket instead. She had to do some washing, so if it had to be primitive and back to nature, then so be it. She rooted again in the back of the cupboard and came up with a packet of soapflakes. The damp had got to them and they were congealed in a solid lump at the bottom of the packet.

'One lump or two?' wondered Cat, breaking off a handful and dropping it into the bucket. She stood it in the sink and turned on the water. The tap spat at her, made several obscene noises and grudgingly produced a trickle of something resembling strong gravy. She was standing staring at it when Fen came in from the stables.

'Oh, is the water going off again?' she said cheerfully.

'It's not going off, it's gone. Does it often do this?'

'It's moor water; we're not on the mains here so we do have problems. I'll go and switch off the heater on the hot-water tank upstairs, else there'll be a bang.' When she came back downstairs, Fen found Cat still standing by the sink with a horrified expression.

'Water from the moor? Fen, d'you mean that you've been letting me drink water that sheep have pooped in? I'll probably develop something nasty any minute now.'

Fen laughed at her. 'No, you won't. It's probably better for you than London water. At least it won't have been through six people before you.'

'Maybe not but it will be full of nitrates from the fields and the odd dead frog. I can't wash my knickers in gravy. What am I supposed to do? Where d'you do your washing anyway?'

'Sally usually does it for me over at the Hall with hers in the big washer.' Fen buttered herself a slice of bread and spread honey on it. 'Tell you what, use the water from the hot water tap to wash them, then rinse them in the water from the rain water tub in the garden.'

'Oh lovely. Maybe I should hop in with them and tread out the dirt with my feet.'

'No love, that's grapes. Listen, something odd has happened.'

'What?' Cat swung round on her, looking worried.

'It's okay, nothing bad. It's just that Michael wasn't over at the stables. He's never not turned up before. I'll have to see him to find out what's gone wrong with the water. He knows where to dig it out on the moor when it gets blocked.'

'You weren't on your own with Ash? Oh Fen, you should have come back for me.'

'No, he wasn't there either.'

'So Michael still doesn't know we're leaving?'

'No – don't look so worried. We're still going on Friday.'

Standing in the garden, sloshing her knickers in and out of a tub of cold water, Cat decided that launderettes were a wonderful invention. She hadn't expected the water in the tub to be so cold. It had a nasty habit of running up her arms when she lifted out her washing. One pair of black lace pants was sitting firmly at the bottom of the tub, out of Cat's reach. They could stay there, she thought, peering in. What could they eat for lunch that didn't involve using that water? Beans on toast and two glasses of milk. Country living was getting worse by the minute.

Fen went back across to the stables and found Michael there, looking red-eyed and weary. He gave no excuse for where he'd been earlier and was so vague and off-hand with her that she couldn't bring herself to tell him she was leaving. It didn't seem the right time for news like that. He already knew about the water – it was off in his cottage as well. He promised he'd go up on the moor to check it out later, when he had time. He was very busy, he said, and then a car drove into the yard with the three women from the village in it. They sat and watched Fen as Michael brusquely told her she could go, there was nothing for her to do here. He strode across the yard and, bending down to the open car window, began to talk urgently to the women. Fen left them to it.

Michael sent the women up into the larch wood to gather wood for the fire. There was plenty of dry wood lying about there, but it was heavy work dragging it to the Bridestone.

'I feel old today,' said Olivia gloomily as they paused for breath, dragging the rotten hollow of trunk along the narrow path through the wood.

'Oh, I feel old lots of days, ' said Amy. 'You just have to ignore it and keep going. Keep on sticking on the patches and be grateful for HRT.'

'Sometimes when I pull off the old patch I have this fear of deflating, like an old balloon,' confessed Olivia. 'Seeing those two down there in the garden sunbathing doesn't help either. They have no idea how lucky they are, having skin like that with no wrinkles.'

Abbey looked at them both in alarm. 'Hey, come on you two – don't go getting depressed now. Cheer up, it's only the tension getting to you. And this wood is heavy but Michael needs it for the fire. And those two will get wrinkles as well, in the end. We all do. But we've got the experience. We've got the power. We're Hecate, remember? We're the triple-headed one with the magic.'

'Hecate,' repeated the other two nodding, then getting stiffly to their feet they began to haul the dead wood towards the Bridestone.

Michael saw them come out of the wood below him as he climbed wearily up the steep hillside to the water tank. He turned to stare back at the cottages and saw Cat and Fen lying like young offerings in the garden. His wise crones were bent with their burden like something out of a fairy tale at the edge of the wood. He felt comforted at seeing all his women together, all in the right place. Nothing could go wrong now.

He bent to the water tank. There was no water running into it – it must be blocked higher up. He came to the water source where it bubbled up out of the rock and saw what had happened. A boulder had slid forward and blocked the entrance to the pipe leading down to the tank. Probably the sun, drying out the peaty soil, had loosened it. He heaved the stone to one side and saw with a grunt of satisfaction how the water gathered itself and at once began to spill into the narrow mouth of the pipe again. As soon as the tank lower down the hillside filled up, there would be water at the cottages again.

He was tired and thirsty. Scrambling over the rocks he bent to where the water broke silver from them. He cupped his hands and gulped at the cold liquid, splashing it on to his eyes. He shook his dark head and blinked dizzily. He was seeing double. He sank to his knees and gazed into the clear spring.

The shaman dipped his cupped hands into the water and brought them to his lips, lifted his arms and gave a spray of drops to the sun to taste. Light sparkled red and blue as it fell. He sat back on his heels and stared up at the sky. There was a hawk, hanging by a thread high above the moor. The shaman shape-shifted into it, circled the wood where the women looked up and greeted him, hung high over the garden where Cat and Fen lay with closed eyes. He felt the air holding him and knew the wind through his feathers. His round, golden eye scanned moor and rock below him as he flew back to the water source and hovered there, pinned in the blue. There was something down there: not blood and bone in fur, not the black, empty shape of the man crouching empty by the water. There was something in the rocks above him, something hidden and shining.

The shaman fell through the warm air currents, dropped with spread talons into the empty cave of his head and pulled on his skin and bones. He sat and waited; yes, he could still feel it pulling at him. There was something in the rocks above him, and it was for him. He got to his feet and clambered over the grey boulders and he could hear it singing to him now. He moved aside some of the smaller pieces of rock and found a slit in the peat dark soil. He slid his hand into it, forced in his arm as the earth opened and hollowed under his fingers. He touched something old and holy, and his hand knew it by the burning. It was warm and curved to his touch, earth caked and muffled. He lifted it carefully into the sun and took it to the water to cleanse and purify. The water stained, clouded and flowed clear again and the shaman stood and held the silver torc, as perfect now as the day that it had been so carefully hidden. The twisted silver collar to go around the neck of the king lay inside Michael's shirt as he came wearily down from the moor.

Fen and Cat were sitting at the kitchen table when Michael shouted from the porch and came in.

'Can I check your tap? The water should start coming through again now. I sorted the trouble – there was nothing getting into the tank at the top.' He leaned against the sink and turned on the tap, his arms filthy with soil and clay. 'There was a dead ewe up on the moor at the Bridestone,' he said suddenly. 'I rang old John in the village about it. Must have been one of his, but he wasn't that bothered. He doesn't check them often enough to know how many he has up on his stray. I dug a hole and buried it for him. It was a nasty sight. Wicked things, foxes.' He turned to stare at them both.

'Foxes?' said Cat.

'Aye. Rip out a sheep's throat as if it had been cut. Then they go for the softest bits, see. They can eat them faster than the rest.'

Cat was glad they'd finished their tomato soup before Michael came in. 'It didn't look like a fox had done it to us. It looked as if something else had done it.'

'You saw it then? What else could have done it? We've no wolves left round here, not any more.' And his dark eyes on her said what would Londoners know about foxes anyway, or about sheep.

She waited for him to mention Ash.

'Now and again you get a fox that seems to go bad, like this one. Kills for the fun of it. I'll be in trouble with Sally when she gets back. I forgot to lock up her hens and it's taken the lot. Her Welsummer cock and hens that she thought so much of.'

'Is she away, then?' Fen looked surprised. Sally never went very far without Michael.

'Aye. She's taken Patsy to stay with her mother for a few days.'

'Everyone's going,' said Cat lightly. 'Did you know Fen and I were going as well?'

He had his back to her, watching for the water to flow, and she was watching him carefully. He stiffened and swung round on them, his face dark with anger. 'What? You never said a word to me, Fen. You're not going now, not today?'

'I'm sorry Michael. We've only just decided. No, we're not going today. Not until Friday when I've seen Mrs Barton.' Fen looked very uncomfortable, anxious as to what he would say next.

He turned back to the sink again and stood with his head bent, then said very softly under his breath so that they only just caught his words, 'Maybe better if you do go then.'

There was a loud gurgling noise and water began to gush from the tap, dark brown and thick. 'There we go. Let it run now until it comes clear. I'll just rinse my hands off if that's okay?'

'Yes, of course. The soap's in that dish. I'll get you a towel. We can't offer you a coffee until the water clears. Sorry.'

He grinned slyly at Fen. 'I could do with summat a bit stronger than water. It was hot work up there.' He smelled of sweat and the moor, and Fen saw how pale he was under his tan.

'What have we got, Cat? Oh, I know. There's that bottle of mead I won at the jumble sale. I'll get it. There should be some glasses in the sideboard.'

Michael sank down into her chair as she hurried off. He yawned and reached across to Cat, stroking her cheek. 'It's not been what you expected, coming here, has it?' he said. 'It's going to be all right, there's nothing to be afraid of. You just stop your worrying and we three will have a drink to celebrate.'

'Celebrate what?' Cat smiled at him as he leant towards her and kissed her.

'Lammas of course. Didn't you know? Today is Lammas Eve. There's Samhain and there's Beltane and there's Lammas. The festival of renewal of the crops.'

The liquid in the glasses swirled and glittered in the firelight and things began to slide. It went down easy as sin, honey sweet and bee sharp, and Cat licked her lips and sucked up the last drops from her glass. Halfway across the long room she wavered to a stop and stared round her. How long had the fire been lit? And the light had changed. They'd been sitting drinking with Michael . . . somewhere else . . . where had it been? Not in this room. When had they come in here? But it was later now, much later.

Michael was standing by the fire with a woman in a black gown with a hood. The hood was pulled back and Cat knew that red hair. 'Abbey National,' she said wisely to herself, nodding gravely. Who had asked her to come? It wasn't her house here, it belonged to . . . it belonged to someone else. Silly cow, looking at Michael like that as if she owned him. Cat had as much right to him as anyone, she'd made love with him, she'd opened her legs for him and he was the best lover. The best lover. There was someone knocking on the door. Cat remembered now. That's where she was going, to answer the door. They kept it locked because of the bad things, but Michael was here now with them, so it was quite safe to open it.

She turned sharply, almost overbalanced and swayed her way over to it. There were two more women in the porch, their arms full of flowers and leaves. They were wearing long black gowns as well. And one had the face of a crow and the other a wolf. Cat stepped back as they pushed their way in past her. 'Are we having a fancy-dress party?' she asked loudly. She pronounced each word very carefully, as for some reason they seemed slippery and went sliding from her all over the place.

And there had been three women dancing in the patch of light from the kitchen window and one had a crow face and one a wolf and the knife came down into the small shape on the stool.

Cat shook her head and blinked, wondering why she felt frightened. After some difficulty she managed to make the door stay shut. The women had gone straight across to Michael by the fire. There was someone missing, thought Cat. Someone who was very important to Cat and who she loved dearly. Michael would know where she was. Swimming through the unsteady air she brushed up against him, tugging at his shirt sleeve until he turned and put his arms round her and kissed her. He stroked her breast and pulled her in close to him so that she could feel his erection. He filled up her glass again and whispered to her, then turned from her to watch the women pulling something white from a carrier bag. They were unfolding it slowly, carefully, pulling down the long skirt. Cat was looking everywhere for someone she'd lost. Lost. All gone away. She stared at the three bent heads.

And they had carried the little body on their linked hands over to the window and Cat spread out her hands on the glass because she didn't want to see and they pressed the bloody face in its pink frilled bonnet against the glass.

The women were holding up a dress. It was a wedding dress but it was wrong: wedding dresses don't have black feathers all round the hem, don't have snail shells round the neck. Cat gulped at the liquid in her glass, and pulled a face at the bitter aftertaste. Fen wouldn't like this . . . Fen! It was Fen she'd lost, Fen she was looking for. Cat swung round to look for her and fell back on to the sofa. Then there was a gap. A hole she fell into. She was Alice falling down the rabbit hole, falling and falling until she hit the bottom with a thump. She opened her eyes slowly and focused unsteadily on the group in front of the fire.

There was a bride in a wedding dress standing there. The black feathers on the hem brushed the floor, the snail shells gleamed in the firelight and circling each small breast was a ring of yellow flower heads. Tufts of fur, knots of grasses, bunches of ribbons patterned the white lace. Round each wrist a ring of black and white fur lay like a bracelet. One of the women was standing on a stool.

And three times the bone handled knife glittered in the light and plunged into the bundle on the stool and came out painted red.

Behind Fen, behind the bride, the tall frozen bride, brushing out the thick cloud of her hair. And Cat squinted at the fair strands, which seemed to have a faint rainbow of light edging each long tendril.

It was story-time. Michael was telling the women a story. The other two were kneeling at his feet, listening to him. It was about a queen. Some ancient, long-dead queen. Something to do with horses. And a baby. But who was going to marry Fen? For the bride was her Fen. Michael musn't marry her. He couldn't, he already had a wife called . . . called . . .

The room reeled and juddered round Cat and she was running down a long tunnel whose red sides were breathing, opening and closing on her, then everything was black. When the darkness cleared, the crow and the wolf were pulling her to her feet and Abbey was pulling off Cat's shorts. She let her pull off her T-shirt and giggled as she thought how silly she must look, standing there with just a tiny pair of white pants on. She pulled those off as well and dropped them to the floor. She wanted to sit down again but the women pulled roughly at her arms and slipped a dress over her head. It smelled strange, of old-fashioned patchouli oil, of another woman. Cat wrinkled her nose and looked down at herself. The dress was made of soft cotton, deep blue with beads sewn across the bodice. The sleeves came down to the tips of her fingers and all round the edge of the wide cuffs there were sewn fragments of mirrors.

'I'm a happy,' Cat said in surprise. 'A hoppy. A hippy.' She began to giggle again and looked for Fen to show her the hippy dress. Fen was standing by the window looking out into the dark and her hair was plaited in a tight binding, spraying down her back in a mare's tail. It was dark; how was it dark so soon? The women were kneeling at Cat's feet, pinning little bunches of flowers round the hem of her dress. They fastened a ring of grasses on her short hair and handed her a lipstick. One of them pushed something round and hard into Cat's hand. 'Thank you so much,' she said politely and saw that it was something she should know. She brought it up to her eyes and squinted at it. It fell open in two parts and there was an eye caught in it, staring up at her. She twisted the powder compact and the broken mirror caught the light, refracted it and splintered it round the room, illuminating here a hand, there a scarlet mouth (for the other women all had mouths red as wounds), here a flash of pink skin. She tilted it to catch her own fast-melting face and drew a big scarlet mouth nearly where it should have been. She dropped the lipstick at her feet and lifted the powder compact. Michael's face appeared in it, segmented and distorted. Cat shut him inside it quickly and dropped him on the floor.

'It's time,' said Michael. Time for what? Time, ladies

please. Cat curled up on the sofa and yawned. But they were all going to the door, crow and wolf and hare. Who was the hare-face?

And the three women pressed the bloody face against the window. Then they were gone, leaving a faint, red smear on the glass. Wolf and crow and hare.

Cat shivered and looked round for Fen. She was going over to the door with the women. 'Wait for me, wait for me!' cried Cat and ran after her. She reached out and touched Fen's arm and her head turned stiff as a doll's to look at Cat. But it wasn't Fen any more; Fen didn't have eyes made of pieces of blue glass. What had they done to her? The women were holding their toy horses, ribboned and garlanded with flowers. Cat looked at them and saw flesh on them, saw the great sweating bulk of them and for an instant the room was full of their wild neighing. Then they were nothing but toy horses again. 'Here's a horse for you,' said Michael gently, holding out to her the little horse she and Fen had found in the porch. '"The glory of his nostrils is terrible,"' said Cat, and he laughed at her and kissed her. He had a glass bottle of an amber liquid and he stroked the bride's forehead with it, whispering to himself. He touched and anointed wolf and crow and hare and came at last to Cat. The oil felt warm on her skin and the smell of it turned her into one big erogenous zone as his fingers stroked her skin. She purred happily to him and lifted up her arms so that the little mirrors of her sleeves splintered into white and pink, orange and purple as she hugged him. She pulled a knot of flowers from her dress and gave it to him. He nodded gravely and tucked it behind one ear. Then he led them through the porch and opened the door on to the night.

Chapter Twenty-one

Silent as ghosts, the women walked down the flagged path, only Fen's dress scratching and rustling like a small mouse where the feathers brushed the stone. Cat stretched out a hand to her to keep herself safe, then she remembered: this wasn't Fen. This was someone else. One by one the women followed Michael down the path. Cat wondered how the darkness could seem thicker round him. He was like the man in the fairy tale with the goose tucked under one arm, and everyone who touched him had to follow. He knew what was going to happen to them all. He would see that it was good. But Cat felt sick and dizzy and clouds were swirling across the sky, wheeling above her head. There were stars, bobbing like silver balloons, and a moon. Such a great, round moon. Cat stopped to look at it and in the cottage behind them, there was a noise.

In the long room they had left the fire flickered and the heavy musk smell of the oil which Michael had used to anoint the women was stronger than ever. There was a sense of waiting, of time unreeling, then through the empty room shrilled the sound of the phone, out of place and in the wrong time. It rang on and on insistently, long after it had been obvious that there was no one there to answer. At the other end of the umbilical cord, Alice Denby stood and waited, holding the receiver pressed tightly to her ear, listening to the burring of her heartbeat throbbing across the dark unanswered.

She wondered why she was so afraid now, why she'd woken and crept to ring Cat at this hour? She'd been dreaming of horses, but surely there was nothing about horses to frighten her so much? And Cat was coming home on Friday and bringing Fen with her, so there was nothing at all to worry about.

There was still no answer.

But where could they both be, at this time of night? She let the phone ring on and on, not being able to bring herself to put it down and break the thin thread which fastened her to Cat, not being able to admit there was going to be no answer.

Cat knew who it was. She turned unsteadily and wanted to go back to answer it but there was hare-face close behind her and beyond her the crow and the wolf grinned and pushed forward. They had Cat by the arms and she was going down the path again, going the wrong way, and behind her in the cottage the phone rang on and on and on. 'But it's my mother!' she wailed and a long-fingered hand closed over her mouth to silence her and the gate closed behind them.

The road ran away silver in the moonlight and Cat tried to follow it, but at each side of her walked a black-gowned figure with the third following closely on her heels. They went under the archway and light was spilling from the stable across the cobbled yard. They stood in the doorway and looked at Bel. The light shone on the great stallion standing with his head uplifted and nostrils flaring as he caught the smell of the women. His oiled coat was patterned with red clay in spirals whorling his chest and flanks. His mane was plaited with strings of small beads and his tail threaded with ribbons and flowers. He arched his thick neck and screamed until Cat leant against the wall and closed her eyes, for the sound went roaring through her sick head. Time slipped, went fast-forward in a black wave.

When she forced open her blurred eyes with a feeling

of missing something, of things happening without her, the three women were standing in front of the stallion, and they were naked. They were smeared and marked with red circling their breasts and round their necks hung their amulet bags. One by one they dropped to their haunches at Bel's head and offered themselves to him, wolf-face, crow and hare lifting to him. And in their pubic hair were knotted tufts of Bel's wiry tail hairs, threaded with beads. They came to where Cat crouched in the straw, watching and led her over to the stallion, pulled her long dress up above her waist and forced her to her haunches in front of him. She stared up at the mass of the horse above her and thought that he could step forward and crush her. She tried to get to her feet and slipped sideways at the feet of the man standing by Bel's shoulder. He lifted her to her feet and he was wearing the head of another horse, he had the bone-white skull of a horse over the top half of his face and she could see his eyes shining darkly at her through the hollow, empty eye sockets. She reached out her hands to push him away and touched skin. He was wearing a cloak of soft mareskin, falling to his feet. He caught hold of her hands and turned his head to the bride beside him and the horse's tail fixed on top of his mask swished and hissed through the air.

'Are you ready, my lady?' the shaman asked and the tall bride nodded, stared with her blue-glass eyes at Cat and walked towards the door. The black robes were on again, the white flesh covered and the three women gathered up Cat and she followed, for what if Fen came back into herself again and needed her? The shaman untied the horse and, picking up a sack, was following them. The sack fluttered as Cat turned her head to watch them. Then the road ran beneath her feet again and turned to grass and they were climbing in the moonlight up towards the moor. The bride's white dress glimmered among the trees in the larch wood and the branches dipped and clawed at Cat as she scrambled after her until the trees fell away behind them and there ahead was the Bridestone.

The heavy fall of Bel's feet behind her drove Cat on across the moor after the pale dress. The three women were up ahead now, hurrying towards a black mass which loomed against the skyline next to the Bridestone. Cat saw a red flash, a spurt of flame and realized it was a huge bonfire next to the stone. A thin, grey plume of smoke rose up into the dark. Flame leapt and shone on hare-face, wolf and crow, on the white-faced bride, caught itself in the little mirrors on Cat's long sleeves. The shaman stood on the flat slab of stone in front of the Bridestone and where was Bel now? Cat looked round for him but he was gone. The shaman raised his arms to the Bridestone.

'It is the time,' he called. 'It is the Feast of Lammas. I call on you to come to me out of the darkness. Come to the light of the fire.' He paused and listened, but nothing moved. He cried again, 'I call on you out of the mists of time long past to come to us here. Lord of the Sun, show yourselves to us.'

The fire crackled and the flames leapt and a low grieving broke from the three women, for the shaman had promised to bring down the god for them and they had worked and waited for this day. The shaman hushed them and took the bride by the hand. He led her to the Bridestone. 'We have brought a virgin bride to the stone,' he cried. 'We have blessed the stone with the women's breasts. Is this not enough? Then we shall give blood on the killing stone for you.'

His hand was in the sack and he stood again on the flat slab and he held something fluttering and banging and screaming. He lifted the golden feathered hen above his head by its feet, its wings flailing wildly, then dashed it down, breaking its neck and spattering blood across the killing stone. He threw the dead bird down at his feet where it lay flapping and jerking in a terrible puppet parody of life.

It was dead, thought Cat, but it was still moving, still beating its wings. She watched in a dull horror as the shaman bent to it and rubbed his hands in the bloody mess which had been its head. He went to the Bridestone and spread his hands on it, taking them slowly away to leave a perfect imprint. 'We have given the Bridestone a bride. We have given it fresh blood. For the third time I call on you to come to us.'

For a terrible, still moment, nothing.

Then out of the moor came the sound of hoofbeats and out of the shadows the stallion came with a rider on his back. The firelight caught the horse and made blood-red patches flame along his flanks as he strode. Still as a statue he stood by the Bridestone as from his back the rider leapt. He stood with his back to the women and the smoke from the fire billowed and swirled about him, wrapping him thickly in a grey cloak. And they waited.

'Do you know what this place was then, in the old time?'

At the sound of the shaman, the naked, horned figure turned and began to speak in a chanting, singing voice. 'I know that,' he began. 'It was yellow; it was blossoming; it was green. It was hilly; it was a place for drinking; it was holy. I knew this place when I went through it as a stag with branching horns; when I was a swimming, dappled salmon; when I was a solitary wild dog with no pack to follow me, then I knew it. Now I know not father or mother or tribe. I speak here to you and to the dead.'

He paused and the shaman called to him again. 'And now? Who are you now?'

He swung his head from side to side before he answered, and the long mane of his hair flickered in the firelight.

'Who are you now?' demanded the shaman more urgently.

'I am the god-king!' screamed Ash, raising his arms exultantly above his head. And the silver torc round his neck burned in the firelight, and the red clay on his skin was black as blood in the shadows. 'I am Lord of the animals. I am the Horned One,' he screamed into the silence.

'What can you tell us?' said the shaman softly.

'I have some news for you. The fox barks on the long hill; the land blossoms sweetly; summer is high. Wind warm and soft; the sun rides high and red; the sea runs smooth with small waves. Young green the bracken; the trees in full leaf; the wild goose gathers her brood. The stallion has covered his mares; the seed is deep planted; the mating is done. This is my news.'

'Who do you seek here?'

'I seek a summer bride. I seek Epona. I seek the Great Mare herself.'

'And you shall have her.' The shaman held out his hand and the bride came towards him from the edge of the fire, stiff and stately with her three black attendants. They knelt at her feet and caught hold of her skirt, lifting the dress from her to leave her naked. Now they stood one at each side of the shaman, bride and groom.

But they shouldn't have done that, shouldn't have taken Fen's dress off her. And this couldn't be a wedding because Fen had never even been with a man. Weddings were in church with a party afterwards. Yes, nodded Cat wisely to herself, and there was always a big cake with white icing on it and on the top of it, two little figures. Bride and groom.

'Are you then the shaman?' asked the god-king.

The shaman pulled open his cloak and they saw the figure of a running horse, tattooed blue across his chest. 'When I was young,' he said, 'and I sat by the fire with you all, then a mare came to me out of the darkness and leaped the flames to come to me with her mane licked with fire. The mare chose me that night. And the old man who had been your shaman before me got to his feet and went out of the ring of firelight and into the dark forest. He did not return. He knew that his time had come and gone. The mare made the choice. I have her drawn upon my skin and my cloak is mareskin. Do you know me for your shaman?'

'Yes, yes, yes,' hissed the three black figures crouching at his feet. 'We know you for the shaman.'

A gust of wind took the fire so that the bitter smoke stung at Cat's eyes. She rubbed them fretfully and wanted to be with Fen. This was all some bad dream, she decided. How could they all be having the same dream? There was no past here and no present, only this terrible dreaming. She tried to push past the women to get to Fen, but they caught her hands and pulled her down to her knees with them.

'Then is it your wish we make the ceremony?' cried the shaman.

'It is my wish,' agreed the god-king, and, 'Make it now, make it now!' urged the kneeling women.

It began with a story.

'Listen to me,' said the shaman. There was no sound but the crackling of the fire as he began to speak, staring over the women's heads out into the dark. 'I am the shaman of the horse, the stallion man. Since time was I have had that name. I am the one who knows your dreams. I am the one who reads the signs in the rocks, in the death of animals, in the blood and guts. I am the one who has brought you here together today to give the groom to his bride. I will give you the god-king's renewal and the harvest of his seed. I will tell you a story of the queen.

'Once, long, long ago there was a holy abbot who set out from the court on important business. What it was is not known, only that he travelled alone through the woods. He was a modest man and a holy one; needing a quiet place where he could piss he looked for somewhere off the beaten track where no one could see him. He pushed deep in among the trees and there in a small glade he came upon the queen, Epona.'

Wolf and crow and hare faces swung to stare up at the bride standing so still next to the shaman, then back to him.

'She was making a magic potion which she drank as he watched her. And then, to his amazement, she changed into a mare. She began to leap and run and then the abbot saw, for the first time, that deep among the trees was a group of horses watching her. She showed herself to them most lewdly, baring her body to them all without shame. And by doing this, by acting out the lustful mare for them, she brought them all fertility. And the holy abbot crept quietly away and later wrote down all that he'd seen, so that everyone could know of the queen's magic. And as he wrote, so has it always been with the queen. So is it still.'

Cat listened to this story very carefully. It made little sense to her but nothing made any sense to her any more. She thought that the story meant that Fen was a queen as well as a bride. Queen for the king. But the king was Ash somewhere as well, and Cat had been the one who played the mare for him, not Fen. 'Me,' she muttered crossly. 'My Ash.' Knocking aside the women's hands clutching at her, she went to him to claim him, reaching out for him.

The god-king stared blankly at her as she lurched towards him, then, as her fingers touched his skin, screamed angrily at her and hit out wildly, catching her face and knocking her off her feet. She lay crumpled in a heap on the short-cropped turf and the stars streamed and sparkled round her and went out, one by one. As she dropped down into dark she knew that she'd been set up: she'd never been any more than the Teaser for Ash, the mare to ready the stallion for the true mating. Fen had been the chosen one all along. Cat groaned and for a long time, knew nothing more.

Chapter Twenty-two

RED. Behind her eyes, leaping streaks of red. Cat forced them wearily open. The women were piling more branches on to the blazing fire and something terrible was standing now by the head of the stallion. Cat groaned and sat up. A gust of wind took the fire so that it flared and shone on the white mare's head of the bride. She was wearing a horse's skull for a head, like the one the shaman wore, terrifying as she swung her heavy head from side to side, her eyes glittering in the hollow sockets of the long-dead mare. Her thick mane of hair was threaded through the top of it, pale as the bone in the moonlight. Round her shoulders there was a soft skin, fastened at her throat with a pin of bone. The stallion swung his head and blew softly at her; she stroked his long nose and he whickered, flaring his nostrils and moving his feet restlessly.

'Now I give you your bride-queen; I give you Epona. She wears the mask of the Great Mare; she wears the skin of one of her unborn children. The ceremony demands that she dance. The dance of the Great Mare for the stallion, for Bel the Shining One.' The women at the shaman's feet nodded their masks and whispered to one another. It would not be long now, the mating they had waited for so anxiously.

Epona knelt in front of the horse and he stamped a foreleg, grunting his deep stallion's call as he smelt the rank and musky smell of her. She got languorously to her feet, as if the flesh was heavy on her bones, and began to dance. She dipped her long mane of hair for him, stroked her long thighs, her hair hissing and slashing the air as her movements became more lewd, more explicit. She slowed and came to a shivering halt, sweat glistening on her like oil. Reaching forward she touched the flaring nostrils of the stallion with the bone skull of her mask. He screamed again, throwing up his head and swinging round excitedly. The shaman caught at his head and a long sigh went through the watchers as they saw that the stallion was erect and ready to take her.

'Come to her now,' cried the shaman. 'Your seed will bring the chosen child. Give us renewal.'

He came from behind Bel and round his shoulders now he wore a cloak like Epona's, and the silver torc of kingship shone at his throat. 'Epona, I give you the god-king,' said the shaman and the night swirled and sparkled round them and when it steadied again, Epona and the god-king were standing on the flat killing stone facing one another.

'Look at how beautiful the god-king is,' said the shaman in a quiet, almost conversational tone. 'Don't you agree that he's a fine mate for you? Look at his thick head of hair, his clear eyes and his strong white teeth. Look at the way he holds his head high, at the deep chest of him, the long back. At the tight curve of his haunches. Such a mate will give you strong, sturdy youngsters.' The shaman turned to the women. 'Is this the one you chose to give Epona the child?'

'This is the one,' groaned the women, crouching by the killing stone and pointing their long fingers at the god-king.

'They have chosen you.' The shaman's voice was soft and reassuring. 'And just look at the woman we've got for you. All that flaxen hair, and the strong, long bones of her arms and legs. Look at her high love-mound ready for you. You saw her dance for Bel the stallion and how

233

he rose for her. Do you want her to make the dance now for you?'

The god-king raised his hands to the torc at his throat and held it. 'I want that,' he agreed.

'Then listen to the women,' said the shaman, as Epona began the second dance.

Wolf-face, hare and crow rose to their feet. Wolf began it, her voice high and eerie over the fire crackle. 'This is Epona. She is both mare and woman. She is times past and time to come: your past but our future. She is empty for you to fill. Look at her strong body. Look at her firm breasts – they will fill with milk for the coming child. Look at her corn hair, her red mouth, her cunt and her womb. She is young and beautiful and she is yours.' The wolf-head tipped back to the swollen moon and howled her loss that the god-king would never need her body.

And the sharp-beaked crow cawed a long screech and croaked at him. 'This is Epona. She is both mare and woman. She is almost ready for you, god-king. See how smoothly she moves in the dance; she flows like a river for you. Her nipples taste of honey and her skin of summer flowers. She is widening, swelling to take in your great prick. She will take you all in. She is opening wide enough to take in all the world and spit it out in brightness. She is the one who can bear your child.' The crow flapped the black wings of her robe and cawed her loss harshly into the night.

Then the soft-voiced hare, full of her own moon-magic, finished it for him. 'This is Epona. She is both mare and woman. She is ready now to take your seed inside her. She will take you in so deep that your prick will cry out in the red passages; it will cry out in the unknown land. Her womb is ready and the banquet is laid out. It lies at the world centre and you are the invited guest. Come

234

feast on her, my lord. Take the bride to the stone and cover her. She is young and she is beautiful and she is yours.' And the hare's great eyes shone with tears because it was too late for her to be the chosen one.

The dance was finished. Epona dropped to her haunches and, sliding her hands down her legs, presented herself to him as a gift. Then she stood and moved in towards him, touching him delicately with the bone mask on his chest, running her hands down his sides, stroking the blue-veined centre of him. His erection jerked and swelled as she touched him and he caught hold of her hands and turned her to face the Bridestone, shadowed blood-red from the flames. Hand in hand, bride and groom, they stepped from the flat slab of the killing stone and walked towards it. Epona bent from the waist and fitted her palms into the bloody hand-prints left by the shaman and the power stored in the Bridestone crashed through her. She screamed out at the force of it and, behind her, the god-king caught her by the waist, leaning along the length of her arching back for a moment, covering her body with his.

'No, no!' moaned Cat, covering her ears at the sound. She turned and saw the two-backed beast they were making but didn't make any sense of it. The Bridestone glittered and shone tall above their white flesh: someone was hurting, and it should be stopped. But it was no use her trying to do anything because no one was taking any notice of her any more. She wasn't even sure that she was still there. She was wandering in the heather on the edge of the firelight looking for something. She'd been carrying it when she came up here and she had to find it or else her mother would be very cross with her. Her face hurt her where Harry had hit her. But that was a long time ago in another place – how could it still hurt her so much now? It had been someone else who hit her. And now he was hurting that woman at the Bridestone, whoever she was. Cat gave a cry of pleasure and picked up her toy horse from where it lay, half-hidden, under a gorse bush.

She hurried with it to where the other three women were standing beside the fire, watching the two-backed beast intently. They were holding their horses as well. They would be pleased that she'd found hers. 'Look, look,' she said happily. They turned to hush her, to catch hold of her and keep her with them. She could feel the tension tight in their hard fingers on her arms. 'Mother?' she said, peering from wolf to crow to hare.

The god-king lifted himself and touched the tip of his prick against Epona and she shuddered and moaned with pleasure, beginning to swing her haunches from side to side. He went into her slowly, furrowing his way in until the bush of her fair hair flattened under him. Then he caught her tight and dug his nails into her and began his own dance in her. He came in her with a blood-curdling yell as the power from the stone spread through her body and into his. The stallion reared and screamed, almost pulling the reins from the shaman's hands. He steadied the frenzied horse, walking him in a circle, soothing him until Bel was calmer. When the shaman turned back to the Bridestone, the god-king was straightening himself, turning to face the women with a shining, joyful face. He held out his open hands to them and they called their praise to him, then lifting up their totems, their fetish horses which had meant so much to them, one by one they threw them into the heart of the fire, calling for fertility for Epona. Sacrificing for the coming child. The ribbons and flowers on the horses flamed and burnt. The plastic horses caught alight and melted into a blackened, twisting mass. The smell of burning plastic swept bitter over them all.

Cat was horrified. Why had they done that? She wasn't going to burn her little horse. She wrapped it up safely in her skirt, but crow-face saw her doing it and wrenched it from her. She threw it with the others into the red eye of the fire. Cat wept as she saw it burn. Now she had nothing left.

The shaman led the horse towards the stone. The god-king turned to greet him but it was not him the shaman wanted. He pushed past him with a blank, dark face to where Epona leant against the stone. He knelt at her feet and kissed them, then pulled her to him and kissed her cheek. He helped her up on to Bel's wide back where she took the reins and waited. The god-king moved to where she sat, smiling up at her, but her head was turned from him. The shaman caught him by the shoulder, pulling him back away from her and a long, mourning cry broke from the god-king as the shaman tore off his cloak and torc of kingship, his horns, and gave them to the women. 'It is done,' he whispered wearily. 'He is yours now. Take him.'

Bel moved heavily to the flat surface of the killing stone, where he let the shaman scramble up behind Epona. She turned the stallion's head and they moved off slowly away from the Bridestone. The shaman held her tightly to him, his hands crossed across her stomach. Nine months, he thought, and the child would be born. The final sacrifice, magical and holy, which would give him all the shaman's powers and more. Behind them, god-king no longer, Ash shook his head and stared after the stallion.

'Michael?' he called hesitantly, and again, more loudly, 'Michael?' But Michael did not turn his head. The stallion disappeared among the trees. Ash tried to follow, but the three women held his arms. Hare-face looked at where Cat still stared into the dying embers of the fire, grieving for her lost toy. 'There's no place for you here. Get off after the horse. Quick now. Go and look after Fen.'

Cat looked up, startled, just catching sight of Bel before the trees swallowed him. 'Fen?' she repeated and began to run.

Then there were only the three women left, and Ash.

One in front, one at each side, they led him off across the moor away from the Bridestone in the changing light: it was a new day now. Ash went to his chosen death willingly for he knew no better. They led him across the moor to the edge of the peat bog where the grass grew lush and green. He knelt to face the rising sun and bent his head. Three pairs of hands picked up a piece of grey stone and brought it smashing down on him, cracking his skull like a breaking egg. He rolled unconscious to the spongy ground, blood clotting his long, fair hair. Hare-face took out her sharp little knife and sliced a bloody line around his throat from ear to ear. She lifted the red blade and the sun ran down it as she passed it on to the crow-faced woman. A second bloody cut and then to wolf-face for the third. Three lines carved in the royal throat. Three times a death: the last one now, by drowning.

They pulled and tugged at arms and legs across the bog to where brown water oozed and laid him face down in it; the greedy bog licked and sucked above their ankles as they worked. They pulled off their amulet bags and one, two and three laid them down his back to keep him safe. Their feet heaved and squelched their anxious bodies back to solid, firmer earth. There was a wind rising now as the morning light grew stronger. It fluttered the muddy black skirts as the women faced out across the bog to the royal grave.

'We have given him the triple death which is due to

the husband of the goddess,' said Abbey. 'His death was needed for the final consummation of our ceremony. His life was given to make sure the bride is fertile.'

'We had no choice,' said Amy. 'He's safe out there, back in the earth.'

Taking off their masks the three women pulled the hoods of their gowns about their faces and left the moor. Behind them, Ash's fingers opened and closed just once on a handful of the black, wet peat where he lay face down, then there was no more movement.

Chapter Twenty-three

A YEAR had passed; it was Lammas Eve again and the three women were dancing round the Bridestone. Michael stood on the killing stone dreamily watching as their long robes flittered like bats in the blue dusk, watching as the white round arms rose and fell out of the long black sleeves. Round and round they danced, wolf and hare and crow presenting their mask-faces to the Bridestone. Each time round the stone they drew a little closer to it, spinning wildly out, only to creep in tighter to it until, at last, they circled it round, finger touching finger so that the ring of three was complete and the Bridestone enclosed. They stood silent in their black knot, leaning to press their bodies close against it in a final blessing before turning to come to Michael.

It was the first time that they had all been together at the Bridestone since the last Lammas Eve. It had been the women's idea to come here tonight. Michael shivered for the place was full of ghosts for him and he half-turned, thinking he heard the heavy footsteps of the stallion behind him on the empty moor. The women knelt at his feet, pulling and tugging him down with them to the flat stone until he was lying spread like a sacrifice for them. Then their hands were busy on him and their three mouths sucked and kissed at him. Their black robes covered him over and he lay and stared up at the sky and in the end was not even sure which of them it was who sat herself astride him and witch-rode him dry.

They left him lying there, used and spent, and only a

faint wolf howl came back to him as they pattered away through the wood. It took him a long time to gather himself together and make his own way down from the moor. He let himself into his cottage and stood listening to the silence. There was no Sally. No Patsy. A year ago on Lammas Eve, he'd had a wife and daughter living here with him. Now there was only himself.

He went heavily into the kitchen and made a mug of coffee. There was a half-eaten meal still on the littered table from earlier in the day. He pushed the plate wearily away. Food had little interest for him, these days. A year ago, he thought, and in a series of bleak snapshots saw Sally's face as she told him that she'd packed her bags and was leaving him. Saw the look on Patsy's face as she turned and stared back at him out of the bus window when they left him. Off to live with Sally's mother.

He didn't blame Sally. She'd come back last year from a few days away and found everything changed. The place was crawling with police, poking into everything, looking for the missing Ash. Cat and Fen had gone off to London and Michael was spending most of his time over at the stables. Calming down Mrs Barton. Sally knew he'd had something to do with Ash disappearing. She didn't know what had been going on, but she never trusted him again. Only the three women knew what Ash's end had been and where he was, and were bound to Michael because of it. The police never did find his body – the bog had swallowed it. And a couple of days of heavy rain washed out all the signs at the Bridestone. Michael had made sure of that. Dave at the pub hadn't even bothered to report his son missing for forty-eight hours so it was a cold trail for anyone to follow. Being Dave, he hadn't grieved long for Ash. Michael still mourned him, felt the loss of him every day that passed and woke at night howling at the memory of that last cry Ash made across the moor after Michael. And he hadn't turned his head; he'd ridden off and left him to his death. But his hands had been on Fen's stomach and it was the coming child that mattered then. Fen's face swam up at him out of the gathering dark, as white and frightened as she'd been that night in the pub when he thought she'd cut off her hair.

Cat's face, her mouth stained with raspberry juice the time she came to him in the garden. Pretty little pussy cat. They hadn't remembered anything of what had happened next day, either Cat or Fen. They accepted what Michael told them – that they'd drunk too much at a party which went wrong. They believed him. Ash and Cat and Fen. He reached across the table where something white glimmered and picked it up. It was the drawing Cat had done of Bel with Ash – Michael had found it hanging, dusty and forgotten, in the tack room and had brought it back with him. All he had left now was Bel.

Michael thought endlessly of what could have happened to Fen, if she'd carried the baby full-term, if the child had lived. It would be three months old now. He didn't know: there'd been no word from either of them since they went. He wondered sadly if it had all been worth it, the price they'd all had to pay. The shaman was still there with him but in the background now. Was it finished, whatever he'd chosen Michael for, that night? Michael didn't think so but he couldn't fit any ending on to it. Not yet.

He was so very tired and it was late now. He rested his head on his arms. He didn't like sleeping in that bed upstairs without Sally. He missed her more than he'd imagined. And Patsy. He needn't sleep alone unless he chose to, for the three in the village were there for him if he needed them. Sometimes one of them came to spend the night with him, sometimes they all three came on bad nights when they needed each other's company. Michael closed his eyes.

The shaman was sitting cross-legged in his hut when he was startled to hear the noise his people were making, laughing and shouting. Had they caught something, to make them so excited? He listened but could make no sense of the voices. He got stiffly to his feet and wrapped his cloak round himself, pulled his horse-mask on to his head and ducked under the skins hanging across the entrance to the hut. And the noise stopped, cut off like a held breath, as they stared at him.

It was a young boy that was causing so much noise. He was walking slowly across the clearing past the fire and there was some creature following at his heels. The people fell back as the boy came walking towards the shaman's hut and he saw what it was. It was a young wolf cub trotting beside the boy. But wolves were wild things out of the wood, they were killers who snatched up small children from the village edge in winter dusk. This one was jumping up now, leaping up to lick at the boy's hand with a red tongue. The boy walked steadily to stand in front of the shaman. He said nothing to the old man, made no challenge, only stared at him as if he were nothing, now. A child in the crowd laughed as the wolf cub sat down and scratched its ear, and the mother hushed it quickly. The boy looked back at the sound, then walked past the shaman, ducking under the skins and going into the sacred hut. The wolf cub scrambled to its feet and ran in after him. The skins fell silently into place behind them.

There was a long, frightened sigh from the people as they saw the boy and the cub go into the holy place.

They backed away from the shaman, afraid of his anger, of what he would do. But the shaman knew that his time was over. The wolf cub had chosen the boy and marked him as the one to follow. The horse would no longer be the totem, but the howling wolf. Just as the mare had come to the shaman with the sign, so long ago, so had this wild creature come. The shaman sighed, for the boy was very young to lead the tribe, with little knowledge. He turned and walked through his tribe for the last time and their silent heads turned from his dead stride. He went from them into the trees and there he hung his cloak on a low branch, his mask from another. He had no more need of them. Wearing only the running horse tattooed blue across his chest he went deeper into the trees.

There in the deep shadows the wolf mother crouched. Her teats were aching with milk for her lost cub and she snarled softly at the first faint scent of the man. She got to her feet and followed him. He knew she was there; he could feel her breath hot at his heels, hear her feet pad, pad, padding over the crackling twigs. He led her on away from his people until he came to a small clearing where the sun broke through the dense canopy of leaves over his head to make a bright circle of light. He stopped here and turned to face her. He opened his arms and she came to him like a lover, her shaggy pelt covering the running horse as she sprang at him and took him to the ground where she lay on his chest and closed her white fangs on his throat, ripping it out in a spurt of scarlet blood. The shaman left his body and moved out into the dark for the last journey of all, the one from which there would be no return, and in his death called into himself the man from the future.

Michael screamed at the pain, leaping howling from his

chair to clutch at his bloody, broken throat, stumbling back in an agony of terror. He crouched in the room corner, rubbing his hands over and over at his neck, staring in disbelief that there was no blood. No wound. Only a terrible smell of animal in the room. He could hardly breathe for the banging of his heart and sweat was pouring from him. As soon as his legs could carry him he went crawling up the stairs, sick and shaken.

What had just happened to the shaman?

He was there now in Michael's head, stronger than he'd ever been, but something had changed. Michael went unsteadily into the bathroom, switched on the light and, going over to the wash-basin let cold water run on his trembling hands and wrists, splashing his wet face. He rubbed himself dry on the towel and straightened, seeing himself in the mirror over the basin. He caught his breath and grabbed at the edge of it with shock. It wasn't him looking back out of the mirror. The glowing red eyes stared at him from out of a brown and wrinkled face, awesome and holy. The shaman's face. He stood and stared at his changed self, hardly breathing, and heard the sharp slam of a car door outside the cottage. He stood and listened. His gate clicked, then there was the sound of footsteps coming up the path. Woman's steps. Then a loud banging on the front door. Still he stood, listening, watching that old face in the mirror. He didn't want to see any of the women from the village if it was one of them. And it would hardly be Sally coming back to him. She would never come back, not now. If he didn't answer, perhaps the do-gooder or whoever it was would go away again and leave him alone.

But there was a different sound now, so frail and thin that at first he couldn't make out what it was. It grew louder and now he knew it for the sound of a baby crying. He moved heavily away from the mirror to stand in the window. Light from the bathroom spilled faintly down to the path below. There was someone standing there with a bundle in her arms. She lifted her head and her long hair fell pale as ripe corn down her back. It was Fen. The bride had come back. She'd brought the Lammas child for him. She'd brought him the sacrifice. The shaman's teeth bared in a white snarl of delight. He wondered for a moment if she was really there or just something he'd made up out of his imagination, but there was her car parked at the gate, and she had seen him standing there. She was staring blank-faced up at him now, then she lifted the baby and held it up in her arms towards him. Louder and louder the noise grew then, until there was nothing but the sound of the baby, crying on and on in the dark.

The shaman turned and went downstairs to open the door for Fen and her daughter.

creed

○

SIGNET

NIGHTRIDER

Only her desire would allow him to live ...

In London, photographer Rose Thorpe has reached a crossroads in her life – and finds herself ready for escape. Haggabacks is a godsend – a cottage high on the Yorkshire moors, the final strange bequest from a father she'd last seen as a child.

But here the dreams turn to shadows and Rose's nightmare begins. As an outsider, she is viewed by the locals with mistrust and scorn. And inside the four damp walls, something is watching her ... following her ... *wanting* to make love to her: a creature of animal passion that has come from beyond the grave, forcing her to respond with a hunger she has never known before ...